'This tongue-in-cheek, heart-in-the-right-place thriller brings a whole new meaning to domestic noir'
The Times

'Insightful, moving, dramatic and darkly funny'
Daily Mail

'Highly original and darkly humorous'
Woman's Own

'A character study in which the best of British comedy is underlined by sadness and grit'
Buzz

'A dark delight that takes the most mundane of realities, soaks it, wrings it out and shakes it into a thoroughly absorbing ride. Funny, violent, real and with characters you love to love – and hate...'
Janice Hallett, author of *The Appeal*

'Funny, grim and very touching'
Harriet Tyce, author of *Blood Orange*

'Beautifully drawn characters with a deftly woven plot, *Make Me Clean* is Tina Baker's best yet'
Alice Clark-Platts, author of *The Flower Girls*

'Dark, sharp, shocking, funny and sad. Tina Baker has a unique voice in the blackest depths of domestic noir'
Kate Griffin, author of *Fyneshade*

'She has topped even her first two novels. Brilliant'
Eddie Mair

'Quirky, dark and delicious'
Caroline England, author of *My Husband's Lies*

'I love the characters that Tina Baker creates, so flawed and undeniably human. *Make Me Clean* is a heart stopper of a book'
J. M. Hewitt, author of *The Life She Wants*

'Dark, disturbing, funny, brilliant'
Guy Morpuss, author of *Five Minds*

Tina Baker was brought up in a caravan after her mother, a fairground traveller, fell pregnant by a window cleaner. After leaving the bright lights of Coalville, she came to London and worked as a journalist and broadcaster for thirty years. She's probably best known as a television critic for the BBC and GMTV, and for winning *Celebrity Fit Club*. Her debut novel, *Call Me Mummy*, was a #1 Kindle bestseller, and featured on *Lorraine*. Her second novel, *Nasty Little Cuts*, was published in 2022. Her fourth novel, *What We Did in the Storm*, will be published by Viper in 2024.

MAKE ME CLEAN

TINA BAKER

 VIPER

This paperback edition published 2023
First published in Great Britain in 2023 by
VIPER, part of Serpent's Tail
an imprint of Profile Books Ltd
29 Cloth Fair
London
EC1A 7JQ
www.serpentstail.com

1 3 5 7 9 10 8 6 4 2

Typeset by Crow Books

Printed and bound in Great Britain by
CPI Group (UK) Ltd, Croydon, CR0 4YY

A CIP catalogue record for this book is available from the British Library.

ISBN 978 1 800 81182 9
eISBN 978 1 800 81183 6

For my dad, window cleaner Pete Baker.
And all the cleaners and carers.

1

Maria takes the cloth from the bucket and wrings it, knuckles white, water red. The hot tap scalds her skin as she rinses and wrings, and rinses and wrings again, attempting to steady herself with the repetition. Her hands are strong, stronger than they have ever been, calluses along the palms. When Maria first started cleaning, she wore rubber gloves, as if she were a princess – a thought that makes her want to both laugh and cry.

On her hands and knees, frantically scrubbing, panting with the effort. The tiles are cold but sweat trickles down her neck. She reaches up to wipe it away and is startled by the absence – the buzzcut always a shock.

She hears Elsie cry out in her old office where she sleeps now, too frail to manage the stairs any longer, and hurries through from the kitchen to calm her, perhaps to beg her forgiveness, but the old woman's eyes are closed. She's curled into herself like a kitten, whimpering under the veil of sleep, creviced lips moving, her scrawny hands clawing at her pillow. Maria strokes the sparse silver hair and kisses Elsie's temple, as she might do to soothe a child, if she had such a thing.

She picks up the empty glass from the floor where Elsie threw it and checks the carpet for bloodstains. She has already cleaned it, furious, frenzied, but she will need to repeat the process after she has dealt with the worse thing. Back in the kitchen, flinching at the sight that greets her there, she runs the tap cold to refill the glass. She places the water next to the old woman in case she wakes in the night, although, thank God, she seems to have settled again, which is something of a miracle in the circumstances.

She ignores the frantic scratching at the door, the desolate pleas for freedom.

Three deep breaths and she returns to finish cleaning the kitchen floor, pouring away another bowlful of filthy water, wiping down the sink, and stuffing the cloth in with the ruined towels. She will need to bleach the surfaces again later, scour the corners with a toothbrush.

She swills round the dregs of sherry in the chipped *God Save The Queen* mug, the only alcohol she could find, and downs it. Then she rolls back her shoulders and faces the old man. She lifts him from his chair, light as a bird, scoops him up into a tender embrace, holding him close to her heart as she elbows open the back door, careful with the step. Then she carries him out to the garden, into the chill of the night air, laying him down on the wet

2

grass next to the ruined flowerbed alongside the gaping hole in the black earth where she will bury his bloodied, battered body.

2

That morning had been a normal day – a different life . . .

Her first regular job of the week is number 43. It is never a flying start.

'Here, HERE, yes?' The woman points, reaching up to mime wiping the top of the doorframe. She beckons Maria through to the dining room and points to the skirting board, dips like she's receiving a damehood, and runs her finger along one of the grooves before holding it aloft accusingly.

'See? Here, too.' She thrusts the can of Mr Sheen in Maria's face. 'All around.' She sweeps her arm in a circle, signifying the entirety of the house. 'And I want you gone by nine thirty today, yes?'

Maria brings some basic cleaning materials, but they are not deemed good enough for number 43.

The woman turns on her heel, but cranes back to say louder, 'No later than NINE THIRTY!' as if Maria is deaf.

5

Her first client of the day and the first time she bites back a comment.

While not deaf, Maria has affected dumbness in most of the homes she cleans – 'creeping round like a bleeding mouse', as Elsie put it. Easier that way. Maria gives a thumbs-up and flashes what she hopes is a cheery acquiescence, but when Nine-Thirty Woman rushes away to make a *very important phone call* (in this house every phone call is *very important*), Maria lets her face fall – resting bitch face, she's been told.

After another half-hour stretching high and stooping low, Maria's back aches. She stands, rubbing her knuckles into her lumbar region before heading upstairs. The throb intensifies with the mopping. Her ankle's also playing up, as it often does when the weather's cold. It's February, a gnawing damp early in the mornings, a slicing wind in the afternoons. Where's global warming when you need it?

She's on her knees trying to remove splatters of dried-on shit from the rim of the toilet bowl when the woman opens the bathroom door and startles to see her.

'God, aren't you done in here yet?' she exclaims and tuts, shamed into scuttling away to the downstairs loo. The people who live in these lovely homes do not like to be reminded of their own filth.

They must notice this dirt. How hard would it be to clean it up as soon as it happens, rather than letting it dry on hard? Maria realises she's muttering to herself.

The woman exacts her revenge when Maria is about to leave, blocking her way out of the front door.

'Next week you can make up this half-hour,' she

announces. 'I want a deep clean of the en-suite tiles. I can see mould starting on the grouting by the shower head.' This is said as if Maria herself might have summoned the spores to grow.

'And you really must manage your time better. I need you to do some ironing next week.'

Perhaps I could shove a broom up my bum and do the floor at the same time? Although she doesn't say this, Maria's face must do something of its own accord because her employer sighs loudly and adds, 'You know, I don't appreciate having to watch you scowl. Thousands of people like you would be glad of a job like this.'

Maria wonders who *people like her* are supposed to be. Swallowing a retort is harder work than the mopping.

It can take her forty-five minutes to travel between the first two jobs, due to the unpredictability of the bus. The number 91 usually arrives in pairs, with an average wait of around a fortnight in-between. She might be better walking – it would probably be quicker – but it's a heavy day, it's just started to drizzle, and any opportunity to take the load off is welcome. She gets on at Russell Square and eats her late breakfast, a cheese and pickle sandwich, as she sits on the top deck. If she was a different sort of person, this might qualify as brunch. She washes it down with a swig of bottled water that came with the meal deal – special offer, half price – and pops in a chewing gum. God knows what she'd do if she needed a dentist.

She does the sums in her head – how much has she got

left from last week's wages for something to eat this evening? With the extra jobs she's doing, will she manage to get to the food bank tomorrow before everything's gone? Will the biscuits and tea her next client occasionally provides be enough to stop her belly rumbling? Will she go to bed hungry again?

There's not a day goes by when Maria isn't doing these calculations, worrying about pennies pretty much every waking hour. It is both terrifying and boring as fuck.

She alights at Carnegie Street and walks through to Cloudesley Square – a home here in Islington's leafy oasis could buy an entire street where she grew up.

She hears a familiar *thud thud thud* as she approaches the door to the house. When Maria gets the keys out of the pocket of her fleece body warmer, the sound gets more frenetic, and as soon as she opens the door, Minty's soft wet muzzle is pushing against her hand, the rest of the dog wiggling a delirious greeting accompanied by joyful yelps. Sometimes the animal does a wee of delight when she arrives, but Maria doesn't mind cleaning that up because nothing on God's earth has ever been so pleased to see her.

Minty makes Maria smile – a real smile, not the one offered to new clients to signal that she will be a benign presence in their homes, the forced professional smile reassuring, *you can trust me with your property and possessions, with your animals and children.* Those smiles are wearing.

She walks through to the kitchen and opens the back door so Minty can run wild. The dog does a single manic lap of the garden, squats briefly, then thunders back in to lean the whole of her weight against Maria's thigh.

This is true love, pure love, total joy. She feels sorry for the animal, so often left alone all day.

'Oh, please don't call her that!' gasped the owner, Mrs Santos, when she first referred to the animal as 'a good bitch'. It was intended as praise.

'I meant she's a good bitch to breed with?' explained Maria, attempting to make conversation.

But no, Minty is to be referred to as a 'girl dog' and she will never have puppies.

The real bitch in this house is the soon-to-be-teenage daughter who eyes Maria suspiciously when there's no school, telling her mother loudly, to make sure she's overheard, that 'the cleaner hasn't done under the bed', although her room is so messy it's a wonder she can find any place to sleep. The girl knows Maria's name, but never uses it.

There's also a boy in the house. Maria finds it difficult to look at him – he has dimples like Joby, which dredges up complicated emotions from her past.

She has never encountered the man of the house, although there are male clothes and shoes around the bedroom, aftershave in the bathroom. Her line of work – licence to snoop.

The dog adores the two children, a feeling not obviously reciprocated. Minty seems at her happiest when they're at home in the school holidays, lying as close to them as she's allowed, yet she always finds time to fuss Maria just the same, trotting over as if to say, *You're not my pack, but you are kind to me, therefore I love you*.

Maria is no one's family any more. Elsie is the nearest thing she's got.

She would love a dog. One day, she promises herself, she'll live in a flat that doesn't ban animals, perhaps somewhere she doesn't need earplugs and chains on her door; a place that more resembles a home.

Small ambitions.

Unusually, today Mrs Santos is at home because she has, 'an appointment at the hairdresser later this morning and it's really not worth travelling all the way into work and back again for only two hours at my desk, you know'. They sometimes tell her details like this, these people who pay for her to tidy up after them. Maria's presence makes women uncomfortable, as if she might be judging them within the sanctuary of their own homes. Well, she is but . . .

Men don't suffer the same guilt. They can easily ignore her cleaning while they sit at their computers or play on their Xboxes. She has to ask some of them to move their legs out of the way as she mops, or she might have to dust around them. Some covertly observe her as she works, checking her, or her finishes, and Maria does not like to be watched.

She is busy hoovering beneath the sideboard when Mrs Santos appears, making her jump.

'Hello! *Hello*?' She's beckoned. Maria switches off the vacuum and hurries after her employer to the kitchen.

'Can you give me a hand with this?'

The woman is struggling with the top of a mayonnaise jar. Maria takes it from her and twists off the lid in one swift movement.

'You're a godsend,' smiles Mrs Santos.

She is one of the nicer employers. She paid Maria cash

in hand when the family went to Dorset for two weeks last year. Maria was tasked with watering the plants in both the house and the garden, as well as giving the interiors of the cupboards a 'spring clean', even though it was the middle of August.

'Just to keep an eye on the place, really,' trilled Mrs Santos. 'Of course, there won't be very much to do with us away, but I'll still pay you the same amount.' Her expression was one befitting Mother Teresa.

Finally, thankfully, her employer leaves for the hair appointment and Maria gets on with it.

As she tackles the hob, she's so tired she tunes out of what she's doing and finds herself back cleaning the caravan – but that's a dangerous place to be. She shakes her head to clear the images and refocuses on the stainless steel beneath her fingers. But that transports her to the clinical surfaces from her times in hospital, so she bends to stroke the dog again, to ground herself, to feel something benign. She cannot allow herself to slip into any thoughts involving Joby, or the aftermath.

When Maria finishes, she gives Minty a handful of dog treats as she leaves. She can't bear to hear the dog's piteous whines as she abandons her.

There are three more Monday jobs to go, including a new flat to clean, and by the time she finishes up at Elsie's and gets back to the poky bedsit in the arse end of Wood Green that in no way resembles a home, Maria will be shattered. She calibrates her tiredness, looks forwards to a certain degree of exhaustion. If she's lucky, she might crash out, sleep a few hours before she's sliced awake once more by dark dreams.

Maria never willingly takes time off. Since Spain, she's never had a holiday. Since Spain has she ever really relaxed?

The new job is a three-bedroom round the back of the big Sainsbury's near Hornsey overground. She finds it stressful meeting new clients, although often this preliminary vetting is the only time Maria will ever see the homeowner.

The door is opened by an angular middle-aged man wearing a grubby tracksuit and Crocs.

'What pronouns would you like me to use?' he enquires.

'Sorry?'

'How should I refer to you? What should I call you – he-she-they, et cetera?'

'*Et cetera*?'

'I don't want to cause offence.'

'I'm sorry. I don't understand?'

'He or she? Chap or *chap-ess*? You know, shepherd, shepherdess, actor, actress, although, I suppose they're all *ac-tors* these days . . .'

Maria reacts with a blank stare.

The man can't hold her gaze and flusters, 'So . . . where are you from?'

'Haringey.'

'And,' he sighs heavily, apparently exhausted by small talk, 'before that?'

'Sheffield.'

Maria never says where she's really from. One of her

irrational fears is that, if she talks about her real home or says Joby's name out loud, he, or his family, might suddenly materialise in a puff of smoke. She's superstitious like that. She's constantly looking over her shoulder, even here in London, tortured by a foreboding that one of Joby's relatives will somehow find her and exact a terrible revenge.

This new client seems irritated by her presence already. He walks briskly, guiding her through to the kitchenette where not a single surface is clear of debris.

'My wife usually deals with all this . . .' (*Burglary? Explosion?* considers Maria.) 'But she's away.'

Along with the pile of chaotic dirty dishes there are two pans on the cooker – one featuring burned beans, by the look of it – which she'll probably need to chisel off, and another with a growth that might be a penicillin experiment.

'Have you been cleaning long?' he asks, as if this is a cocktail party.

'Long enough,' she replies. *Far too long* is the truth.

She guesses some of his other unasked questions. Has the agency sent someone who'll turn up on time, work hard and keep their mouth shut, or someone who could hack into the computer and steal the contents of the bank accounts?

She lets the homeowner make of her what he will. She will slide from his mind soon enough and he'll most likely make sure to be out this time next week.

'Can you just crack on in here, please?'

'Of course.'

He turns his back.

'Excuse me? Where's the stuff for the dishwasher?'

The man harrumphs around the kitchen, scrabbles under

the sink until he finds a bottle of Fairy Liquid, waving it aloft triumphantly before plonking it on the table. 'Just holler if there's anything else you need,' he calls as he retreats.

She's about to point out the mistake with the washing-up liquid, but by the tone of his voice guesses that she is never to disturb him again.

Upstairs, a single pubic hair greets her in the bath.

So many cleaning jobs.

Maria didn't have the energy to hate this life exactly; all the same, she deeply resented it. It was gruelling, soul-sapping.

But what she wouldn't give to have that boring old life back again right now.

Because her *new improved* skills surpass everyday scouring and tidying and taking out the rubbish. Her special *deep* cleans now run to the removal of violent husbands and bodies rather than basic waste disposal.

Perhaps she should bill Elsie for the overtime.

3

Elsie's garden is a meagre piece of land, shaded by a tall lime tree on one side and an overgrown tangle of hazel on the other. Narrow, although Elsie brags that for London it's a fair old size.

Maria has been encouraged to plant herbs in one corner, and a smattering of jolly bulbs – daffodils, frayed tulips and grape hyacinths. 'The forget-me-knots seed themselves,' crowed Elsie, grinning, like this was a fabulous gift from Mother Nature herself.

The vegetable patch, Elsie's pride and joy, has yielded enough tomatoes for perhaps two meals in as many years.

Four years Maria's worked here – no, five. Time gets away from her.

There's been too much else to deal with for Maria to garden much recently, but now she digs. No moon, but she can see well enough with the kitchen light and the glow from the streetlights to the side of the fence. She needs to make the grave deeper. Hard to estimate this sort of thing.

Hours of digging, muscles straining. Deep, deeper, deepest. There are foxes here.

Her eyes keep flicking up to the neighbours' window to her left. Students. For once it is quiet next door. Hopefully they've partied themselves out over the weekend, or they might be away at an all-night party now, or something. She's not entirely sure how many lads officially live there – there always seem to be new faces. It would only take one to look out . . .

The widow in the house to her right goes to bed early. *Let her sleep deeply*, prays Maria.

What would she say if anyone saw her? 'Hi! Me? Night gardening. Yes, it's a thing! This dark shape you can't quite make out? Big bag of fertiliser. Ha ha. Huge.'

She's probably sweating as much from anxiety as from the work, and her hands are filthied from the digging along with the seepages from the old man. The night air is dank, and her ankle feels the cold deep within the bone – old injuries reminding her of their origin story.

Perhaps a metre more to be on the safe side and then she will roll the body into the pit, shovelling soil on top of his battered face and skull, stuffing earth into his nasty mouth.

Her body is shaking with fatigue, but she urges herself on. She knows she must keep going. As soon as she stops, she might collapse.

An owl hoots nearby, the cry soft as a caress.

And instantly she's back there, back with Joby—

Nights of campfires sparking high into a blue-black sky and dancing under endless stars and Joby burrowing into her hair, telling her how much he loved her, and the fucking, so much fucking at the start, and laughter and then screams, and the yearning cry of a solitary owl on a night with a moon so bright she saw her own shadow as she dug another grave—

She drives the spade hard into the ground to rid herself of the memories – that's a place she dare not revisit.

The owl calls again.

She was surprised to hear owls in the city when she first came to London. Elsie said they lived in the high trees, feeding on rats who grew plump on litter discarded by the kebab shops along Green Lanes.

'But they're not the same as country owls, this lot,' explained Elsie with her serious face on. 'Their calls are different. If you listen carefully, they hoot, "T'wit t'whoo-you-lookin-at!"' She cackled her lovely low laugh.

Maria stretches up, squeezing her shoulders to loosen them, and returns to the kitchen.

She had shut Elsie's cats in the living room to keep them out of the way and they're now frantically scratching at the door, desperate to investigate, sensing blood. They can't escape their basic natures – but who can?

She wraps two dishcloths around her palms so she can continue digging and heads back out into the cold night air.

Maria has often been surprised by her body's resilience.

It keeps going, some deep spark pushing her onwards, forwards: when she stumbled down the mountain, down and down, despite feeling she could not take one single step more; when she summoned all her strength to fight back against the man looming above her with an axe . . . This basic life force does not let her lie down and give up; it does not let her rest. But in her opinion, this doesn't make her a survivor, and it doesn't make her brave – it just makes her a glutton for punishment.

She sets to digging again, the soil heavy. A stone clashes against the metal of the spade, the shock jolting up the handle and through her spine. It's bigger than it first appears, and she struggles to manoeuvre the tip of the spade underneath, trying to lever it away from the cold earth clinging to it in protest. Her arms rebel as she attempts to prise it out, and she loses her hold on the spade, slips, falls back, bruising her tailbone on the hard ground at the bottom of the hole.

She could lie here a moment, catch her breath, but the wetness of the earth is soaking through her trousers, icy fingers on her skin.

Silently she tells herself to get a grip, reminds herself why she's doing this, picks up the spade and starts again, heaving leaden dirt into a pile next to the crater.

Eventually she climbs out of the pit and stands, swaying a moment, then she braces and pushes the old man hard with the sole of her foot to roll him over. Her ankle protests at the kick but there's a satisfying 'whoomph' as he hits the bottom of the grave.

She throws his walking stick in after him and the bedroom

rug because she'll never get the blood out of that.

Another sound makes her pause. A cry. She wheels round but sees nothing at the neighbours' windows. It might be the fox family she's seen over by the garages round the back of the gardens. They loll on top of the flat roofs on sunny days, like an urban lion pride.

In some ways it's harder filling in the hole than it was digging it, although gravity is now on her side. She was terrified that someone would see the old man lying on the grass, although it's hardly less suspicious filling in a giant body-shaped trench in the middle of the night than it is digging one. She hurries, desperate to be done with it.

Finally, she flattens down the loose earth by walking up and down, then stamping on top of it. The idea of dancing on his grave does not horrify her. She shovels the last of the dirt over the top, kneeling to replant the shrubs, hastily shoving them in and squashing down the moist soil around the roots. The sweat cooling on her back makes her shiver. She pushes some unearthed stones between the plants, making a half-arsed rockery around the six sad rose bushes – more than the old bastard deserves.

She says no words over the small mound. The owl alone sends a plaintive blessing.

Maria's mind shoots ahead, worrying. How will Elsie be in the morning? How might she react when she wakes? What on earth can Maria say to her? How can she soothe her, given what's happened? The old girl does not like change of any kind. Dementia makes her reactions unpredictable at the best of times, let alone after a night of screams and blows, when her husband has been

19

clubbed over the head with his own walking stick, dying in a puddle of blood on the bedside rug right in front of her.

4

She stands under Elsie's shower letting the water wash away dirt and worse, the warmth easing the shrieks along her shoulders, her arms now as floppy as cooked spaghetti. Scrubbing the nailbrush into the ingrained mud and blood beneath her nails, she tries to rid herself of the guilt and shame and anger of the night. And she allows herself to sniffle a little, for all she's lost and all she still might lose – for Elsie and Joby, for her mother and father, for her old life. Not one of those tears is for what now lies beneath the heavy soil in the back garden.

Elsie doesn't have a spare dressing gown, so Maria wraps a bath towel around her chest, switches on the heating, takes the load out of the washing machine and pushes in her own fouled clothes. She drapes the clean towels across the clotheshorse next to the radiator and puts on the kettle, trying to think what might happen next.

Her hands tremble like an alkie's.

The scratching at the door becomes more demented and is now accompanied by a chorus of pathetic yowls. When she lets the cats out of the living room they charge at her, pushing at her legs with demanding whiskers, like a shoal of furry sharks.

'Come on then, you lot.' She gets the large Tupperware container out of the bottom cupboard and starts scooping the crunchy cat food into the four dishes.

When Maria first started work at Elsie's she'd asked if they each had their own dish. Elsie snorted. 'You've never had cats, have you.' It wasn't a question.

Before the feeding frenzy gets underway, Maria strokes each animal and puts a bowl in front of it. Boris always gets his first. 'He's a right greedy bastard,' says Elsie fondly. The girls get theirs next – Spotty and Sweetie – sisters, both built like tanks, followed by the gentle ginger, Harry, who never knows what day it is.

Sweetie is Maria's favourite. She greets her gently, patting Maria's hand with the pads of her paw, then rolling on to her back, exposing her soft speckled belly. She suspects Sweetie is also Elsie's favourite, although she swears she loves them 'all the same, with all my heart'.

Elsie never had kids.

Maria likes to watch the old woman with her animals. The tender moments where she sits and strokes them are like a meditation.

Maria has always wanted a pet, but she's never had the chance, not since she was a kid. Dog or cat, she wouldn't mind. With Elsie's decline over the last twelve months, Maria worries what might happen to her cats.

By the time Elsie stirs, the sky has lightened but Maria's heart has not. She's heaved the washing machine away from the wall and is frantically scouring underneath it. Even though she can't see any bloodstains, she's afraid molecules of the old man might have found their way into the nooks and crannies, clinging to the handfuls of cat fur which collect under all the appliances and furniture in the house like tumbleweed.

When she hears the flush of the downstairs toilet, she pours Elsie her mug of builders' tea: strong, with two heaped spoonfuls of sugar. Maria's been trying to get Elsie to cut down on sweet things – it's not that she's overweight, but it can't be good for her. This morning, however, is not the time to sweat the small stuff.

By the sound of Elsie's voice humming her favourite songs – fragments of 'Let Me Call You Sweetheart' and 'Hit Me with Your Rhythm Stick' (she has an eclectic playlist, has Elsie) – the horrors of last night have obviously not yet surfaced.

Maria calls through, her voice strained: 'Do you need a hand?'

'No, darlin',' Elsie shouts back. 'All fine and dandy this end.'

A good day, then. Maria lets out a breath. The one positive thing about the state of Elsie's brain is the likelihood of her having forgotten what happened last night.

Elsie comes through to the kitchen in her bunny-ears dressing gown and plonks down at the table with a soft groan. Maria kisses the top of her head and the cats swarm around the old woman's legs as she fusses them. She chomps down on a mouthful of the toast and Marmite Maria's laid out for her and starts in the middle of a sentence, talking with her mouth full.

'We met on a course in Oxford, you know. Ruskin College. Young trade unionists, and all that malarkey.'

'Who?' asks Maria, who is used to joining in conversations halfway through. She's also used to Elsie trailing off without warning, giant leaps between topics, or the more disturbing silences.

'Richard. Richard somebody . . . He smoked those little cigars. Stunk of them. Ooh, I loved the smell of them.' There's a long pause. 'Should've married him.' She glugs her tea. 'Hamlet!'

Unlikely, thinks Maria. 'What happened?' she asks.

Elsie seems to properly register Maria for the first time and smiles up at her. 'Life, darlin'. Life.' She sighs and her face crumples. Then suddenly, she adds, 'Happiness is a cigar called Hamlet!' She beams up at Maria. 'Are you having any . . . any . . .?'

Maria watches Elsie's fingers, which are in constant motion, carving emotions and expressions out of the air in place of the words and thought fragments she's now missing. They're covered in rings like Joby's mother's hands were, although Elsie's rings are tiny in comparison and the stones more likely to be chips of glass.

'Bought them all myself,' Elsie once told her. 'Apart from that one,' she nodded, indicating the thin band of her wedding ring. Elsie's husband, Nick, hadn't even bought her an engagement ring – a portent of what was to come.

24

Maria has been worried about what they'd do if they needed to get the rings off, swollen as Elsie's knuckles are.

'Call the fire brigade to cut 'em off,' suggested Elsie. 'And get 'em to do one of those calendars with their tops off while they're here!'

Elsie nods for Maria to sit with her. 'Have a brew,' she encourages. Then, clocking Maria is only wearing a bath towel, she asks, 'What have you come as?'

Elsie has always insisted on tea breaks. Maria felt flustered when she first started cleaning for Elsie, embarrassed to take the Mr Kipling Cherry Bakewell being thrust towards her. By the time she met Elsie, she'd already spent five years cleaning in London, and she was worn down with it.

'Used to be a union rep, dint I?' Elsie smiled, flashing teeth and gaps. 'Tea and a nice bit of cake and a fag, back in the days when it was okay to smoke and okay to have a bit of meat on your bones. The good old days before calories.' She laughed. 'Your breaks are obligatory, darlin'. You can't let the bosses take the piss. Work through one break as a favour and they come to expect it. Give 'em an inch and the next minute they'll have you bent over a table shoving it up your Blackwall Tunnel.'

Elsie had loved her job and only retired at seventy. 'Worked all my life at that clothes factory. Only gave it up so the young 'uns could have a go,' she explained with pride in her voice. 'I've bought all my own things with my own money. Independent woman, me. That Beyoncé and me? Sisters, we are!'

'You're white and you haven't got a bum,' teased Maria. 'How can you be Beyoncé's sister?'

'I'm adopted,' grinned Elsie.

Maria now watches the old woman eat her breakfast. Elsie smiles at her and gives her a little wave. It makes Maria happy to see Elsie smile, but it's also worrying that she doesn't recall last night's horror show. But what is Maria supposed to do – remind her?

Elsie's been forgetting more things lately, although she reckons she's always been absent-minded. 'Even before my brain turned into that whatchamacallit cheese with all them holes in.'

It comes in waves – the gaps in her memory, the mood swings, the *absence*. Sometimes Elsie will sit stirring her tea like a broken-down robot, swirling the spoon round and round, staring at nothing. She can also lash out, hitting and swearing, slump into sobs, panic, confuse strangers with long dead family members. She can no longer be trusted to go to the local shops alone in case she gets lost.

Occasionally she forgets who Maria is, which cuts deep. Maria can't bear to lose someone else.

When Elsie's finished her toast, Maria takes the plate and puts it in the washing-up bowl. Elsie's always refused a dishwasher. 'Don't need one,' she declared. 'Don't want that Greta bleedin' Iceberg round here duffing me up.'

'Do you want the radio on?' asks Maria.

The old woman seems not to have heard. She sits daydreaming, a million miles away, but her face looks blank rather than pained, so Maria hopes her thoughts are easy ones. She switches on the radio because Elsie often responds to music.

Then she phones around trying to arrange cover for the next day. No one wants to do her overnight job, so she asks the cleaning agency to rearrange it for Wednesday, if the client's happy. Elsie's various trips to the doctor and other emergencies over the past few months have occasionally led to these last-minute changes of plan, but the other cleaners are usually more than happy to take on her jobs for the extra money. As far as her colleagues are concerned, nothing much has changed.

For Maria and Elsie everything has.

When she returns to the kitchen, Elsie is sitting quietly stroking Sweetie's ears until Spotty tries to join her sister on Elsie's lap and there's a kerfuffle about who gets possession, resulting in both cats jumping down in a huff.

She sits a while longer, then joins Maria at the sink, reaching up to pat her shoulder.

'Where have you put your pills?' asks Maria. She doesn't get a reply.

It's only when she's making Elsie a second mug of tea that Maria finds the pill bottle in the fridge next to the milk.

The news comes on the radio – a story about 'the rise of sourdough'.

'Ooh, I love new bread,' muses Elsie. 'Fresh bread straight from the oven . . . that smell! Shall we have toast for breakfast?' she asks, her voice high like a little girl's.

Perhaps forgetfulness is a blessing.

5

Elsie's nephew Del arrives mid-morning on his way into work.

Elsie looks up from the puzzle book she's tackling. Word searches are good for her brain, according to the Admiral nurse who specialises in 'cases' like Elsie's.

Maria is bleaching the kitchen cupboard doors. Again.

Elsie calls through to the hall, 'All right, Del?'

A fragile peace exists between the two of them. She says to Maria, 'Let's have a brew.'

'How's she been?' Del asks Maria, placing his briefcase on the side. He gives off harried-accountant vibes. Balding; crooked teeth; hardly any lips – not blessed in the looks department is Del.

'She had a bad night,' she replies, which hardly covers it.

Elsie likes her tea brewed in the ancient brown teapot then sloshed into her favourite Sex Pistols mug. 'Love me a bit of anarchy,' she grinned when Maria first commented on it. 'Love winding Del up. One of the capitalist elite, my darling nephew,' she sniffed.

The delightful Derek has been round much more often since Elsie's needs and mishaps have increased. He does indeed *bang on about money*, which is one of Elsie's main complaints, but he works for Barclays, so he's hardly Elon Musk.

When Maria first made tea for Del, Elsie whispered, 'Give him that decaf bollocks, babe. Me and you'll have the good teabags.' Said decaf was a mistake buy – Elsie had picked them up in a two-for-one deal. The best-before date had long expired.

Maria was taken aback by the way Elsie treated Del, although when he threw his Coke can in the bin rather than the recycling, she clocked at least one of the reasons Elsie didn't like him.

The other, more incendiary, reason is that, as Elsie often complains, 'He's forever on at us to sell up and move to them warden flats down Archway.' Elsie screwed up her face, as if the flats stank. 'Either that or he wants to ship me off to some bloody care home. The shifty little git's just after a slice of the proceeds from selling this gaff. And I will not be told where to end my days, by him or any other bugger, thank you very much. I'm staying put. It's mine, this place. *Mine.*'

Maria wasn't sure where Nick, the estranged husband, featured regarding ownership of the house. He had lived with Elsie when she first started cleaning for her, but he'd disappeared more or less completely about a year ago, around the time Elsie's health started deteriorating.

This was a blessing, as far as Maria could work out. Elsie always confided more information than she really wanted to know.

'Separate lives, babe. Suits me down to the ground. No love lost there. Can't be in the same room as him for five minutes without a blow-up. Biggest mistake of my bleedin' life, *him*. I blame the libido, darlin. *Rioting* it was in them days.'

Nick's side of the wardrobe was emptied and there was only the one photo of him left – a black-and-white shot from his semi-pro boxing days which resided in the lounge, a room Elsie rarely used.

On one of his rare visits, Maria witnessed a row – a high-decibel slanging match liberally peppered with the C-word on both sides which kicked off over Marcus Rashford. Elsie was left panting as her soon-to-be ex-husband stomped out of the house, shooting Maria a furious look as he slammed the door behind him.

'I'd take the knee to rub his smug face in it, but I'd never get up again,' Elsie said with a grimace.

Until he'd materialised on the warpath last night, Nick had been living with his sister. 'He's split up with his bit on the side and gone to stay with that snooty-arsed cow. If I was the girlfriend I'd think good riddance,' said Elsie.

Nick hasn't been party to the many discussions about Elsie's 'state of mind'. Del is the one involved these days. He irritates Maria almost as much as he does Elsie. There's nothing much she can put her finger on, although he smells of cigarettes, which sets Maria's teeth on edge, conjuring up echoes of Joby.

On a regular basis Del will say something like, 'I reckon it's time, don't you?' – trying to enlist Maria to his side, keen to see Elsie moved out of her home and be done with it.

But if Elsie hears anything of the sort, she goes *off on one*. A couple of weeks ago there was a huge barney.

'You mercenary little toerag,' she'd spat, lunging at Del with a fork.

'See?' squeaked Del, as if Maria hadn't noticed. 'She should be bloody well locked up.'

He backed away round the kitchen table as Maria grabbed the fork out of Elsie's hand.

'She just forgot she was holding it, that's all,' tried Maria.

'No. This is different league bollocks,' declared Del.

When he'd gone, Elsie sneered, 'Where there's a will there's a bunch of bastard relatives.'

Sharp as a tack sometimes.

Now Del makes his voice singsong, like he's talking to a five-year-old. 'You okay, Auntie Elsie?' he asks. 'You feeling okay?'

Elsie rolls her eyes.

'You had a bad night, yeah?'

Maria's heart plunges. What might she say?

'Nah. It was okay.' Elsie smiles. 'Had that Tom Hardy round. Begging me to marry him again he was. Won't leave me alone that lad. Going to have to get a restraining order.'

Del looks appalled.

'She's joking,' says Maria, as if it needs clarification. 'She had a few bad dreams, that's all. But I've taken the day off anyway to be on the safe side. Just to keep an eye on her.'

'Good, good,' says Del. 'And you'll be here for the nurse tomorrow morning?'

'Yeah.'

Del and Maria make sure at least one of them is around when the Admiral nurse visits.

'Well, I'll be making tracks, seeing as you're here,' he says, keen to be off. 'Bye, ladies.' He leaves his mug on the table rather than putting it on the side to be washed.

After he's gone, Maria fishes his discarded cigarette packet out of the bin and puts it in the recycling. Elsie nods a *told you so*.

'I'm just going to change your bed,' says Maria.

'What you going to change it into?' says Elsie.

Maria has to steel herself to go back into Elsie's room. She scrubbed the carpet like a maniac last night, but now she sees there's still a tiny smear of blood left on the duvet cover. She'll go over every surface again with the bleach spray after she's put the bedclothes on for the hottest wash.

6

Maria was messy as a kid. Frankie, her dad's girlfriend, was constantly on at her about her bedroom. 'Clean this tip up!' she'd nag, and Maria would say nothing, but she'd think, *What's it got to do with you? You don't even live here* – although Frankie was itching to move in with them.

Her dad rarely had a go at Maria, but he took Frankie's side on this topic. 'Shift some of it, yeah, love. We'll have mice if you don't tidy up a bit.' But he said it with a smile, so she never took him seriously. And he bought her one, when she answered back that once, saying that she'd 'really like a mouse, actually'. They called it Houdini for obvious reasons.

She cleaned for her gran, who bunged her a couple of quid every time she ran a duster half-heartedly over her surfaces. Maria wasn't a good cleaner back then, always keen to get away to netball practice, or hang out with her mates. It made her feel bad, taking the money. Her gran lived off her pension, if it could be called living – survived, might describe it better – haunting Morrisons at the end of play when they did the reductions; having her hair done on the Pensioners' Special afternoons when they let the trainees loose at the college up on Thornborough Road, which accounted for the shock of bright acid-yellow frizz one April.

Still, Maria took the cash and then she'd skip off with her friends as soon as she could. If she stayed, her gran would only start wittering on about boring stuff, like how to put vinegar and olive oil on your hair to make it shine, but Maria said she wasn't a bloody salad, and her gran told her not to swear.

Maria couldn't wait to escape.

She'd skipped off early with her mates the day her gran took a tumble. That's how her dad put it: 'took a tumble', as if it was a gentle trip, not a terrifying plunge that smashed both her knees and one cheekbone to smithereens.

When Maria went to visit and saw her gran's face – a kaleidoscope of wrong colours against the off-white hospital pillow – she thought she might heave. She confessed to her dad in great gulping sobs, admitting that she'd left her gran's house early.

As the old woman was lying at the bottom of her stairs, twisted in agony, bleeding into the ancient Axminster carpet, Maria was titivating, getting ready for a pointless party, and she'd never be able to change that.

He said not to worry. 'Even if you had been there, there's nowt much you could have done to stop her going over,' he reasoned as he patted Maria's head like she was a dog. And that was probably true, although she could have called for the ambulance a damn sight sooner.

For one brief week it looked like her gran might come home, albeit in a wheelchair, but then the pneumonia saw her off.

Maria wondered if she might be struck down in the church during the funeral, the full-on bum-numbing affair her gran had wanted. Her dad did his best to make the day okay, but then it wasn't his mother and he'd not loved the old girl like Maria did – the only blood connection to her mum, a woman she'd never met.

She used to ask her dad things about her mother when she was little. She'd badger him until he gave up titbits: her mum had been good at school; she'd wanted to travel, perhaps teach. She'd wanted a big family, too.

She didn't get a single one of her wishes.

The family never had a foreign holiday, although Maria banged on about going somewhere *abroad* for ages, until her dad's face told her to shut up about it, in the same way her dad stopped mentioning her mum so much because of what Frankie's face did.

Maria can still blush to remember the one time, years ago, when she asked Frankie, 'Are you my mum now?' Her dad's *girlfriend* (she was nearing forty at the time and it was hard to imagine Frankie had ever been a girl) just smiled an embarrassed smile and shook her head.

Her dad had smiled a different sort of smile and said, 'In her dreams.' He never considered it might be in Maria's dreams, but seeing as she'd killed one mother, she probably didn't deserve another.

Her gran had told her how her mum died. 'She bled to death, chick. When you were born.'

A massive haemorrhage killed her, right after her daughter, her only child, battled her way into the world. Maria learned that word from her gran early on, before she even went to school – 'cat', 'dog', 'ball', '*haem-orr-hage*'.

There was no one to ask about her mum after her gran died.

She helped her dad clear out her gran's house. She gave him a hand cleaning the windows and mopping the floors, but they never managed to get the blood out of the carpet at the bottom of the stairs. It had to be prised up and taken down the tip with the rest of the rubbish.

Now Maria knows better. She can get blood out of a carpet these days. She has professional liquids.

She has had to learn how to clean. The guilt always came naturally.

7

After Del leaves, Maria is on edge, jumping at every noise. The lack of sleep makes it harder to guard against the vile images clouding her mind and it takes all her energy not to go over and over what happened the previous night. She feels sick and sweaty, and when she catches sight of herself in the bathroom mirror she looks haunted.

She watches Elsie for any signs of trauma. The only difference seems to be that she's quieter than usual. Maria isn't sure if this is a sign of a deeper wound, or is she just worn out?

Maria herself is dog tired. And she's horrified by the night's violence – furious at the assault on Elsie; shocked by her own actions; terrified at the consequences that might ruin both their lives. She's reeling with it all. She can't make sense of it. Perhaps she never will. It feels unreal – a living nightmare.

By the time Maria has done the rest of the laundry and finished the housework, made Elsie soup for lunch, and popped to the shops to replenish the biscuits and buy something for Elsie's tea, she's too exhausted to go back to her bedsit. She needs to be back at Elsie's first thing in the morning for the nurse's visit anyway.

She asks Elsie if she can stay.

'Don't be daft, darlin', of course you can.' Elsie gives her a bony bear hug.

Elsie always seemed happy when Maria slept over, but she was afraid of outstaying her welcome. She knew she needed to have the conversation with Del about her role caring for his aunt, but each time she saw him, she bottled it, afraid it would catalyse the end of the unofficial arrangement. In an ideal world, Maria would move in with Elsie and look after her full time. Perhaps, with a small wage and no rent to pay, she could give up her other cleaning jobs and just care for Elsie. It might stop her worrying so much when she had to leave her.

Maria is on her last legs by early evening. After their tea of fish fingers and beans (Elsie had reverted to her favourite childhood foods), they watch a bit of telly and she goes to bed at the same time as Elsie. She barely manages to read for half an hour before she slips into a deep, thankfully dreamless, sleep.

Loud music from the students' house wakes her at two. She is just about to march round there and give them what for, but it quietens again, allowing her to slip back to her night terrors.

When her eyes are open she refuses to look too closely

at what she has done; works hard to distract herself. But as soon as her eyes close, her subconscious tries to unravel her clashing emotions – fear and fury, a sense of both righteousness and despair. Her dreams replay, forcing her to relive sickening scenes.

She jolts awake again long before the dawn to panic about what might happen next.

The doorbell rings as Maria is scrubbing the kitchen floor, which is already spotless, but . . .

The Admiral nurse's name is Comfort. There's a Faith and a Charity in her family back home in Nigeria and a Hope in Cockfosters. Sadly, the Joy died as a child – malaria. Elsie took to the nurse immediately and, while she often forgets exactly who the woman is, she takes to her again on most of her visits.

Maria greets the nurse, taking her umbrella as Comfort shakes out her sodden coat on the doorstep before hanging it up in the hallway. She leaves her hat on, although that too looks waterlogged.

Today, Elsie seems to be having a good day. She obviously remembers Comfort, although she's forgotten her name. Usually, a good day would make Maria happy, but now she's afraid Elsie might blab something she shouldn't, so she hovers in the kitchen after she's made the tea, in case she needs to distract her. So far, she hasn't said a word about her erstwhile husband, or the manner of his untimely death. Maria is anxious it doesn't happen now.

Comfort chats to Elsie, holding the old woman's hand as

it squeezes and grips her own. Thankfully the topic of conversation is the weather rather than more taxing subjects.

'Yes, it is *sooo* wet,' says Comfort, as they all gaze out of the window at the incessant rain, agreeing on the degree of wetness.

'Cats and dogs,' supplies Elsie.

Comfort looks round in case one of the actual cats appears. She is not at all keen on them, so Maria has shut them in the living room – all except Sweetie, who was nowhere to be found.

Maria's belly contracts as she looks out at the rain and notices that what was a slight mound in the garden, until the heavens opened last night, is now looking more than a little concave.

Comfort is smiley as the chat continues; but then, she's always smiley. She was smiley as she discussed the trajectory of Elsie's condition with Del and Elsie some months back as Maria sat alongside and listened. They were told how parts of Elsie's mind would shut down; the person they knew would slowly disappear. She might become furious or terrified by things she didn't recognise. Her world would shrink. She might begin to fear anything outside of her home, her room, until eventually she would be imprisoned within the confines of her skull. 'The light will be on but there'll be no one at home. I'll be totally doolally,' as Elsie herself put it. Of course, Comfort didn't put it exactly like that, although her professional words amounted to pretty much the same thing.

Today Comfort attempts to reassure Maria that Elsie doesn't seem to have had a further decline with a cheery

'Nothing to worry about', but despite Comfort's wonderful enunciation, Maria's worries continue on high alert through several rounds of tea. The good biscuits make an appearance. On other days, this would constitute a successful visit.

Elsie tunes out of the conversation at some point. She sits staring through the window. Maria realises she's gazing at Sweetie, who's jumped up on the garden fence, sheltering under a branch. The soggy cat stares back, the thoughts of both the woman and the feline unfathomable.

When she finally closes the door behind the nurse, Maria leans her head against the wall and exhales. Her jaw unclenches a little. The first of many trials overcome.

But what might happen next? What will she do when Elsie is finally deemed 'too doolally' and whisked away into care despite her protestations? The old woman has threatened to chain herself to a tree rather than leave this house and even before the new imperative beneath the rose bushes, Maria has been campaigning to keep Elsie at home for as long as possible, knowing the upheaval of a move would really upset her. So far Del has agreed, but only because Elsie frequently swears that she'll top herself if she's forced into 'one of those bloody places'.

Now it's essential that no one buys the house and digs up the garden. You could say, a matter of life and death, thinks Maria grimly.

Her belly is sloshing with the three mugs of tea she's consumed, and she pops to the loo. The blisters on her palms from the night dig are sore and she puts plasters on them. When she comes out of the bathroom, the kitchen door is swinging open. She hurries into the garden after Elsie, who's made her escape through the back gate twice – even though it's locked, she always seems to remember where the key's kept in the kitchen drawer.

This time Elsie hasn't made a bid for freedom. Instead, she's wandered down to the bottom of the garden, the downpour making her hair transparent so her skull shows through. She looks back to the house, where Maria is frozen, framed by the kitchen doorway, watching with horror as Elsie stands in the middle of the flowerbed – the rose bushes and rocks and pile of sodden earth on top of her husband's makeshift grave.

Elsie stares down at her feet.

Maria rushes out into the garden and takes hold of the old woman's arm, trying to drag her out of the rain. Elsie resists with a sharp, 'No!'

The snarl on her face makes Maria let go and take a step back. Elsie's had a few of these temper tantrums over the past months. She threw a mug across the kitchen a couple of weeks ago, although Piers Morgan was being interviewed on the radio at the time. The moods can flare up out of the blue, but they usually die down again within seconds.

Maria softens her voice and tries, 'Come on, love. You're soaked. Let's get you inside.'

Again, 'NO!'

'What do want us to do out here, then?' asks Maria. 'Synchronised swimming?'

Elsie turns her face up to the heavens and grins.

Maria runs back to the house and ferrets out an umbrella, although Elsie seems happy enough standing in the deluge. She'll warm her up and dry her off as soon as she gets her back inside. But when she tries to cover Elsie's head with the brolly, Elsie pushes her away, stepping to the side and slipping a little on the wet grass of the shabby lawn.

'These . . .' Elsie indicates the rose bushes, frantically pointing – the word for roses eluding her. '*These* aren't *here.*'

'I moved them,' says Maria quietly. She's not sure if Elsie can hear over the rain battering down on the umbrella.

She inches towards her but Elsie dodges from under the brim and reaches out her arms, palms up to the sky.

Maria tries again: 'What about some warm water, hey? A nice hot shower?'

Elsie doesn't move, but this time when Maria gently takes hold of her arm, she doesn't pull away. Maria starts slowly steering her towards the kitchen and they're almost at the door when Elsie makes another dash, scuttling back towards the one bit of the garden Maria doesn't want her anywhere near. For a seventy-six-year-old who struggles with stairs, she can be surprisingly fast on the flat. She skids a little near the disturbed earth, halts, then kicks out at one of the rose bushes, the other slippered foot sinking into the mud. And she cackles.

'Elsie! Elsie? What are you doing?'

The laugh turns nasty, higher – a yelp, a yowl.

The noise stops as suddenly as it had started, and Elsie turns to Maria. '*Him.* Most people . . .' Eyes intense, her hands frantically trying to carve the words out of the air and the rain, then jabbing her finger down towards the grave. '*Him!* Most people just have . . . garden gnomes!'

She beams.

Then she turns and shuffle-trots past Maria back inside the kitchen.

8

Apart from Elsie, the only other person who regularly makes Maria tea is Brian, who lives in one of the side roads near the Crouch End Clock Tower. She wishes he wouldn't. His concoctions are likely to be exotic combinations of things like fennel and blackcurrant and possibly dandruff – organic, naturally. Not a normal teabag to be found in the flat, no hope of Tetley or (heaven forbid) cow's milk.

Maria likes the Clock Tower because it reminds her of her hometown, although the streets of Coalville never featured tiny pictures drawn on pieces of discarded chewing gum. Artistic, Crouch End. Also, seemingly, the spiritual birthplace of sourdough and artisan coffee, given the number of places that sell both.

She usually does Brian on Tuesday afternoons, after the early-doors office block in Finsbury Park and the *Casualty* actress's flat on the 'Highgate Borders' – a place entirely

47

made up by estate agents – but there's been a rejig this week due to the recent *unforeseen circumstances*.

One of Elsie's friends from the community centre is sitting with her this afternoon while Maria is out cleaning, then Del will take over when he gets back from the bank. Despite Elsie's antipathy, it's Del who'll stay overnight when Maria's working, or if she's back at her bedsit, so fair play to him. It makes her feel sick to think of what Elsie might say to Del, or anyone else, but what can she do? She has to work. She still has to buy her travel card and cleaning materials and her own food and pay rent on the bedsit, although she hardly stays there these days. Even if Del agreed that she should move in with Elsie full time, she'd still need to give her landlord notice.

Even without the added terror of the new garden feature, these worries are too big to wield, so Maria forces herself to focus on walking.

Maria first met Brian just before he was 'signed off with stress' six months ago, and ever after he's been at home when she arrives. Sadly, this means a 'tisane' of some sort will be offered, plus a variety of pastries from Dunns Bakery. Brian regularly enthuses, 'Their cakes have been on *Killing Eve*!' but the only thing that matters to her is the sugar kick.

Sometimes, when it's warm enough, she'll be invited to go outside with Brian to sit on the 'bijou' patio together. It's the size of a shopping trolley and their knees bump when they face each other. Then, as Maria perches on the uncomfortable designer seat that leaves a lattice pattern imprint on her bum, he'll tell her things.

Brian didn't ask much about Maria's life at first – thankfully no one ever did, and she could bat away the few bland questions directed her way. Yet within three sessions, Maria knew all about Brian's mother (nerves, like him), his sister (planning a gastric band), his brother (working in Singapore) and the former boyfriend (the love of his life, who sadly realised he wasn't yet ready to settle down, but only after he'd been inside half the Royal Vauxhall Tavern). Brian talks very fast, and Maria missed some of it, but she learned how people in general 'took advantage' of him, especially his 'vile' boss at the start-up company where he works, who 'does everyone's head in'. In light of this slew of information, when Brian announced that he was worried about his heart it was hardly surprising.

He confided in her, 'I think the stress of it all is going to kill me!' And when she nodded and listened some more, he said, 'It's easy to talk to you, Maria. You'd make a good counsellor.'

Maria had no real idea what Brian's start-up company did, nor what qualifications she might need to become a counsellor.

Once, in the middle of a convoluted story about his boss's 'insane demands', Brian grabbed Maria's hand and she thought she might lash out, but as she swallowed back her cry he said, 'Here, feel this,' and he placed her palm in the middle of his chest where she felt a furious fluttering. 'That's just what *talking* about the bastard does to me,' he whimpered.

49

Maria nodded and made the right noises and continued listening while she tried to control the manic palpitations under her own sternum.

Now she feels more comfortable with Brian – as relaxed as she ever can be in someone else's home. It is a lovely flat, with so many plants it's like a greenhouse. She finds his constant chatter soothing, almost. He has smiley eyes. He's kind – and that's a rare and highly prized commodity as far as Maria's concerned.

A couple of weeks ago, Brian asked her to help him or-ganise a get-together. He's been planning to invite a few work colleagues to his flat for a drink one Friday night. His therapist suggested this might be a good step forwards, gar-nering support in the office before he goes back in part time.

'But *he'll* get wind of it and make my life a misery once he finds he's not invited,' he sighed.

'Your boss?'

'Who else?'

'Why don't you invite him and be done with it? He might not come.'

'Oh, he'll come all right. He'd not miss it for the world.' Brian shook his head and sank into himself, looking like a small boy. Any mention of his boss had this debilitating effect on him.

'Then leave your job,' she suggested. 'Surely it's not worth all this aggro?'

'Don't think I'm not looking,' said Brian. 'I don't want to be doing this all my life.'

Maria hasn't a clue what Brian's job actually entails, although he describes himself as *a creative*.

'Anyway, you don't want to be doing *this* for ever, do you?' He indicated Maria's mop, drying on the patio. 'What are your long-term plans?'

Maria gave a mirthless laugh and said she didn't have any, but he wouldn't take the answer at face value.

'I mean, what are your ambitions?'

'Ambitions?' She tried the word in her mouth.

'What would you like to do if you could wave a magic wand?'

'Travel the world and live in a big fuck-off house near the sea!' She smiled at the thought.

'What about a job, just in case you don't win the lottery?'

She shrugged. 'I thought I wanted to be a teacher when I was a kid.' That feels like a million years ago.

'You could go for it now.'

'I didn't do my exams.' She fiddled with her spoon.

'So? You could go back and do them as a mature student.'

'You think I'm mature?' She laughed.

'Seriously,' he said, 'what's stopping you going back to study? You're clever, Maria. You'd make a good teacher.'

Any sort of praise made her feel uncomfortable, yet she liked the fact that he thought she'd be a good teacher – based on absolutely nothing, but still.

It has been a long time since anyone saw potential in Maria. Brian's comments reminded her of the teachers who praised her at school; those who gave her hopes for her future – before she threw it all away on Joby. She worked hard to make them proud of her and when she pleased them, it made her glow.

She works hard for all her clients, but she takes extra care cleaning for Brian because she wants to please him; in his own way he's trying to help her, and it makes her want to help him too. Perhaps, if she'd had a brother, she might have felt something like this.

Today, when he asks how she is, she replies, 'Fine,' which is her usual response, because she can hardly tell him the truth. She's not sure how the hell she is.

'Really?' He raises his eyebrows, but he's sensitive enough not to push.

She makes a start on his home office. As she's polishing his desk he comes through with a pale purple T-shirt and says, 'I thought you might like this.'

'Are you sure?' This is the fourth time Brian has given her clothes, because they're a similar size. He offers her things he's got bored of; things that have gone out of fashion – but she's pretty sure she hasn't seen this particular T-shirt before. Perhaps it's an unwanted gift. She hopes he hasn't bought it especially for her because that would be too much and then she won't be able to take it and it is really lovely. She's never had anything this colour before.

'Can I give you something for it?' She steels herself for him saying yes.

'Don't be silly.' He smiles.

After an hour, he presents her with a drink – lemongrass and ginseng! – and settles down for a chat, her on the sofa, him on his bizarre retro beanbag affair.

'So, what's the gossip?' he asks.

'You really don't want to know,' she replies.

He thinks she's joking.

Keen to steer him on to easier topics than herself, she asks, 'What's new with you?'

Brian's news is that his boss has indeed got wind of his proposed event and has predictably invited himself to what is now to be 'a full-on soirée', whatever that might be.

Maria doesn't understand. 'But it's your party. He can't come round to your home if you don't want him here!'

Evidently he can, and he will.

Brian says he's now trying to 'reframe' the party after discussing it with his therapist – looking on the less-than-desirable circumstances as an 'opportunity' rather than a home invasion. He's resolved to 'have a talk' with his boss about the incessant list of unreasonable demands, but only on the proviso that Maria is there to 'provide back-up'.

'What do you want me to do?' she asks. She hasn't been to a party for years.

'I want the drinks and nibbles to be just right, so he can't sneer about those. Could you help with that, and perhaps provide a shoulder for me to sob on if it all goes tits up?' he flusters, before finally admitting, 'I just need someone here for moral support.'

'Can't someone else do it?' she replies.

'No. I want you to come. You can intervene if the boss gets a bit much.'

'Like a guard dog?' she jokes.

But a jolly get-together is the last thing Maria feels able to deal with after the night of the unfortunate . . . what? Accident? Manslaughter? Murder?

'You might have fun,' says Brian.

She shakes her head and says, 'I can't really cope with a

53

party right now, Brian. Not with Elsie how she is.' Which is true, but only partially so.

He looks disappointed, but she's far too preoccupied trying to forget that awful night, trying to work out what she'll do next, and trying to scrub certain images out of her mind to worry about *fun*.

9

After she finishes at Brian's, Maria buys some bits and bobs for herself (Simple soap and moisturiser on offer at Superdrug) before walking back to Elsie's. The morning deluge has given way to bright sunshine and for a brief period London feels fresh, the pavements washed clean. The house is up on the Haringey Ladder – Roseberry Gardens. It sounds more glamorous than it is, although, to be fair, there are a fair few rose bushes in some of the tiny front gardens. Maria generally walks between jobs when she can. Cheaper. Only when she's knackered, and the rain makes things grim, does she hop on a bus, but often there are no sensible connections and rush hours are impossible. She will not use the underground if at all possible – too much like being interred.

She doesn't take up much space on pavements. She walks across the road rather than encounter two mums walking together with pushchairs. If she can, she'll take evasive action, stepping into the gutter rather than face off someone coming the other way, but sometimes that's not possible and she feels her shoulders contract as she presses against parked cars or shop fronts, applying a strained expression that she hopes is a smile, although few people notice whether she smiles or not.

If it's a hot day and she's forced to remove her hat (a cheap beanie which makes her head sweat even on cold days), a few more people might observe her – as if her shorn skull is some form of fashion statement, as if she might be *trendy* – but not many. At thirty – or is it twenty-nine? Maria doesn't really keep track of her birthdays – she is much older than the girls who attract most of those looks and her demeanour does not deliberately court attention. Her clothes are generally charity-shop trousers and T-shirts, fleeces and trainers, muted colours. She dresses entirely without vanity – look where vanity had got her! Function, not fashion, these days. Although thanks to Brian she does now possess one particularly lovely pale purple T-shirt.

Along with the neutral wardrobe and weary expression of the manual worker, she carries a heavy backpack with extra cloths and sprays for the properties that run out of cleaning fluids and polish. If someone mugged her, they would be disappointed to find no credit cards and only the most basic of mobile phones. There are generally only coins and a travel card in her purse. No home address, no In Case of Emergency.

As she walks, she thinks about the party. Poor Brian. She can't understand why he feels compelled to have someone he hates in his home. She's not sure what she can do to help him. But it is nice to feel needed.

The sun disappears and it's suddenly very cold again. She crosses Wightman Road, the rush-hour traffic (which can last two or three hours) heavy.

Often, she doesn't think of herself as *Maria*, an individual – she blends in, making her set patterns between the homes she cleans, her bedsit and Elsie's house, like a worker bee.

Once, Joby said she was a queen, but she never really felt like one. Yes, he bought her lovely clothes and jewellery, but he totally controlled her life. And she was never allowed to walk tall.

Del intercepts her in the hall as soon as she gets back.

'She's told me!' is the first thing he says to her, before she's even taken off her jacket. He might as well have thrown a bucket of cold water in her face.

Maria closes the front door and walks through to the kitchen in slow motion. Are there police inside waiting to drag her off to jail? What the hell will happen to Elsie if she's not around to look after her? Will they arrest her, too?

Elsie is thankfully unflanked by armed officers. She sits quietly, looking like a child who's been caught pinching apples. Harry's cleaning his paw on the kitchen table in front of her, which isn't exactly hygienic, but Maria's given up on that. Elsie's stroking him under his chin and the cat is ecstatic.

Maria puts down her backpack, all her muscles tense.

'Tea, anyone?' she asks, concentrating on keeping her hands still as she pours water into the kettle from the filter jug.

What has Elsie told him? Is everything about to come crashing down? She feels sick.

Del starts pacing up and down the kitchen floor, anger radiating off his shoulders.

Maria steals a glance outside, just in case he's dug up the garden, but nothing seems disturbed.

'What's she said, then?' Her heart is hammering, but she somehow manages to keep her voice level.

'It's time, if you ask me. I keep telling you, it's time,' says Del. 'She is winding me up good and proper.'

Maria doesn't know exactly what he means, so she stays silent, bracing for what might come next. Although, come to think of it, being *wound up* would hardly cover discovering a relative had recently been slaughtered and was now languishing under the rose bushes. Perhaps this isn't the end of everything.

'Waste of bloody time and energy,' splutters Del. 'It'll make no bloody difference. She's a bloody liability. She shouldn't be living here by herself. Bloody *dancing*! And I suppose muggins here will need to ferry her there and back and pay for it.'

Maria gasps. A reprieve! She has to turn away so he can't see the relief on her face and she struggles to focus on what he says next. She makes the tea on automatic pilot and eventually gathers what seems to have riled him.

What Elsie has told Del is that yesterday Comfort suggested she take part in a series of special exercise classes for people with dementia. Music and lots of repetitive movements. Comfort showed them stuff from YouTube on her phone. Elsie joined in, waving her arms about to 'Sweet Caroline', singing along with the right words and the *do-doo doo doos*.

'I can't take any more bloody time off bloody work,' Del says.

And I can? thinks Maria.

She tries to soothe him, saying, 'I'll take her. I'll try and rearrange my days – swap a job. And the classes are free. The council and the charity cover the cost.'

Her offer doesn't seem to calm him because the classes are the least of it. What's really angered him, it transpires, are the other things – yet another rant from Elsie about him never getting his hands on 'a single penny' of her money. Plus, as soon as his back was turned ('I was only on the bloody phone for two minutes, max!'), she poured half a mug of tea in his briefcase.

Maria smiles – as much from relief as from Elsie's naughtiness. It doesn't go down well with Del, who glares at her before carrying on.

'She needs more help than I can give her,' he moans, not unreasonably. 'I've got my own life, you know!'

Maria repeats her litany that they need to keep Elsie in her own home where she feels secure and happy for as long as possible, in familiar surroundings; where she can keep the cats, where Maria can help look after her – that's what Comfort recommends, that's what Elsie wants – while at regular intervals, whenever the words 'care home' pop up, Elsie tells Del to 'fuck right off'.

In the middle of this heated discussion, Maria winces, but

not due to Elsie's language. She's putting the cutlery away when she drops a spoon, bends to retrieve it and spots a very small, but very obvious smear of blood at the bottom of the washing machine. Jesus! She struggles to keep the shock off her face.

Is she going mad? She's sure – absolutely sure! – she cleaned up every speck after Monday night. She knows she did a good job cleaning Elsie's bedroom and the kitchen, she's a professional! But evidence to the contrary is right there in front of her.

Surely she would have spotted it before now – when Comfort came round or when she did the laundry? Is she seeing things? Has she turned into Lady Macbeth?

She daren't bend down to wipe the smear off while Del is in the room, so she stands and shields it with her leg.

Del gets out his cigarettes, which provokes another round of Elsie telling him he can't smoke in the house and Del saying he'll smoke wherever he wants, although, to be fair, he always goes outside for a fag. That slides into another row when Elsie refuses a final plea for her to give him a loan to *tide him over*.

He steps into the garden, cashless, sulking, throwing a, 'We'll see what Nick has to say about this,' over his shoulder as he lights up.

But Nick, snug in his shallow grave, mouldering down quietly with the worms ready to fertilise the roses, keeps his opinions to himself.

As soon as he's out of the kitchen, Maria grabs a cloth and the bleach spray and starts rubbing at the streak of blood. On her knees as she scrubs, she sees fragments of fur

60

and the tiny skull of something that once might have been a mouse or a vole; something that has been eviscerated and wedged under the washing machine.

Thank Christ! Never has she been so pleased to see a rodent corpse. As she prises the bones and squelchy remains from their resting place, Del comes in and tuts. She wraps the dead thing in kitchen towel before laying the creature to rest in the bin outside, and when she comes back, she notices she's being observed by two pairs of inscrutable eyes as Spotty and Sweetie nestle together in their hammock, glaring at her as if to say, *Find your own playthings; find your own things to kill.*

10

She cleaned for her dad, of course, but Maria's housework back then was slipshod and slapdash. When you're young you aren't interested in scouring the bath, are you? Cleaning is for those who've given up all hope of adventure; chores are for when you've settled down in a nice house or flat, with some nice little knick-knacks. You yearn for anything new and exciting when you're young. You desire *experiences* as much as *stuff*. You want fun not furniture. And if you're lucky, you don't need the soothing repetition of simple tasks.

There was always something more interesting to do than clean back then – like netball. Tall for her age, Maria shone on court. She was an excellent Wing Attack and she loved visiting other schools for games, thrilled to be somewhere – anywhere – *different*. She was always keen to be out, away from her dad's poky house, away to her future. She didn't just want to read about places, she wanted to *be* there and taste the food and smell the smells. And she didn't want passion confined to the pages of novels – thrilling though some of those descriptions were – she was desperate to experience it for herself.

'Ants in her pants, that one,' pronounced Frankie, perhaps somewhat jealously.

Her first professional cleaning job was for Murad, who owned the local Mini Mart, both in the shop and in his cluttered flat above it. She got the job at thirteen, after she'd been on at her dad to give her some pocket money and was told in no uncertain terms, 'You graft for your money in this house.'

Murad was her dad's mate – both used to play football in the Sunday league; both were widowed before they were forty, although Murad's wife died of cancer. There was a photo of her in his flat. She was wearing a lovely red dress, looking young and glamorous, and there was a bunch of plastic flowers in front of it like a shrine. Maria thought it was wonderful. She told her mates, 'I want my picture in a frame. I want someone to love me for ever after I'm gone.' She sighed, adding, with no sense of irony, 'It's dead romantic.'

She learned how to wield the big mop, swishing it up and down the aisles late on Sunday afternoons, plus two nights a week. It wasn't often busy. Murad blamed the big Morrisons that had opened on the edge of town.

You learn a lot about people by the way they treat cleaners. Most don't even notice you; a few might smile a greeting, and some take great delight in wheeling their dirty trolley wheels over the bit you've just done. Classmates who popped into the shop would take the piss – 'You've missed a bit!' the hilarious joke Maria heard at least twice a week.

Her arms and shoulders became muscled with the work. It helped with the netball.

When she peeled off her rubber gloves after she'd finished cleaning the shelves and mopping, her hands would be sweaty, her fingertips wrinkled.

'It is honourable to earn your living by the sweat of your brow,' said Murad. He might have even meant it.

Honourable or not, Maria envisioned something better for herself when she left school. She hoped to stay on, do her A levels, perhaps go into teaching. She liked school.

When she discussed her future plans with her dad, he'd say, 'We'll see,' but she knew he was proud of her. The issue would be if she wanted to go to university. He was dead set against any form of debt.

Murad was a nice enough boss. As well as the fiver he gave her, he'd let her take anything coming up to its sell-by date that she fancied. Inevitably, some kids from school started on at her to pinch stuff for them – cigarettes and booze, mainly. She refused. Then they'd call after her on the way to school, 'Oi, scrubber!' and laugh.

Eventually, Murad showed her how to do the till and, if he had to pop out, he left her minding the shop. He didn't go out often but she was dead chuffed when he left her in charge. The money was never short when he cashed up. He told her dad,'You've got a good girl there,' and her dad smiled and said he knew, and she felt proud.

She sometimes dreamed of opening her own shop, perhaps somewhere warm, like Italy.

Small ambitions.

She never achieved a single one.

11

Del goes upstairs for 'a bit of peace' while Elsie settles to her soaps and Maria sits alongside her reading. Chapters are occasionally interrupted when Elsie pipes up, 'Fancy him? She'd never give him the time of day! He looks like Mr bloody Potato Head.' The comments are accurate, and Maria takes this as a positive.

When she gets her to bed, Elsie snuggles down soon enough, which has to be another good sign, doesn't it? Surely she can't be traumatised if she's sleeping?

Maria is more anxious about Elsie's feelings than her own. She daren't even start to unpick how she feels. She forces herself to concentrate on cleaning, struggling to push down thoughts of the burial, fears of discovery. But the images keep flashing into her mind and a sickly guilt pervades everything she does.

She has an hour to herself before she has to get off to

her overnight clean. Usually she would nap, but there is no hope of sleep right now, so she sets about cleaning the oven. She leaves Elsie quietly snoring and doesn't bother saying goodbye to Del.

Depending on buses, she usually arrives at the luxury flat near the South Bank between midnight and one o'clock, when the owner is at work. The agency briefing notes informed her that the man, a Balogan (it wasn't specified if this was his surname or first name), ran nightclubs and consequently slept during the day, not that it was of much interest to her.

It's a blessing, truth be told, this single night when she's left to her own devices, pushing through her fatigue until she is so dazed she can stagger back to her bedsit and collapse into a brief, dreamless sleep in the thin hours. She imagines the feeling must be what jetlag is like, but how would she know? She's never been on a plane in her life.

Never have I ever flown, bought a Mother's Day card, got a qualification, felt safe since . . .

What does she usually think of as she cleans? Money. Food. Elsie. But different thoughts swirl in these small hours. Silly notions.

Perhaps there's a sense of how she might make things a little nicer in the world, one flat at a time. To clean away filth and restore some portion of order. Retribution and reparation in microscopic increments. Atonement.

How many clean surfaces, how many dust motes, equal a life?

She works harder tonight, almost manic. The harder she scrubs and vacuums the less energy she has to worry about what lies in Elsie's back garden. The faster she polishes and scours, the less likely she is to think about what she's turned into.

This is one of her best nights, in the lovely flat on the top floor, and she's high in the sky, far away from the sounds of traffic, gazing down on all the London lights, which look so pretty from that vantage point, so full of promise. It thrills her that she can see The Shard.

Sometimes she wonders what it might have been like to leave home and come here to the city when she was young and full of hope, instead of what she ended up doing: running away from a small town desperate to see the world, but fleeing to a life even more constrained – from a terrace to a caravan.

She also imagines what it might be like to live in a place like this. She loves the space and the panoramic view which somehow makes her thoughts expand, as if they might fly away on the night air outside the window.

Only the issues with the neighbours took the shine off.

The people in the flat next door had moved in a few months ago. There were piles of packing boxes littering the corridor for several weeks.

They usually returned home around two or three in the morning and the cacophony – parties and ridiculously loud music (a mad mix of jazz and hip hop and other weird discordant sounds) stopped Maria's daydreams. When it kicked off, the revelling was often accompanied by some sort of argument – raised voices muffled against heavy bass beats, shouts, slamming doors, banging and clattering – sometimes followed by noisy make-up sex noises through the bedroom wall.

She didn't have headphones to drown it out. The cries rattled her as the bassline throbbed through her skull.

She guessed few of the other flats were occupied. These palatial developments were generally bought as investment properties, according to the agency. They sent cleaners to spruce them up when overseas owners 'popped into town' from somewhere exotic on the way to somewhere else exotic.

It wasn't Maria's place to complain about the noise.

Tonight, around two, there'd been laughter, the neighbours' door opening and closing as people came and went, a constant pounding music. It quietened eventually. But as Maria is finishing off in the bathroom there are suddenly shouts, two voices, something smashing.

Then a wail – a fox's scream? But you don't get foxes ten storeys high, do you?

The shriek stops Maria in her tracks as she's scouring the bathroom taps. She catches sight of herself in the mirror above the sink and sees her own terrors superimposed over her reflection – a pulse of horror from her past; a stab of violence from the other night; a glimpse of something darker within her.

She marches around to the neighbours' and batters on the door for so long, if there's anyone else in the complex they must be able to hear the commotion.

She springs back as the door in front of her is wrenched open.

'What?' snarls the sweaty face before her.

The man pushes blond floppy hair out of his face as he tries to focus on Maria. Fine features, almost girlish, although he looks much older than the hair suggests. Not what she imagined.

'Is everything all right?' She forces out the question, despite her throat tightening around the words. She plants her feet under her hips to counter the instinct to run, although she is quite a bit taller than this man.

'Yeah, yeah. All good here. Just partying, you know?' He smiles with too many teeth.

She is not taken in. His eyes are full of chemicals. She doesn't move.

'Whaddya want?' he demands, leaning his shoulder against the door frame, crossing his arms like a bouncer.

She tries to peer around him into the room down the hallway. In the gap she sees a guitar on the coffee table, a double bass propped against the window, an overflowing ashtray, discarded pizza boxes on the sofa, two bottles scattered on the carpet. It pains her to see such a beautiful space made so grubby.

'Is everything okay? I heard a scream.'

'No. All cool, all cool.' Posh-boy accent, feral vibes, his jaw grinding and gurning, his lips curling into a snarl rather than a smile. Deep lines exaggerate the expression, making him appear more animal than human.

'Are you sure?'

'Yeah. Yeah. All—'

'Is someone hurt?' She can't stop herself. 'Did you hurt her?'

'Fuck off!'

The door whooshes towards her and she's forced to take a step back as it slams in her face.

She listens for a long time, but there's nothing more. She returns to Balogan's flat, finishes the clean, and packs up her things. She does not call the police. She doesn't want to get involved, can't afford to – not with what's under Elsie's rose bushes. She thinks of Nick as she puts out the rubbish.

After she leaves, she berates herself. She should have done more. What, exactly, she isn't sure. What if someone's hurt? She feels ashamed of herself.

She walks part of the way back to Wood Green until her legs ache, then she catches a night bus. Lights trail past the window, and she watches a shop opening up for a delivery, yawning early commuters. She yawns in response.

She feels no relief when she opens the door to the bedsit. The house has been butchered into six rooms without any thought for what might *feel* right. Mean, ugly rooms. Even before she spent so much time at Elsie's, Maria made little effort to make this place . . . nice. It is clean – that's pretty much all you could say about it. But it would never be her home, so what's the point?

Maria rarely sleeps well. She falls to sleep easily enough, but the dreams often make uninterrupted rest impossible, forcing her awake.

And the recent night of violence has triggered deeper fragments from her subconscious. Nick might lie well hidden under the soil, but his burial has unearthed worse memories, and as weak dawn light filters through the thin curtains of her bedsit, the cry of the fox is her own.

12

She wakes groggy on the Thursday afternoon, disorientated by the change in her routine.

The rest of the day passes in a blur of hoovering and bin emptying and mopping and polishing, around Islington, Hackney and Haringey, and by the time she collects her overnight things and returns to Elsie's, Del is keen to be off, saying, 'I've already put her to bed.'

At least he's not put her to sleep, thinks Maria, ungenerously.

She should feel relieved that today Elsie hasn't blabbed, that Del hasn't done a spot of gardening, that she's not been struck by lightning. But if anything, her dread intensifies. It will happen at some point – discovery. She got away with it once, but she will be punished for these recent sins.

Maria gets up twice in the night and creeps downstairs to check on Elsie, who's tossing and turning. She stands looking through the kitchen window to check on the garden, where Elsie's husband is the only one sleeping the sleep of the dead.

She's already had two strong coffees by the time Elsie wakes at six on Friday morning.

'Ding dong merrily on high,' Elsie starts singing at the top of her voice as Maria helps her dress. The lyrics morph into Chuck Berry's 'Ding-a-Ling' and back to the carol. She is beyond perky.

'Are we having turkey?' says Elsie, clapping her hands together.

'Perhaps,' says Maria. Surely no one has ever been this excited by turkey.

Christmas was weeks ago, but sometimes it's easier to go along with Elsie's train of thought rather than attempting to force her into the present reality.

Maria has spent every Christmas with Elsie since she started cleaning for her. 'You can't be on your own at Christmas. It's illegal,' Elsie had declared.

But the first meal she ever had in this house was one Easter Sunday. Elsie asked Maria if she had anywhere to go for the Bank Holiday. The question took her by surprise, so she didn't have time to think of a lie.

'Come here, then.'

'Oh, thanks but—'

'Don't be daft.'

Maria and Elsie had immediately hit it off, but spending a whole Sunday together was another level.

'Are you sure? Can I bring anything?' Maria tensed for a request that she'd be unable to fulfil.

'Just bring yourself, babe. It means I'll have someone on my side for once, rather than that miserable bugger scowling at me with his ugly mush.'

Maria assumed Elsie meant her husband. At that time, he had never been present when Maria cleaned. 'Do you two not get on?' she asked.

'Me and Nick? Jesus, no!' exclaimed Elsie, like the very thought of *getting on* with your husband was hilarious. 'To be honest, I can't remember if we ever did.'

'But at the start?'

'Must have,' said Elsie, helping herself to another Garibaldi. Maria mirrored her. 'I do remember . . . the sex was good at the start. Blinding. But after the change I turned to dust downstairs and that knocked that on the head.'

Maria didn't know where to look.

'You've got all that to come, love. You make the best of it while you can!'

Maria took a gulp of tea that was too hot.

'You got anyone, darlin'? Bird? Bloke?'

'No, no,' flustered Maria.

'Don't like to assume with the hair, like,' wittered Elsie. 'Fine by me either way. It's nice to have someone . . .' She nodded at Maria's buzzcut. 'Although I did think you might have nits.'

On that Easter Sunday, Maria arrived at eleven to lend a hand. It had taken her almost two hours to walk from where she was staying back then, in a tiny crappy flat near King's Cross, because there were few buses and she didn't want to

75

be late. Elsie opened the door wearing a frilly yellow pinny over a bright red dress. She'd daubed two pink circles on her cheeks, so she looked like a little Russian doll. Her eyes were very bright, and her hair had been freshly cut, and by the looks of it professionally fluffed.

'Come in, come in. Let's have a tipple and a nibble before old grumpy drawers comes back from the pub. I'm already in good spirits!' she joked, toasting Maria with her sherry glass.

She was delighted with the two big bags of Dreamies Maria had bought for the 'fur faces', as Elsie referred to her brood of cats.

'Ooh, they'll bloody love them!' said Elsie. She reached for an old tea tin and brought out a roll of cash held together with elastic bands. She tried to give Maria a twenty-pound note.

'No! Elsie, it's a present!'

'If you're sure you can afford it?'

Maria nodded. A white lie.

'I reckon they put feline crack cocaine is in these. And they'll be up for what's left of the lamb later.'

Elsie gave each cat a couple of treats anyway, supervising with her toe to ensure Boris didn't steal more than his fair share, then she set about making mint sauce. 'I never did that, you know,' she said with a sigh. 'All the rest, but not that. Probably too late now.'

'Never did what?' asked Maria, confused by Elsie's train of thought.

'Crack cocaine,' said Elsie.

Maria was dumbfounded.

'I'm joking!' she cackled.

Twice Elsie told Maria to stop trying to help with the veg, making her sit at the kitchen table.

'Take a load off, love. Today I don't want you lifting a finger. Have a bloody break.'

Maria sat and the ginger boy cat jumped up on her lap for the first time. The cats usually disappeared when the hoover emerged.

'Ooh, he likes you, don't you, Harry?' Elsie smiled. 'Good taste! I trust people that cats like.'

Sweetie and Spotty were curled around each other on their hammock bed-thing which hung against the radiator. No sign of Boris, who'd disappeared as soon as he'd wolfed down his snack. 'Probably out murdering baby birds now,' smiled Elsie fondly.

Nick eventually arrived, noticeably unfocused, a small compact man with the air of a belligerent Jack Russell. The remaining felines fled. He grunted but didn't say hello to either woman, barrelling through to slump on the big old armchair in the corner of the kitchen that looked like it had come out of the ark. He balanced his walking stick next to him – an ugly twisted thing with a silver wolf's head on top which put Maria in mind of Bill Sikes.

Elsie acknowledged his arrival with a, 'Look what the cat's dragged in.' Then she whispered to Maria, 'Thinks that's his bloody throne.'

Maria noticed Elsie had forgotten to turn on the carrots, so she suggested, 'Do you want me to microwave these?'

'Jesus! Yes, okay, love.' said Elsie, shaking her head in disbelief.

Elsie had always seemed a bit scatty to Maria. She often

forgot what day she'd booked the clean and when Maria arrived she might say something like, 'Bloody hell! Is it Friday already? Where's the week gone?', although she always looked pleased to see her.

As Maria helped dish up, Elsie whispered, 'You know they say the way to a man's heart is through his stomach? It's not, though.' She paused as she ladled potatoes on to the three plates. 'It's straight through his ribcage with a bloody great pickaxe!' She giggled, gazing down at her hands, as if surprised to see the spoon.

'Grub's up,' called Elsie and Nick harrumphed, heaved himself from his chair and made his way to the dining table in the other room. Maria brought the plates through.

It was a nice meal, interspersed with an occasional appreciative grunt from Nick. He didn't say much to Maria, or actually thank his wife, but he nodded at her when he'd finished, then tottered over to switch on the telly, taking his hot-cross-bun bread-and-butter pudding with him as he settled back on the sofa with his second can of Special Brew.

When Elsie popped to the loo, Nick rose from his seat and came through to stand by Maria as she did the washing-up. She thought he'd come to lend a hand, but very quietly he said, 'You can fuck off now.'

'Sorry?' She wasn't sure she'd heard right.

He hissed, 'Sling your hook. You've had your scran, now fuck off.' He glowered at her, his mouth loose, breathing alcoholic fumes in her face.

He was back on the sofa by the time Elsie returned to the kitchen. Maria made her excuses and left, feeling guilty for hurrying off and leaving her with the rest of the dishes.

That night her dreams were filled with memories of the bad things, superimposed with new images of Elsie's gravy with lumps like blood clots.

13

Maria never forgave her dad after Frankie moved in.

The house became a soup of dangerous female hormones – a hysterectomy on Frankie's side catapulting her into a riot of menopausal angst, and Maria's puberty making her 'a right mardy cow', according to Frankie. Her dad spent more time down the pub.

Maria escaped by taking on two extra house cleans. She had more jobs than any of her friends, who might do a paper round or wash the family car for a bit of cash.

'You'll be paying tax soon,' laughed her dad, but she knew he was pleased really.

He didn't realise she was saving up to leave home. She couldn't wait to get away. She talked to her friends about them getting a flat together, although that wasn't likely to happen any time soon, and she vowed to go off to university as soon as she could, but that seemed an age away.

In the meantime, Maria stoked her hatred of Frankie. She was furious most of the time.

One Saturday morning, playing a much better netball team over in Ashby, Maria was pushed in the back by their Wing Defence and went flying, although the referee didn't notice. However, she couldn't miss the retaliation, when, instead of passing the ball to her teammate, Maria took aim and smashed the ball right into her opponent's face. She claimed it was an accident, but she was sent off and the girl taken to hospital with a suspected broken nose.

Her dad was called to the school to discuss her behaviour and Frankie bloody loved that. Maria spent a lot of time plotting how she might contrive to smash a netball into Frankie's smug face, or stave in her skull with her dad's monkey wrench.

So, when she thinks of it, she has always had violent tendencies.

All those years cleaning for her dad, for Murad and for Joby – her husband; a man who insisted everything in the caravan was gleaming – stood Maria in good stead when she had the trial for this job, although the other girls told her the agency basically took on anyone and everyone who applied, as people were always leaving for better things.

'No one wants to do this for the rest of their lives, do they?' sighed the cleaner who was sent round with her to 'supervise' Maria on her first week. 'No one wants to do it at all, really. The money's crap. Whose ambition is it to be a cleaner when they're a kid? I wanted to be a dancer, but at least this saves on gym membership. What do you want to do?' she asked Maria.

It was a question Maria had rarely asked herself since she left school. She tried to forget her old ambitions, kept her head down and just got on with it. Otherwise the regrets crowded in on her.

The work was fair enough. She took any jobs the agency offered, and covered for the other girls whenever she could, even if it meant ridiculously early starts or doing overnights. She grafted hard, never complained.

She was respectful of other people's homes, handled their possessions with care. Each item had a memory attached to it, just as much as the photos showing smiling families evoked happy times. Sometimes those images made Maria turn away as she dusted.

After six months the agency printed out the comments from their website and handed them to her for her first 'performance review'.

FEEDBACK

The girl came on time, cleaned, and left on time. (***)

Maria is very nice and although she doesn't stay to chat, she has been very kind and always strokes my Muffin. (****)

I need new hoover bags and could she swap Tuesdays for Fridays for the next three weeks as I have a Zoom course on the artists of the Italian Neoclassical movement. I need the organic spray, please, because of my asthma and I don't like the smell of the other one. Kindly obliged. (No stars)

Your cleaner is OK. Please stop sending these emails as they clutter up my inbox. (****)

Excellent, efficient, punctual. Would recommend. (****)

Maria always goes above and beyond my expectations. We all adore her! My surfaces have never been so sparkling! She even managed to get the dog sick stains off the sofa!! She's trustworthy and efficient and works very hard. A delight! (*****)

I never know she's here, but I always know she's been. All I want in a cleaner. (****)

After Maria read the printout, she was asked to complete a 'self-assessment' form highlighting areas for improvement, as if she worked for NASA. She did it at the agency office because she had to admit, *Never ever have I owned a computer.*

Perhaps she might have fostered new ambitions then – trained to be a supervisor of a team of cleaners at one of the big city office blocks or studied part time and tried to better her prospects. But the nature of the work was wearing. It sapped her energy and gnawed at her resilience against the bad memories. And so much of her time was taken up feeling guilty, going over and over what had happened in Spain, trying to envision a different outcome. So many nights were fractured with nightmares.

These days she had thought she might have come to an uneasy, fragile truce with her past. Elsie and Brian looked at her and saw a basically good person. It gave her hope. But the recent night of savagery has exhumed the old fears, a bitterness, a suppressed fury.

When she walks between jobs, as she cleans, when she stews in her rumpled bed, Maria has the urge to lash out and scream until her throat is raw.

14

The following Tuesday, Maria is spritzing the impressive greenery in Brian's flat. Only filtered water is good enough for his 'emotional-support pot plants'. Each one has a name. His favourite his Chesney the giant cheese plant, with Fenella fern a close second. 'Good for oxygenation and they lower the blood pressure,' explained Brian when she first commented on his lush indoor jungle.

Brian is currently working on some 'proposal' or other, which always seems to involve a lot of sighing and gazing out of the window. They are interrupted by an incoming FaceTime call on his laptop.

'Jesus! It's him!' squeaks Brian.

Instead of leaving the room, as she usually would, Maria dawdles, intrigued to see what the nightmare boss looks like.

She's surprised to see a classically handsome face appear above a tight logoed vest, impressive, sculpted arms and chest (he obviously works out), eyebrows groomed within an inch of their lives, and he seems both tanned and Botoxed.

She's less surprised by the tone and the harshness of some of the words which causes Brian's shoulders to slump. She notices the slight tremor in Brian's fingers as he grips his pen tighter and tighter as the call progresses. Whenever he tries to explain – the project hasn't been completed because his deadline was next Thursday; it had always been due next week – he's shut down by the sneering voice emanating from the face on the screen.

More than once the phrase 'don't be so fucking gay about it' is employed. The man laughs like a donkey.

Even though it's supposed to be a work call, the boss is incredibly personal.

'You been hitting the doughnuts, mate? Or have the happy pills chunked you up? I thought you lot were supposed to be into the body beautiful.' *HAW HAW HAW.*

'Still feeling a fragile delicate flower, are you? Deliver me from fucking snowflakes! Hope you're not watching the news, mate, that would really give you something to worry about!' *HAW HAW HAW.* 'Mental health? Yeah, right. Get a fucking grip, sunshine!

'Just so you know, we're interviewing some new blood in the next couple of weeks – some super-keen youngsters who won't flake out on me. The quick and the dead in this business. Shape up or ship out.' *HAW HAW HAW.*

When the call is terminated, Brian looks broken. He turns to her, eyes teary and says, 'You see?'

'He can't talk to you like that, Brian. It's not right. He's putting too much pressure on you. You're supposed to be signed off sick.'

Maria might work in a gig economy – she doesn't get paid if she doesn't work and her bosses are hardly supportive – but the way Brian's boss mocks and belittles him gets right under her skin.

'He's just a total control freak with this new project,' sighs Brian. 'He's got investors on his back.'

'Don't make excuses for him!' she says, but when she sees Brian wince, she changes tack. 'Is he still coming to your drinks do?'

'Of course he is!' wails Brain. 'He'd never let an opportunity go by to humiliate me. And, before you say it, I know I shouldn't put up with this, this . . . bullying, but I just can't seem to . . .' He hurries away to the kitchen to make some organic chamomile and lavender nonsense – a brew Maria feels might only be 'enhanced' by adding some of the debris she's hoovered up from beneath Brian's sofa.

By the time Maria's finished in his office Brian still hasn't returned from the kitchen. She finds him out on the patio, silently sobbing.

'What's up, chuck?' she tries, in an attempt to make light of the situation. 'Do you want to stroke Patsy?' (Patsy is the peace lily in Brian's bedroom.)

He gives her a weak smile. 'Alex wants to come to the drinks party.' He sniffs. 'He's insisted on it. I've begged him not to because that bastard will have a field day if Alex turns up.'

'Who's this Alex when he's at home?'

Brian actually blushes.

'Aha! A new love interest.' She smiles. The smile today surprises her; she has so little to smile about.

She manages to winkle out more information about Alex: tree surgeon; bear; sings in the London Gay Men's Chorus; adores Cher; can take or leave Saint Judy. The relationship is in the very early stages but it's obvious Brian is smitten.

'Please come to the party,' pleads Brian. 'Please help me.'

'How can I help you? What can I do?'

'Be there for me if I need to hide and cry in my bedroom. Help me cater because I can't cope with all that on top of everything else. And keep an eye on Alex. Steer him away from my boss. I can't bear the thought of those two *chatting*. Alex will kick off big time if he hears that man say half the things he usually says to me. And I don't want Alex to think I'm a wuss, which I am, but . . .'

'Okay. I'll think about it,' promises Maria.

She helps him compile a lengthy party shopping list and pins it to his fridge with his Gemma Collins fridge magnet. She gives him a big hug when she leaves.

On the walk back to Elsie's she considers . . .

She'll need to ask Del to stay over with Elsie, but she doesn't think that will be an issue for him. Elsie hasn't said anything about Nick so far, so there's no reason she'll suddenly start talking now. And even if she did, would anyone believe her? Del hasn't noticed anything's changed in the garden – he never goes down that end, just stands and smokes outside the kitchen door.

Plus, she'll be working, and Brian has insisted he'll pay her for the night, so there's that.

And Brian's been good to her. He's asked for her help.

She texts him, saying, *OK. I'll be your waitress for the night.* It's the least she can do.

I WILL ALWAYS LOVE YOUUUUUU!!! comes the immediate reply.

As she shops for Elsie's tea in Green Lanes, an idea comes to her unbidden.

She will help Brian with *the nibbles* as discussed. And while most of the items will come via Waitrose and Cook as requested, she wonders if she should also make something herself.

She can probably get the main ingredient from Elsie's neighbours – the students who are always in a party mood – and then she might make her special mushroom vol-au-vents.

She has Joby to thank for the recipe. She has Joby to thank for so much – a fractured ankle, a missing tooth, and the nightmares that wrench her from sleep at three in the morning.

Maria does not like control freaks. And she hates bullies. She swore to herself she would never put up with anything like that again.

As she carries the shopping up Roseberry Gardens, the idea takes root.

Wouldn't it be fitting if Brian's obnoxious boss had a taste of what it was like to feel totally and utterly out of control. Wouldn't it be great if she could make him feel small and pathetic and terrified.

She smiles to herself as she lets herself back into Elsie's.

15

She met Joby when she was fifteen.

Sitting outside the St John Ambulance Hall on that heady Saturday afternoon, drinking bottles of warm fizzy cider with her mates. A delicious age. A dangerous age. Giddy with hopes and hormones.

Now Maria notices those types of girls outside schools – the loud, giggling gangs, flicking back their hair, hitching up their skirts and burgeoning breasts, self-consciously smoking cigarettes and weed – every action shrieking, LOOK AT ME!

She never suspected that the future she yearned for, full of fun and travel and possibilities, could fall and impale itself on those three words.

These days she sees them for what they are, those girls – silly children. They have not one single clue.

But back then, they were so sure, so brittle-confident.

They knew it *all*. You could not have told them to be cautious, to reel it in a bit, to beware of certain kinds of men.

She had no one who might tell her things like that – no mother to turn to.

A glorious spring day, unseasonably hot. She was sitting with her friends and the cool girls she was so keen to impress, girls who laughed in the face of everything.

They were laughing then, gossiping about who they fancied, who might fancy them, when they noticed the man climb over the low stone wall right at the bottom of the field and walk up towards them, slow, swaggering like he'd just got off a horse. (Maria would discover later that, in fact, he had.)

She remembers quietening as he strode closer, they all did. She felt his power even then. He exuded a sexual magnetism. He was shockingly handsome. Nothing like the youths they knew, who were just daft boys. He walked straight up to them. No whispering to his mates, pretending not to look at them, which happened at school. That wasn't his way.

He smiled. He had . . . a twinkle, you might call it; a shine on him. Despite the ancient, faded T-shirt with the sweat patches under the arms, they all fancied him, wanted him – his attention, his dimples directed towards them, his tongue in their wet greedy little mouths.

He stood before Maria, choosing her, even then. 'Gorgeous hair, girl,' he announced, staring right at her.

She glowed.

'I know,' she sassed, not that she felt at all sure about it with him standing in front of her, but she had the protection of her pack, and the buzz of the cider, so she tried the style of cheek used by the cool girls, adding, 'Grew it myself.'

She caught the look on her friends' faces. Brilliant.

He threw back his head and laughed as if she was hilarious, then stared deep into her eyes as if she was the most fascinating girl in the world.

She had to look away. It was too much.

He nodded to where she was sitting and said, 'You'll get splinters in your arse.' Blunt. But he smiled, as if everything was a joke.

The girls sat on the top of the tables rather than on the benches (of course they did), signalling their rebellion. Maria wore her blonde hair down – so long back then, she could sit on it; hair like a princess in a tower – smudged dark eye make-up that she'd slathered on after she'd left home, glossy lips. What did they think they looked like? Skinny bare legs swinging against the wood, tiny denim shorts, shirts tied up, exposing their pale belly buttons – variations on a single theme; they might as well have worn uniforms.

Thanks to the drink, bathed in his attention, sparkling with sunshine and the awe of her friends, she managed to show no fear. When he asked for a swig of her cider, she didn't meekly hand it over, but countered, 'What's it worth?'

He flashed back, 'A night on the town. Next Saturday. My treat. Fair payment.' He was already reaching for her bottle, expecting compliance.

She's still not sure if he took the drink or she gave it to him.

The same with the kiss. It happened so quickly. A gulp of her cider, then, as he handed back the bottle, he swooped in – a swift press of his lips on hers – and she felt dizzy with shock or excitement or both.

Smoky lips, sweet from the cider, and the roughness of his stubble.

'See you on Saturday.' He laughed, and strode off, throwing back over his shoulder, 'Leave your hair like that. It's beautiful.'

People often remarked on Maria's long blonde hair; only her gran had ever called her beautiful before.

'Where . . .?' she called after him, dazed.

'I'll be in touch,' he shouted back.

'He's off that gyppo site round the back of Morrisons,' said one of her mates as they watched him walk away like a gunslinger. 'They did a story about that lot on the news. They're going to settle them there – plumbing and stuff. They're getting grants. My dad reckons it's a waste of taxpayers' money. And they'll be nicking our stuff before—'

'How come you're the expert all of a sudden?' snapped Maria, annoyed that the spotlight was off her again.

She didn't even know his name, but he was all they talked about for the next week. They analysed what he'd said, what she should wear, how far she might go if it came to it on the date.

She was nervous when she thought of that.

She'd had a couple of boyfriends, nothing serious, but Maria was never a slag at school. She spent more time at netball practice than she did at parties; more time at home than hanging about the precinct and the back of the market car park.

The fact that her suitor was a gypsy made the fantasy

more exciting, or terrifying, she wasn't sure which. Both, probably.

He'd driven by as she walked back from school on the Thursday, pulling up alongside her in a flashy filthy Range Rover, arm hanging out the side. He knew where she went to school! She was a bit embarrassed to be seen in her uniform, but mainly smug that her mates got to see the car when he called her over.

She trotted across the road to him, her hair a pennant in the breeze.

'Fancy coming for a ride?' he grinned.

'I've got to get back for my tea before my dad goes to work.'

'You're no fun, you.' Teasing. 'Well, we'll leave it till Saturday, then.' All dimples, all chat.

Maria looked round to check her mates were watching. They were.

'So, they're calling me Joby.' He left a gap for her name, which she willingly filled.

'Maria.'

After he gave her the details of where to meet for their night out, he leaned out of the car, reached over and wound his hand in her hair, his fingers snaking around the back of her neck, and he pulled her towards him through the window. That kiss with the flicker of tongue was the end of her.

She wore a summery dress – pink, as she recalls – her nails done the same colour, a peony on the slide scooping her hair behind one ear. She'd plaited it overnight, so it fell over her shoulders in waves.

She met him by the cinema as instructed.

He strode up to her like he owned the world. She might have laughed at his swagger, but she was dazzled. He kissed her on her neck and wrapped his arm around her waist.

The pub wasn't the sort of place her dad went to. Rough. No one batted an eye when he ordered her a vodka and coke. She'd only asked for it because that was Frankie's drink. Joby had a pint of lager, licking up the side of the glass to catch a dribble, looking at her as he did it.

He led them to a table in the middle of the room like he was showing her off.

He took up a lot of space, his ankle crossed over his knee, leaning towards her over the table to ask a question. Tight jeans, tight T-shirt, but clean this time. She couldn't take her eyes off him. She felt drunk after two sips of her drink, high on the novelty of it all.

He got them both a refill. When he came back to the table, he slid his hand around her ear, making her shiver, and he took the slide from her hair and put it in his pocket. 'So you'll have to see us again,' he said and winked.

She couldn't help but look and look at him. Blue eyes, like hers, dark wavy hair, builder's arms. And those dimples!

He told her he hung about with Tyson Fury. He said he'd boxed too but he'd 'knocked the fighting on the head' himself because he had better things to do with his hands. A dirty grin aimed at her.

She blushed.

He pulled a packet of Marlboro Reds from his pocket. She watched those hands open it, large workmen's hands, nut-brown like his face. Although— The thought of where he might be paler sent a shivery jolt right through her that made her squirm slightly in her seat.

He popped a fag behind his ear.

When they got outside the pub, he offered her one.

'Oh, no thanks.'

'Clever girl.' He smiled as he lit up.

'It'll kill you,' she joked.

'Nah. If it were dangerous, they'd be putting warnings on the packet.'

'But there are warnings on—' She realised he was mocking her.

They went for a walk down the lane that led to the disused railway line. She noticed she was as tall as him, even in her sandals. They stopped by a tree, and he trailed his hand through her hair and pulled her towards him. The taste of nicotine made her knees weaken as he smoked and kissed and kissed and smoked. Then he laid her beneath him on some dock leaves, which were cool and damp beneath her shoulders and hips. He gnawed on her neck.

'No.' She struggled up, grabbing his wrist to stop him doing anything else. 'I've not done it before.'

'Good girl.' He sighed, running the thumb of his other hand across the wetness of her, making her tremble, making her desperate for his fingers inside her.

'You been smoking?' snapped Frankie when she got back, not late as it turned out. Joby brought her home well before eleven, so if Frankie had been trying to catch her out she was disappointed.

Maria had to finish herself off in the bathroom, the bedroom, once, twice, three times, conjuring the smoky smell of him, his hands, his tongue.

He kept her hairslide.

If her dad noticed she would say she'd lost it, but he never did.

From that night it was like a fever, all she ever thought of – *Joby*.

At school, in lessons, she might forget what had happened for a couple of minutes and then she'd remember again and gasp, as if she'd been stung.

She giggled with her mates like usual as they walked to the school bus, she smiled to herself in classes, she was distracted at netball and Miss Atkinson shouted, 'Get your brain in the game, Wing Attack!' She did her homework and she made her dad's tea and she mopped Murad's floor – and while she was doing all that, going through the motions, she glowed.

He was her heart, the pulse between her legs, the pulse of her blood – *Joby, Joby, Joby*.

16

Anxiety hits her in the gut as soon as she opens her eyes. The owl's hoot outside chills her. Maria has to get up, no matter what time it is, a cold sweat on her back, shaky as she quietly pads around downstairs until it's light enough to shower and dress and see to Elsie. She's keen to get to work because she needs the physical activity to get rid of the curdling tension, although the nature of her job doesn't distract her enough from the thoughts that crowd in on her.

Did Nick have friends? Will they come sniffing round asking questions? Will Del push for more answers? Will he notice that the disturbed rose bushes at the bottom of the garden have obviously carked it? Will the death of her husband hit Elsie at some point? Should Maria feel more guilty?

What the hell is she turning into?

Since the night of the burial this constant thrumming anxiety is now Maria's new normal.

It's a state she's experienced before. The familiarity does not help. She leaves Elsie at the next-door neighbour's house for the morning – the widow, not the students, although she wonders if Elsie wouldn't be happier with them – and sets off for work, cutting across Green Lanes and over the bridge by Harringay Station, scooting through the side roads with the nice gardens, until she crosses the A1 via Suicide Bridge. When she first came to London, she'd thought about that, but they've now put up higher railings to dissuade the half-hearted from jumping. She breathes in traffic fumes until she finally reaches the back of the Whittington and her first job of the day at Bex's flat, a chic paradise full of neon lights and hot-pink cushions.

Maria would love lights and cushions like that.

Bex is one of those clients who will not stop trying to engage her in conversation, as if Maria is a friend, not a servant. But Maria doesn't know what to say at the best of times, let alone now.

How's my day been? The usual hard slog. Would you like tips on getting bloodstains out of a carpet?

It is always difficult if a customer works from home – free-lancers, usually, or writers – all desperate for a break in their day. Now, with more clients only commuting to their offices part time, Maria often finds the demands of conversation harder work than the cleaning.

Bex works in front of a huge computer screen, although she is just as likely to be found scrolling through funny videos of dogs on her phone.

When Maria arrives, she's asked if she fancies a drink. She often powers through long days on coffee and tea alone, so she rarely refuses an offer like this, but when Bex puts on her oversized fake-fur coat, Maria realises they're going out for coffee. She hopes she won't be required to buy anything herself – an everyday mortification for the working poor.

Maria traipses down the stairs behind Bex. She's led across the bustle of Junction Road, and Maria pauses by the Costa, assuming that's where they're going, until she catches the expression of horror on Bex's face, and hurries on after her.

A few doors down, they arrive at a new independent café with the sign *GRRRINDRRR* emblazoned across the window along with several winking emojis. 'It only opened last week!' Bex informs her with a note of excitement in her voice more appropriate to discovering the cure for cancer.

'Flat white?' asks Bex, who, thankfully, seems to be paying. 'Or should we try the dirty chai latte?'

Maria nods, unsure of what she's agreed to. There is nothing under three pounds fifty on the board.

Maria sits, distracted by the dust on the shelves featuring ugly ceramics made by a *local artist*. Bex brings over their drinks and starts wittering about 'Kenyan versus Colombian' as she proceeds to unload and set up her laptop. Why anyone might want to work in a shop with music, chatter and constant interruptions from inquisitive dogs and toddlers, rather than in her own quiet two-bedroom, Maria can't fathom.

If Maria ever has a nice home again – somewhere she might feel cosy, somewhere she might feel safe – she might never leave it.

Bubbly as ever, Bex starts questioning Maria on what

she's planning on doing for Valentine's Day.

'Nothing,' she replies. There's a whole lot of nothing in Maria's life.

Bex seems blissfully unaware that she's blundering into tender spots. She doesn't wait for Maria to say more but launches into her own plans – she and her boyfriend are planning a 'romantic jaunt to the country'.

'I hope they can manage without me in the office,' adds Bex, rambling on about colleagues whose names mean nothing to Maria, then launching into a complaint about the 'latest graduate intake' at her firm. PR. Maria isn't sure what that entails. 'Ethnically diverse, which is a positive step, props to HR, but still unanimously privileged,' grumbles Bex, blithely unaware of any irony.

Maria forces a smile through her expensive foam and tunes out of Bex's witterings – 'The problem is what should I wear for the Valentine's Day tasting menu? I want to look sexy, obvs, but don't want to feel constrained, you know . . .'

Yeah, OBVS that's a real problem, thinks Maria, nodding, but checking her phone.

Along with her own issues, Brian has had another meltdown. He has texted her a dozen times this morning, distraught. *I don't know what to do! I CAN'T BEAR IT!!!*

Brian's company doesn't have an HR department and he isn't in a union. His boss is still pressurising him to come back to the office, even though the doctor has signed him off for another two weeks. Maria doesn't know what to tell him.

The more she thinks about the bastard boss, the more it riles her.

A long, repetitive, grinding day ensues, the highlight of

which is Maria imagining what revenge she might exact on the man bullying someone as nice as Brian.

Back at Roseberry Gardens, Elsie insists on making Maria a cuppa when she comes in, although the tea is always in a mug.

'You're looking a bit peaky, darlin', aintcha? You feeling okay?'

'Yeah,' lies Maria, 'I'm fine, love.'

'Look, not my place or anything, but you need to put the brakes on a bit, you know? Put your feet up. It's too much all this sorting me out on top of all the cleaning jobs. You're not getting any younger.'

'And you are?' teases Maria.

'Cheeky bugger! No, listen, you've got to get your rest. I hear you wandering round the house in the middle of the night, you know?'

'Sorry. I'll try to be quieter.'

'Not the bleedin' point,' says Elsie. 'It's just . . .' The old woman regards her. 'I *know*. I'm worried as well . . . about you-know-what,' she says, nodding her head towards the garden. 'What happens if . . .?'

The *what-ifs* are multiplying in Maria's mind: what if Elsie tells Del or anyone else what lurks at the bottom of the garden? What if Del sells the house? What if the police start looking for Nick?

'I don't know, Elsie,' says Maria. 'I really don't.'

'Oh, darlin'! We'll come up with a plan. No, don't look sad – we *will*!'

She comes over and wraps her arms around Maria. The affection, the '*we* will', is almost too much, as if someone has grabbed what is left of Maria's wizened heart and squeezed too hard. Elsie is the only person to hold her, and, since Joby, the only person to love her.

She misses that physical contact as much as she dreads it.

How she'd craved Joby's touch – couldn't get enough of him.

And look how that had turned out.

When Elsie is in bed, Maria puts the door on the latch and pops over to the neighbours.

The student who looks a bit older than the rest answers. Half-hearted beard, spots; a highly unlikely UCLA sweat-shirt. Maria knows him enough to nod to him if their paths cross coming and going.

'Hi. A problem?' he asks.

'No. Not at all. I just wondered if you have any mush-rooms I could buy?' No point beating around the bush.

He looks startled.

'I'm not the police,' she adds, as if anyone might mistake her for an undercover cop.

'Er . . .' His mouth gapes.

'Please. You'd be really helping me out.'

He says nothing, just looks gormless.

'I smell your dope wafting over,' she tries. There are few places in London where you don't smell dope, but her com-ment does the trick.

'You'd better come in.' He hurries her inside.

The house is a mirror image of Elsie's but it's much neglected. There are bits of plaster missing and one of the windows is cracked. As she expected, the place is filthy. There's an impressive cluster of spider webs in the top corners and burns in the greasy cover of a ramshackle sofa.

The young man looks embarrassed, either by the state of the room or by her request.

'If you don't have any, I thought you might know someone who did? The 'shrooms, not the dope.'

He doesn't reply, so she tries, 'I'm going to a party.' And she smiles in what she hopes is a friendly way. She takes the cash she's borrowed from Elsie's tin out of her pocket. It will take her weeks to pay back, but she can hardly ask Brian to pay for the *special nibbles*.

The money galvanises the youth. He leads her through to the kitchen at the back and for a moment she wonders if he might be about to offer her button mushrooms from the shop, but he bends and burrows to the back of a drawer and brings out a washbag.

The dried 'shrooms are neatly packaged in small food bags.

'Sixty for a quarter. They're my mate's,' he adds, as if she's bothered.

Maria has no idea if she's being ripped off, but hands over the money.

'Good quality,' he enthuses. 'Are you micro dosing?'

'Sort of.' She holds her smile.

'You'll only need a pinch.'

'Yeah. Thanks.'

They are both relieved when she leaves.

Apart from baking Elsie a birthday cake, and making her favourite bread-and-butter pudding, Maria's hasn't done much cooking. She finds she enjoys preparing the vol-au-vents.

Joby taught her about mushrooms. He showed her what to pick in the fields – berries, herbs, leaves, nuts – how to live off the land, what to look for, how much to use. He could catch a rabbit in a snare, hook a brown trout from a stream, cook a squirrel – although, more often than not, he'd just go to McDonald's.

He taught her many things, Joby: how to drive, how to read the tea leaves, how to brush her hair one hundred times every morning and one hundred times every night.

Some lessons were harder.

She considers adding just a pinch as the student suggested, but that's not the effect she's after. She wants the boss totally off his head. She wants him to suffer. She would like him to feel like he's going insane. So she adds the whole packet and stirs.

Hubble bubble, she thinks, and smiles to herself.

17

The night of the party comes round. Maria turns up dressed in a black T-shirt and black leggings as Brian requested, so she looks *professional*.

'Are you sure you don't want me in a French maid's get-up with a cap and frilly apron?' she'd joked, but Brian seemed too nervous about the occasion to smile.

She is also nervous. Will she really offer her special treats to Brian's boss? The man might not come. Or he might not eat a vol-au-vent. Despite all the preparation, she might be disappointed.

Two dozen people have turned up by half eight. Maria walks around topping up drinks and handing out food, clearing up paper plates and emptying the ashtray on the patio at regular intervals. Brian's new boyfriend, Alex, arrives at nine, sweeps Brian into a huge embrace and is glued to his side as Brian starts introducing him to his friends.

Maria meets Alex as she's ladling out more hummus in the kitchen. Brian leads him over and he gives her a kiss on the cheek.

'I'd go in for the hug,' says Alex, 'but it seems you have your hands full.' He grins at her.

She instantly likes him, but she's glad it's only a peck on the cheek. She doesn't really do hugs until she's sure of someone.

'Brian has nothing but good things to say about you,' he beams. 'I'd love you to come and do for me if you're not too busy. Cash in hand so the bosses don't get a cut? Is Hoxton on your patch? And do you mind guinea pigs? I have two – Belle and Cinderella. Absolute monsters! They run me ragged!'

She smiles, but before she can answer, they hear a booming voice from the front door. 'The big bad wolf, I assume?' says Alex.

Maria nods and makes a face.

'Wish us luck,' says Alex, hotfooting it after Brian, but he's waylaid by a girl with green hair on his way out.

Even from the kitchen she can hear the boss crowing, 'Uber Lux. The only way to travel, mate.'

For the next half-hour, Maria keeps her eye on Brian as he studiously avoids his boss, which is quite a skill given the amount of space in the flat. It has filled up with more guests and she walks round offering plates of nibbles.

She's fascinated by the array of fancy eyewear on display, a kaleidoscope of colours and unusual shapes – mostly designer, she guesses. Almost everyone vapes or smokes, which means there's a queue for the patio. *Creatives.*

Brian sends fretful glances her way any time the boss orbits nearby. The man is braying about his forthcoming trip. 'Lads in Ibiza, lads in Split, lads *on the pull*!' He has to be at least forty, reckons Maria; *lads* hardly covers it. 'Jet-skiing, coasteering, all the fucking jollies! The full-on super-yacht experience,' he boasts to anyone who'll listen. Given that he pays the wages of a good proportion of the guests, there's a gaggle of attentive faces surrounding him, hanging on his every word.

The thing that strikes Maria, along with the volume, is the edge to his voice – she's heard that tone with some of Joby's mates and it never led to anything good.

She's blotting a red wine spillage with a kitchen towel, when she spots the boss corral Brian by his aspidistra. Somehow he's been separated from Alex, who's either in the toilet or in the kitchen, leaving Brain exposed.

There is gesticulating and an angry pantomime, all jutting chin and puffed-up chest, and a finger prodding in the general area of Brian's face, and as Brian sinks into himself, as the slurs about his work get louder, harsher, his workmates start melting away lest they be implicated, but not before the boss says loudly enough that anyone might hear, 'You supposed to be drinking on your antidepressants, mate? Won't that send you into another hissy fit? Pity you can't grow a pair and get back on it in the office rather than wafting around here like a fucking princess.' *HAW HAW HAW!*

That grating laugh again. Maria stiffens.

She makes her way closer, ready to intervene at Brian's signal. As the boss's voice lowers, he gets more sibilant, sliding into mockery of Brian's flat, his *lifestyle* – 'a bit pink, mate, a bit pink for me'.

He leans over, placing one hand on the wall, backing Brian into the corner and as he does so, his leg catches the plant pot.

'Avril!' squeaks Brian as the aspidistra topples.

'It's a fucking plant. Get over yourself!' laughs the boss.

Maria rushes forwards to help Brian right the plant and its stand. Thankfully only two stems are broken. As she squishes down the soil, she bristles further when the boss snorts, 'And that big fat fairy over there in the Madonna T-shirt . . .' He points towards Alex, who is beaming and chatting to a group of tipsy girls from Brian's office. 'He your girlfriend, is he?'

That's when Maria decides.

Brian's boss is distracted by the arrival of two young women. He struts away from Brian to greet them, as if this is his party.

'Are you okay?' she asks Brian. He nods and swallows the remains of his wine in one. Alex comes over and Brian seems to gather himself a little.

Her homemade items are on a separate plate, covered in clingfilm, hidden in her rucksack on top of the fridge. She hadn't made up her mind whether or not to offer them until this point. Now she can't bloody wait.

She hurries to the kitchen, checks she's not observed, and retrieves her special treats. She locates Brian's boss in the lounge, presenting the plate with a flourish.

He doesn't register her at first – too busy talking *at* a redhead, listing more of the adventures he's planning on his big willy trip – but Maria stands tall, blocking him into a corner (see how he likes it), staring him down with a forced smile, until he finally glances her way, and she thrusts the vol-au-vents towards him.

He hesitates, so she simpers, 'Would you like to try one? I made these myself.'

He takes one. She hopes he chokes on it.

She has steeped the mushrooms in sherry and cream. The pastry is perfection – ready-made from Waitrose, thanks to Brian giving her money for the shopping.

Maria holds herself very still and swallows a desire to scream as the boss sticks his tongue into the filling, staring at her as he swirls it around obscenely.

He takes a bite and says, 'Yum yum.' He eyes her, leering. 'I like a woman who cooks. What else do you do?'

'I clean,' she answers.

'Oh, I love a woman on her knees!' he smirks.

She forces herself to unclench her jaw. 'Would you like another?' she suggests.

'No, I'm good—'

'I imagine someone like you needs to fuel your workouts. Your muscles are *so* impressive!' She smiles. She is a good liar.

She only fully retreats when he's finished the second pastry, snatching away his empty plate. As she turns to leave he smacks her arse.

It takes a lot of self-control not to turn and punch him in the face, but she goes back to the kitchen and waits until she's alone before putting her special snacks back in the carrier bag and stuffing them deep in her rucksack. She will wash the plate especially carefully back at Elsie's.

And then she waits.

She watches the boss's every move, hoping, at the very least, the man will make a total tit of himself in front of his employees. She hopes he's violently sick, or, better yet, tortured by a really bad trip – she'd like to see him writhing on the kitchen floor in terror, mewling for his mummy.

She has a fleeting image of shoving him into a deep hole and burying him.

But it doesn't happen. Maria is disappointed when the boss leaves only fifteen minutes later.

At least then Brian's face relaxes, and his fingers unclench. He gets out his karaoke machine and sits on Alex's knee – it's Abba time!

She helps Brian and Alex clear up later, long past midnight, chatting about the guests. Brian seems happy. Alex announces that Brian's boss is obviously 'a closet queen'. And Maria has to content herself by imagining the vile man disgracing himself on the tube or in his Uber, or perhaps he's back at home – doubling over with cramp, heaving up his guts into a toilet bowl – or if he's blessed having his third eye opened to the many wonders of the universe, he's terrified, no idea what's happening to him, falling and spiralling into space.

If it had been a different sort of party, at a different time in her life, she might have cut a vol-au-vent into two pieces and offered Brian and Alex half each. That would be more than enough. A whole one is pushing it – two, if she's honest with herself, is probably dangerous. She knows that, but she still did it.

And she's glad.

But she doesn't really hope the trip will be so bad he'll jump off a building. She doesn't hope he'll die.

Does she? No. That would make her a cold-blooded murderer.

18

It wasn't long before Maria was spotted out with Joby, and someone reported back to her dad. It was hardly a surprise as Joby seemed to want them to be seen, yet, foolishly, she hadn't rehearsed her answers for the inevitable interrogation.

'How old is he?' her dad asked one day.

'I'm not sure,' said Maria, which wasn't a lie.

'Because from what Frankie reckons, he's a man, not a lad. And what's a man want with a schoolgirl?'

'I make him laugh,' she replied. That much was true.

'You'll be laughing on the other side of your face, missy,' he shouted out of nowhere, making her jump. Her dad rarely raised his voice. Frankie had obviously been bending his ear.

Then it all came out. Before she'd even closed the door as she came in from school, Frankie spluttered from the sofa,

'Now we know why you kept your mouth shut, don't we? Because he's a bloody gyppo, this bloke, in't he? From that new site up by the petrol station, in't he?'

'He's got a job,' tried Maria, abandoning her jacket and any hopes of a quiet teatime.

'You don't know where that lot have been or what they get up to,' said her dad, obviously narked.

'Some of his family are settled. They've a couple of houses on the Thringstone estate.'

'How they pay for that, then?' challenged Frankie.

'They've got horses and his uncles do roofing and stuff. Repairs and—'

'And rip off pensioners while they're bloody at it!' snapped Frankie, who loved stirring.

It died down a bit, mainly because Maria only saw Joby when her dad was on shift, and they avoided pubs. He drove her out to places – the countryside round Rutland, which she loved. And he promised they'd go to the seaside one day, but he had work and she always had to get back home because Frankie checked up on her.

She couldn't wait to go travelling with him. The annual week in Skeggy was the furthest her dad went.

Then Joby sent her a bunch of white roses, three dozen of the bloody things, which left Frankie spitting feathers, and it all kicked off again.

'There's more to it that this, you know,' she snarked as she watched Maria put them in two vases of water and a pasta jar she had to empty out to house them all. 'Gifts and nights out and stuff – that'll all stop soon enough. And then what?'

Maria couldn't remember the last time her dad had bought Frankie a proper present. She usually got a bog-standard card and a box of chocolates from Murad's for her birthday and that was about it.

'And you know what men want in return for presents,' sniffed Frankie. 'And don't you dare roll your eyes at me, you cheeky little mare. You haven't got a bloody clue.' She barked out a bitter laugh. 'You don't know the half of it!'

'You listen to our Frankie,' said her dad, launching into a long speech about how 'young 'uns like you always think you know better, but life has a way of biting you on the arse', and so on.

All Maria heard was '*our* Frankie'.

'How did you know I loved white roses?' she asked Joby when she met him later, sitting on his lap, snuggling into him.

'I didn't, not till just now.' He smiled, nuzzling into her hair, her neck, tickling his hand up her thigh. Oh, he knew what she liked, all right.

Maria knew she was in love with him – a constant fizzing feeling whenever she saw him – only she wasn't going to be the one who said it first.

She only had the one bust-up with Joby in those early weeks – when he went off to some horse fair. She wasn't invited, and she sulked because she was desperate to go somewhere new.

Joby said there was no way she could come because his family wouldn't be at all pleased that he was seeing a flattie girl, which was what his lot called settled people like her and her dad, and she wouldn't be able to stay in his wagon with him because they weren't wed, so there'd be no point.

Her dad would never have let her go anyway.

'You enjoy yourself,' she sniffed. 'I might not be waiting for you when you get back.'

'Don't even joke about that, girl,' said Joby, pulling her close to him, so she felt how much he was going to miss her.

After a few months when the romance hadn't run its course, a powwow was arranged. Joby met her dad, taking them to the Birch Tree, buying all the drinks with an impressive wodge of cash. Maria sat perched on the edge of her seat, wincing at the awkwardness from her side of the table where she was squashed on to the bench alongside Frankie and her dad, like they were interviewing Joby for the position of boyfriend.

'I will treat her like a queen,' beamed Joby, doing what he did best, talking and smiling.

'And how will you afford that, then?' challenged Frankie.

'I make a good living, see. My family are grafters. We take pride in our work and in our community. There's the building work, the scrap, market stalls, Uncle Nugget's horses – he does the accessories and traps and all – the car repairs, and our Jed's antiques—'

'Into all sorts, then,' interrupted Frankie, determined to be unimpressed. But her dad took to enthusiastic nodding as Joby continued to catalogue the extended family's enterprises and implied wealth.

'We've got good solid businesses. Good prospects, see.'

'And I bet you don't pay it all back in tax,' suggested her

dad, suddenly flushed with booze and high hopes.

'I'm not daft,' laughed Joby, winking like they were in this together.

'But the *culture*,' Frankie tried out the word. 'It's hard on women, isn't it?'

'Ah now, don't you believe everything they say about that nonsense,' said Joby, turning on the twinkle. 'That's racism, that.'

Frankie looked shocked to be accused of such a thing. Her friend Cynthia from the t'ai chi class down the Masons' hall was from Malaysia. Of course, her real name wasn't Cynthia but the other one was unpronounceable, and she was happy enough answering to Cynthia.

'You come to the site any day and have a word with some of the ladies there. See what they say,' offered Joby.

Maria clocked her dad eyeing the Range Rover when they said goodbye in the car park. It had been cleaned and polished for the occasion. There was a hearty handshake. The four pints Joby had bought her dad had helped, while Joby himself had stuck to two halves of lager. He didn't light up a fag and Maria didn't get a proper kiss goodbye, just a chaste peck on the cheek.

Frankie wouldn't talk to her dad on the way home. They walked back in silence. 'He might have that one wrapped around his little finger,' she hissed, indicating her dad as he went up to bed, 'but he don't fool me.'

'He knows Tyson Fury,' tried Maria.

'They're all interbred, that lot,' spat Frankie.

★

When Frankie announced that she'd heard Joby was married, she looked like she'd won the lottery. But that juicy gossip backfired on her big time.

It turned out Joby had been married. But his first wife, Liberty, had died in a car crash, that most ordinary of tragedies, which made Maria's heart swell with tenderness and disposed her dad to like him a tiny bit more.

Not Murad, though. She saw the way Joby looked at Murad when they met, and the way Murad looked back at Joby, and she felt ashamed of them both – casual racism on each side.

Frankie never apologised for getting the wrong end of the stick, but her dad laid off Maria, for a time at least.

But just as that crisis had been averted, another was lurking around the corner. Maria took a funny turn.

She had to stop playing during her Saturday-morning netball and sit on the bench by the side of the court sipping water that tasted metallic, and she tried not to heave as she put her head down between her knees.

On the bus home, Maria realised with a wave of absolute terror that the life she'd dreamed of was over. She had to get off two stops early before she brought up the water.

Her friends were chuffed to bits with all the excitement, but Maria was reeling.

She did a test and told Frankie before telling her dad.

'It's *his*?'

The way Frankie said it, Maria felt even sicker. 'Of course it's Joby's. Jesus!'

'More fool you,' said Frankie, adding, 'And don't think I'll be telling your dad for you. If you're old enough to get yourself in this mess, you're old enough to face the consequences.'

When her dad went back on days, she bought his favourite pie from Jo's Chippy and asked him to turn the telly off because she needed to talk to him about 'something important'. He probably thought it was about what A levels she might do, which, up until then, had been the most important life decision she'd had to face.

She found it hard to get the words out. In fact, she didn't manage. Her dad looked at her pale face and paused with a forkful of beef and onion halfway to his lips.

'You're bloody not, are you?' he asked.

She nodded, her lower lip trembling.

It was worse than she'd feared. He didn't shout or rage or swear or threaten. He put the fork on his plate, his head in his hands, and lowed like livestock.

Joby was the only one pleased.

'I always wanted a babby,' he grinned, stroking her belly, which made her feel even more queasy. He told her how he'd tried with Liberty, but it had never happened. Mind you, they'd only been married six months when she died. 'And we'll get wed!' he said. It didn't seem to be a question.

The next week she met Joby's mother, Lily.

Lily's wagon was like stepping through the looking glass, a little mobile palace: etched windows and mirrors; lovebirds in a cage; bright jewel-like fabrics on the curtains,

123

upholstery, the tablecloth. There was a horseshoe above the gas fire, a statue of the Virgin Mary on the shelf, a huge statue of a dog in a corner, although the actual dogs were kept outside.

Lily looked like she was dressed for a Saturday night out and it was only eleven in the morning. Her dark hair was piled high on top of her head, gold clips holding it up, black and gold around her eyes, gold earrings, blood-red lips, purple dress. She looked magnificent.

Maria was grabbed and hauled in for a huge embrace. Lily squeezed her to her chest, cried a bit, then pushed her back, looking her up and down, placing her hand on Maria's belly, which wasn't showing at all, given that she was only a couple of months gone, and said, 'My first grandchild!'

Joby's family already knew she wasn't a traveller, so Lily didn't bother having a go at her on that front, but she did ask her what church she went to. Maria knew better than to say 'none' because Joby had told her that her gran and mum having been Catholic would go down well.

They'd been doing the getting-to-know-you chat for half an hour when Joby's dad got in from the building site and he nodded a greeting. Maria didn't know where to look when he stripped off his T-shirt then went back outside to wash his face, neck and under his arms with a flannel in a small bowl.

'Does he not want to come inside and do that?' she asked, embarrassed.

Lily snorted. 'Mokadi,' she pronounced. 'We have rules. We like to keep things clean.'

It didn't make sense to Maria.

Lily continued chatting until her husband came back in, then she swapped places and immediately set about getting his lunch on. Maria thought she might face a second round of questioning, but he switched on the telly and totally ignored her. She realised that if her dad was narked about the situation, so was Joby's.

True to his word, Joby did indeed treat her like a queen when she was pregnant. He turned up to her dad's bringing dark leafy greens, *for the iron*, he bought her Guinness when he took her to the pub, and he told her to spread Marmite on her toast *for the laddie*. He was convinced it'd be a boy and announced he wanted to call him Michael, after Lily's late father.

'It's too soon to start thinking about that,' said Maria, panicked as the idea of a baby became more real by the day.

Some nights she wondered if she should have kept her mouth shut, told no one, and gone to Leicester to the clinic to sort things out herself. She knew she was a terrible person for that thought.

When she got heartburn, Joby brewed up comfrey and mint leaves and made a tea for her to sip. He rubbed her feet when she went round to see him, although she wasn't allowed to spend the night in his caravan, even though that was shutting the stable door long after that particular horse had bolted.

Both sides agreed that she'd stay living at home until they wed, but the wedding arrangements, in the circumstance, were fast-tracked.

Her dad seemed resigned to the pregnancy, but Frankie was . . . 'repulsed' was the word that came to mind. 'Never wanted kids, myself,' she admitted, wrinkling her nose. She shrugged, adding, 'You and your dad came as a job lot.'

If it wasn't for the terrifying prospect of a child, it might have been the happiest time of her life, planning her future with Joby, and her escape from Frankie. But as she counted down the weeks to when she'd be leaving school and her mates and her old dreams behind, she felt a weight settle deep in her gut. It wasn't that she didn't want a kid one day, sometime in the far future; she just didn't want one then. But the decision had got away from her.

Joby loved the idea of being a dad and he loved her pregnant body. He constantly told her she was 'blooming'. He was thrilled with how big her breasts got. 'Hand-reared,' he joked when his brother Anthony commented on them, making her blush.

Early on she had told Joby that she didn't like the way Anthony looked at her.

'Ignore the runt,' he laughed, like it was a joke. 'He's forever flirting, our Anthony.' It was hardly reassuring.

Lily and Maria sat outside her wagon one Saturday afternoon, watching Joby and Anthony tinkering with the cars in the yard.

'Joby adores his little brother,' smiled Lily. The term was a joke because Anthony towered over Joby. 'Always been close, them two,' said Lily. 'You got no brothers or sisters?'

'No,' said Maria.

'A shame. I reckon this one's a boy,' said Lily, patting Maria's belly. 'And you'll be wanting a few more and all so he's not lonely, hey?'

Maria felt a wave of nausea.

That afternoon they snuck off to bed for half an hour, locking Joby's door. Joby caressed her breasts then kissed her belly, swearing he could see a bump, although she couldn't see much at all. He was tender, stroking her hair, massaging her back, but when he fucked her, he pinched her bullet-hard nipples until she almost fainted.

Whenever Joby took Maria round to see his mother, as soon as the cups of tea were finished, Lily would read the tea leaves.

'What do they say?' asked Joby.

'Change, son. Change,' she pronounced, poring over her dregs.

As good a bet as any, thought Maria, although she didn't say a word.

Lily read her cups like other folk read their star signs. She told Maria her grandmother had been Bella Lee, a famous Romany fortune teller.

Maria bit back the words, *Aren't they all?*

Maria's readings showed images like a man falling, fire, the devil. Maria couldn't make them out herself and wondered if her mother-in-law-to-be was just telling her scary stories to keep her in line. She should have listened.

But, at the same time, Lily was a hugger. Maria was embarrassed to find she liked it, and she loved Lily stroking her hair, like she was a pet or something. Maria loved Joby but the truth was, within a month, she was also smitten with Lily.

'I always wanted a girl,' sighed Lily. 'But after the lads,

nothing. Joby and Anthony are all I have.'

Maria thought that was plenty.

Joby was thrilled that his mother had taken to her.

She once overheard Anthony laughing about her behind her back, calling her 'a lanky bloody *gorger*, that one', and Lily shot him down.

'Stop it! That's your future sister-in-law!'

Joby told her his mother had doted on Liberty. There was no sign of the dead wife in Joby's trailer, but there was a picture of her on Lily's shelf. In the gold frame, Lily had her arm around the shoulders of a petite girl with long dark hair and dark eyes. Lily made Maria jump as she came up behind her while she was looking at it.

'She was too beautiful to live in this world,' she gulped, big fat tears spilling down her cheeks, taking a good deal of mascara along the way. 'There was a witness you know,' she sobbed. 'But they never found him, the bloke who did it.'

'I thought she'd died in a car crash,' said Maria, confused.

'She did. Some boy racer caused it. Stolen car. Found abandoned later. Never found him, though. Didn't look too hard, if you ask me.'

Maria patted Lily's shoulder. The older woman took her hand and gave it a squeeze.

'The thing is,' said Lily, as she dabbed her cheeks with a tissue, 'they're all scared of us really. They don't trust us, so they try to bring us down. They can't control us, so they try to destroy us.'

'Travellers?' asked Maria, unnerved, unsure of what was really being said. 'Gypsies?'

'Women,' said Lily, gripping her hand so hard it hurt.

19

She hears nothing from Brian after the party night. On the Sunday afternoon she can stand it no longer and texts, *How are things?*

Never better, comes the reply. Nothing else.

She's itching to find out what's happened to his boss, but it might be incriminating if she asks outright, so she forces herself to wait.

As she walks through Crouch End on the Tuesday, an unfamiliar tension builds, which might be fear or excitement or both – but she's disappointed that Brian's not home when she arrives. She expects him to return with pastries from Dunns, but by the time she's spruced up the flat there's no sign of him.

She texts, *I'm at yours. Where are you?*

In the office! he replies.

Oh. He wasn't due back for another week at least.

Are you okay?

Brilliant! He's not here! While the cat's away. I've taken in cupcakes!

Any news?

Britney might be releasing new music!!

Not the information she needs.

It niggles her throughout the overnight clean at Balogan's flat. What happened to Brian's boss?

She speeds through the work.

When she's finished, as she's locking up, she senses a man come up behind her. She jumps, dropping the keys. Bending to pick them up, she brings the longest key between her fingers, making a fist ready to attack if necessary, then she slowly pulls herself up to her full height.

He is much taller than her. He does not move, preventing her from getting past.

'You are the cleaner, yes?' A deep, accented voice.

'Yes. And you are?'

'I am Balogan.'

There is a weird darkness about him, not least because of his size – huge, filling so much space, blocking the light from the corridor. He too has a buzzcut – in this single aspect they might be twins.

'I live here.'

'Oh! Yes. Everything okay?' she asks, thrown, embarrassed.

He nods.

She takes a deep breath and puts the keys away in her bag, to give herself a moment, trying to gather herself, then she attempts to edge her way past him although there's not a lot of room.

They do an awkward shuffle around each other, then he reaches across her to push the door further open and steps inside his flat.

'Come in.' It sounds less an invitation, more an instruction.

She tries, 'Oh. No. Thanks. I'm finished. But . . . sorry. I have to dash. I—'

'Please.' He doesn't look away, his gaze intense.

'Er, just for a moment?'

'Balogan,' he reiterates. He offers his hand. She feels herself flush as she takes it. It is warm and smooth, unlike her own rough knuckles; large, like the rest of him. He reaches across with his left hand and cradles hers in both of his, and they both clock the remains of a deep gash on the back of it. He notices her reaction to the scar and pulls the hand back sharply, all the while smiling.

She takes in his well-fitting suit, which must have been made specially for him to accommodate the size of his arms and chest. Smart. The glimmer of grey hairs show across his scalp and chin, indicating age. A huge silver fox. She notices the faint line of another old scar across his forehead. Startling blue eyes.

He beckons her through to the spacious lounge which she has left in tip-top condition, as always. She stands in the doorway for a couple of seconds, self-conscious, and then follows him in. This had been her space – now he owns it completely.

The glow from artificial lights illuminates the London skyline. She can't help but turn and stare, as she always does.

'You like it here?' He indicates the window.

'Yes.'

'It is beautiful. The lights, yes?'

'Yes.'

'It has taken a long time, this . . .' He gestures around the flat. 'The *penthouse*.' He smiles. 'It is the right word, *penthouse*?'

'Yes.'

He seems genuinely delighted with his home.

His eyes look tired, like her own, yet his smile does not appear worn around the edges like hers. Piercing blue, like the eyes of a husky. She stalls, not sure whether she is required to continue the conversation or to make her excuses and leave.

'Welcome. You are?' His accent is hard to place. Nice manners, though.

'Excuse me? I am what?'

'I am Balogan. You are . . .?' One side of his mouth smiles.

'Oh. Maria.'

'Would you like a drink, Maria?'

'No. No thank you.' She is flustered.

Neither of them says anything for a moment. The drum-beat next door continues pulsing. He gestures towards the sound. 'Annoying this, yes?'

She was about to say it didn't matter but finds herself nodding in agreement. It is unusual for her to be so honest the first time she meets a client.

He says, 'The view makes up for bad neighbours. And I am not usually home so early.'

He walks to the bar in the corner of the room and takes

a vodka bottle out of the small fridge. 'I think, your accent, you are from the north, yes?'

'Sort of,' she replies.

'I am from the north of my country. Kiruna. A small mining town. Sweden. I come here to escape that . . . small-ness. What brings you here to London?'

'I'd never lived in a city before.' Maria is surprised she tells him this. She is surprised that he too is from a mining town, not that there are any working pits left where she comes from.

There is something about his manner, the way he cocks his head as if he is really listening to her.

'Not so many opportunities elsewhere,' he suggests.

She nods. 'No. I—'

A crash from next door makes her flinch.

Balogan holds up one finger. 'A moment.' He places the vodka bottle on top of the bar and leaves the flat. He moves gracefully, despite his size. She stands looking at the sky, unsure of what to do. She hears him bang on the neighbour-ing door, but not what is being said. The music immediately stops.

He returns, striding through the room to pour himself a drink. 'Are you finding everything here satisfactory?' he asks.

What an odd question. She should be asking him if he finds her work satisfactory. She isn't sure what he means and hesitates.

'Hm.' He seems to acknowledge her silence. He puts the vodka bottle back in its place. 'Are you sure?' He gestures to his drink.

'No. I mean, yes, thank you. Everything is fine. I don't want a drink.'

'You do a good job.' The lopsided smile again. 'Thorough.'

The compliment warms her. She finds herself returning his smile.

He comes over to stand near her as they both look out of the window. There's a long silence. He turns to face her, watching her looking at the view. His gaze makes her feel awkward and she blurts out, 'I'll have to go, get on.'

'Of course, of course. I am sorry to delay you. It was good to meet you, Maria. I am impressed with the . . . order you bring to my home. It pleases me. My work occasionally takes me away. It is good to return to this.' He nods at the fresh, tidy surfaces.

Suddenly he reaches forwards, and she quickly takes half a step back, pulling her head away like a baby tortoise retreating into its shell. More slowly he brings his hand to her temple and brushes away something tickly.

'A cobweb, I think,' he explains.

'Oh.' Probably from crawling under his bed to get the hoover around the legs. 'Um, thanks.'

'Goodbye, Maria. I hope we will meet again.'

'Yes.'

She drifts back towards her bedsit, confused about how this encounter has made her feel. She likes the man. He made her feel good about herself. But . . . Something about the conflicting emotions is familiar – any glimmer of some-thing nice also makes her sad and fearful that it will be snatched away from her.

Any hope or desire for something more, something better

than her small life, churns up doubts: she doesn't deserve it; she has no right to want it; there will be a horrible price to pay for *wanting*.

But beneath the confusion is a faint but insistent beat of, *Me, me, me!*

20

Ann, Nick's sour-faced sister, turns up at Elsie's the next afternoon.

'Who are you, then, darlin'?' asks Elsie as Maria leads her through to the kitchen. By the tone, Maria guesses Elsie is deliberately winding Ann up.

'Where's our Nick?' demands the woman, who favours frosted eyeshadows and has her hair set like a helmet. She plonks herself on a kitchen chair, aggressively parking her floral shopping trolley next to it.

In the past, Elsie expressed her fervent hope that, in the event of a divorce, she'd never have to see Ann again. No such luck. And divorce is highly unlikely now, given the circumstances.

When Spotty trots up for a fuss, or more likely sensing meat products in the trolley, Ann shoos the cat away.

Maria busies herself with the kettle, ears alert for anything incriminating Elsie might blurt out.

Nick?' demands Ann.

'Nick . . .?' replies Elsie, shooting Maria a sly look as Ann rummages in her handbag for a tissue.

'Don't you give me that!' snaps Ann before noisily blowing her nose.

'What am I giving you?' says Elsie, all innocence.

By the time Maria has the tea in the mugs, the two older women are sitting glaring at each other like it's a game of Who Blinks First.

'I've not seen him for the best part of two weeks,' says Ann, splashing her tea as she violently stirs in sugars. 'He's left all his stuff at mine, but he's buggered off again.'

Maria avoids eye contact but sets to cleaning the sink so she doesn't miss anything and can step in if things take a dodgy turn.

'His mates haven't heard a peep out of him. He's not even phoned Oggy. He's just disappeared.'

'Good riddance,' sniffs Elsie.

'Look, he's no angel, I know, right, but I'm getting worried about him. Do you know anything?' she calls across to Maria.

'No. I thought he was off with the betting shop woman?'

Elsie had told Maria all about Nick's messy fling with the deputy manager of the William Hill on Green Lanes. The relationship was apparently characterised by week-long benders and epic fights, which involved a brick through Ann's window one time after Nick had gone back to stay with her. It would make sense that Nick wouldn't go near his sister if he was back with the on-off girlfriend.

'She's thick as pig shit, darlin' – all fake tits and fake smiles that one,' Elsie had confided, seemingly unbothered by the affair. 'I get the sex part, I do. He's younger than me and he's always been a randy old sod. But after a couple of months, what? You have to talk to 'em at some point.'

Maria never knew what to say or where to look when Elsie went off on one like this, but the old woman would continue undeterred.

'You've got to have some conversation in a bloody relationship! Or a hobby to share. Pottery. Photography. How else you going to keep it going? How much time does the sex take? Half-hour if you're bloody lucky. And that's including all the pleading first,' she cackled.

'He won't be with her,' sniffs Ann. 'Not after the last time. She's trashed his vintage football card collection! Worth a bob or two, them, and all. He wanted to take them on the *Antiques Roadshow*.' She blows her nose loudly. 'He's not been round?'

'Not as far as I know,' says Maria, trying to keep her voice normal. 'He might have been here while I was at work.'

'When did you last see him, Elsie? Elsie!' demands Ann.

Elsie stares at the kitchen floor, as if she might conjure Nick from the tiles.

Maria intervenes. 'Elsie, didn't Del say Nick was back with the woman from the bookies? Didn't he reckon—'

'Del don't know his arse from his elbow,' snaps Ann. 'No offence. Elsie!' She waves her hand under Elsie's face, forcing her to look up. 'I know our Nick's been a total bastard to you, fair dos. But I need to know where he is.' She juts out her chin. 'He owes me.'

Ah, so that's why you're round here, thinks Maria.

'I hope he's dead,' announces Elsie. 'I hope he's dead and buried—'

'I think I need to get her ready for a nap,' interrupts Maria. 'She gets a bit cranky when she's tired.'

'She's not a bloody baby!' snaps Ann.

'It's part of her condition,' Maria snaps back.

'Well, if he does turn up, tell him I want a word.' Ann addresses Maria rather than Elsie. She mutters, 'Totally bloody unreliable, our Nick. Always was.'

Elsie's fingers clench and unclench whenever Nick's name is mentioned.

It takes another tea and quite a bit more flannel along the lines of Nick turning up someday soon to get the woman moving.

'Better make tracks,' says Ann finally, getting to her feet.

As she rummages in her trolley, Elsie suddenly pipes up with, 'I know! I know something!'

Ann says, 'What?' and Maria says, 'Elsie, no!' and Elsie chirrups, 'I know . . . your trolley's crap.'

When Ann and said trolley have left the building, Maria returns to the kitchen, and sinks to her seat, shattered. Elsie reaches for her hand, gripping it tightly.

'Would she go to the police?' asks Maria.

'Nah,' says Elsie. 'He's been growing weed in her cellar for years – ever since I put my foot down and told him to get it out of here. There's enough ganja in her house to poleaxe the entire darts team. She'll not have the Old Bill anywhere near.'

'But won't she worry where he is?'

'It's not the first time he's gone AWOL, babe. He buggered off to Newcastle once. Gone a month that time, living the high life up there. Went to a casino. She'll think he's off with the cash he owes her.'

It's reassurance of a kind.

'Shall we get your tea on?' asks Maria.

'He owes me and all,' says Elsie, ignoring the question. 'Always into all sorts – anything dodgy, bloody Nick.'

She looks tired, thinks Maria. Ann's visit has taken it out of her.

Halfway through another mug of tea and her poached egg on toast, Elsie suddenly stops eating and looks scared.

'He's not coming back, is he?' she says, her eyes big. 'He's not, is he . . .? He won't . . .?'

Maria gives Elsie's hand a squeeze and says, 'No, love. He's still dead.'

21

The agency calls. Balogan wants to up the night cleans to twice a week – Fridays as well as the usual Tuesday – and he's asked for her to do both. Maria agrees. There isn't really enough work for two cleans, but who is she to look a gift horse in the mouth?

That first Friday night the neighbours are surprisingly quiet, and she whizzes through her work.

The door opens before Maria has put on her coat to leave, making her jump. Balogan stands grinning with his hands behind his back, like he's on parade.

'I have something for you,' he announces.

'Oh. I—'

He steps forwards and thrusts a box towards her.

She's too startled to reach for it.

'Come,' he instructs. He takes another step towards her, so she has no choice but to put her hands out, and he places a package in them. Fancy wrapping.

'For me? Why? I mean . . . Really?'

'Open it. Please.' He gestures, his hands opening like a prayer book.

She unwraps the gold paper, neat corners, artfully tied with string, and finds a pair of bright pink rubber gloves, almost elbow-length, with a large fake emerald ring on one finger, plus shiny green stones and pink feathers around the top.

It is such a daft present, she laughs. It sounds weird to her ears, like it comes from someone else, someone she used to know.

'Perhaps not for the more taxing work?' His eyes crinkle as he says it, 'But your hands,' he reaches for one of them, 'they should be protected.'

Embarrassed, she snatches her fingers away.

Balogan steps back, his shoulders tense and his eyes narrow. He suddenly looks angry.

Shocked by the jarring change in atmosphere, she grabs for her coat. 'Sorry!' She steps round him and scuttles out the door, saying, 'Sorry, I have to go. Thank you.'

She bumps into Balogan's neighbours as she's leaving.

The man is wheeling a huge instrument case up the hall – a double bass by the looks of it, presumably the one she saw in his living room – and she has to stand back against the wall to let him pass. He does so with an icy stare, as if her face offends him. A girl is trailing behind, struggling to carry two guitar cases. As she passes Maria she smiles, eyes dark circles in a pasty face.

She says, 'Hiya!', sounding about twelve.

'Hi,' answers Maria.

'Sorry about the other night. The noise. Is it, like, your bedroom next to us?' She talks quickly, staccato. She seems very nervous.

'I don't live here,' explains Maria. 'I'm just the cleaner.'

'Oh. Right. Sorry, though. We, well, Mal and his mates, well, sometimes we, like, have a jam after a gig, you know how it is?'

Maria does not know.

'A bit of a party. Chill. Gets out of hand.' A short laugh, twitchy. 'Sometimes. You know. Sorry! Just finished a gig tonight. I sing!' She looks delighted with herself. 'But Mal's the musician – he writes all our stuff. Plays, produces, arranges. He's, like, a *genius*!' The girl flicks back her sweaty blonde hair.

'Cass!' calls the genius. He's wearing a baseball cap backwards as if he's a street kid. Trying way too hard to be young and trendy. 'Cass, come on!' he shouts, irritable.

And the girl moves on, throwing a bright, 'See you!' behind her. Then she pauses, turns back to Maria and says, 'Grab a coffee some time?' She looks so hopeful as she says this, Maria nods.

'Cass!'

The girl hurries after him.

On the way back to Elsie's, as she avoids the early shift workers sleepwalking to their jobs, dodging through traffic already queuing at the roadworks on Upper Street with a single horn optimistically tooting to no effect, each time

145

Maria thinks of the gloves in her backpack – a present, for her! – she swallows a smile.

Elsie is always on at her to moisturise her hands. She swears by Vaseline. Perhaps she'll give it a go – start looking after them again. She feels a small shoot of something which might be optimism.

But then she remembers how Balogan's eyes had changed when she pulled her hand away.

She passes a poster of a missing ginger cat which makes her heart sink. God knows what she'd do if one of Elsie's brood went missing.

A van is unloading outside the florist's. The roses make her shudder.

22

She had white roses at her wedding.

They rushed to organise it – a register office job, which Joby's side were not at all thrilled with, followed by a knees-up that her dad chipped in for, which sweetened the pill.

She turned to Lily for help with the arrangements. If that put Frankie's nose out of joint she didn't acknowledge it. Even with a small wedding there were so many things to sort out – the flowers, the shoes, the hairdresser . . . All Joby had to do was get dressed and turn up, while she had to decide on things like *party favours*, whatever they might be.

But despite the endless to-do list, the truth was she was excited to be marrying Joby. Her friends were all jealous and excited for her, and Maria was in love, and she wanted the big day and the big frock – Joby's parents paid for the wedding dress, which was *huge*, a proper princess dress.

'You look gorgeous in it!' enthused Lily as Maria turned like a ballerina in a jewellery box to admire her reflection in the bridal-shop mirrors. 'Our Joby's a lucky man. Your mother would have been so proud.'

Maria teared up hearing that.

Two weeks before the big day, pains started during a chemistry lesson. She hurried home from school, then sat in the kitchen waiting, wondering what to do. She drank tea and waited some more. As it happened her dad was at work and Frankie was out with some mates in Leicester, so at least she didn't have to talk to anyone or fake a happy face.

By morning the pains had stopped, and she realised she was happy about that, a reaction which surprised her. She didn't tell Joby about the scare because he'd only make a fuss. She didn't say a word – not to her friends or her dad or Frankie, let alone to a doctor. Afterwards, that was what she blamed herself for.

The morning of the wedding was a blur of getting ready. So much preparation and the ceremony was over before it started.

She slouched down on to one hip for the wedding photos because Joby said he didn't want her 'towering over' him, even though she was only wearing small heels.

'Hey, short arse!' mocked his brother. 'Have to get you a stepladder to mount her. You be marrying a supermodel with this one.'

Maria wasn't sure if it was meant as a compliment.

'Shut it,' laughed Joby, amused rather than annoyed. It

seemed his brother's digs couldn't reach him on his wedding day. Anthony had been the obvious choice for best man, which meant he squashed himself against her in too many photos.

Joby was all dimples and back slaps and from the moment they got to the reception, she didn't see him without a smile on his face and a bottle in his hand.

Her belly was mauled by Joby's family throughout the party, which made her squirm. So many brothers and sisters on Lily's side, all the uncles twirling her round the room, buying her dad so many drinks he was soft focused before half six.

Maria's family and friends looked like dowdy house sparrows next to the travellers. Their safe navy dresses and cream jackets couldn't hold a candle to the splash of colours on display from Joby's mates and relatives. The travellers' hats were full-on plumage, huge and flashy, the blokes' waistcoats gold and purple and pink. Maria's guests wore sober M&S get-ups, the usual black suits for the men, her dad going all out with a pale blue tie. Frankie, wearing 'dove grey', which is still grey when all's said and done, called Lily's frock 'loud', but not to her face.

Joby's side really went for it on the dancefloor. But as the evening progressed, there was an edge to some of the comments from a couple of the uncles – she could never remember all the names – a whiff of anger, violence. Twice she heard the word '*gorger*'.

One of the gypsy women was sneering to her mate about it only being a 'registry office, not a proper wedding', and Maria shot back that it was a '*register* office, actually', which did her no favours.

Anthony stumbled a little as he spun her round to 'Lady in Red' feeling up her bum in an entirely unbrotherly way until she managed to wriggle him off. Lily told him to, 'Stop mithering the lass.' Then she said to Maria, 'Bear him no mind, girl. Our Anthony's just being affectionate.'

Which was one word for it.

As Maria made her way off the cramped dancefloor, Anthony followed her, grabbing her arm. Thankfully Joby joined them, positioning himself between Maria and his brother.

'Time to start the fuck jar, Joby lad,' Anthony cackled.

Maria piped up, 'What's a—'

Anthony breathed fumes in her face, laughing. 'You be putting a fiver in a jar every time you fuck in the first year of marriage, like. Then you take out a fiver every time you fuck, from then on.'

The brothers laughed in unison.

'The thing is, you *never* run out of them fivers,' he whooped as Joby playfully punched his arm. 'You *never* empty that fuck jar for the rest of your death us do parts!'

She went upstairs to get changed. This was the second hotel they'd tried – when the first venue found out it was a travellers' wedding, they pulled the plug, returning the deposit, claiming a mix-up with the bookings. Lily appeared as she was unlocking the bridal suite, asking if Maria needed a hand.

'What did you say to your Uncle Pat?' she asked as she reached up to help Maria take the flower garland out of her hair – she'd worn it down like Joby wanted.

Maria wasn't sure which one Pat might be. 'I'm not—'

'Best to get down there and dance with him, hey?' Lily gave her a tight-lipped smile. 'Don't want him thinking my Joby's married a stuck-up little *gorger* bitch, hey girl?' Then she laughed, like it was banter, but Maria caught the edge of the words.

She knew Joby's lot didn't like settled people. Some stopped talking when they saw her approach, others gave hard stares. Her side weren't the biggest fan of the gypsies either. Being stuck in the middle, judged by both communities, did not bode well.

But later that night, upstairs in the honeymoon suite, Joby made her forget all that. Again and again and again.

He drove them up to the Lake District for their honeymoon, which was a big disappointment as she'd wanted to go somewhere abroad, and it was pelting down, the rain battering like hail on the caravan roof. But then they were in bed all day, which made up for the weather. Later, she wondered if that had brought it on.

Three days after they got back, the pains started, worse this time. Joby rushed her to hospital, but it was too late.

When her dad visited he didn't know what to say or where to look, but when he left to get them a coffee, Frankie said it was a shame it hadn't happened before the wedding. Maria was so shocked she felt dizzy.

She was still dazed when they got back to the trailer. She kept saying sorry to Joby and he kept saying she had nothing to say sorry for.

But she'd carried on with her netball, she'd had a couple

of drinks with her mates on her hen do, and she'd regretted getting pregnant – thought it was way too soon to be a mother. Did she wish it away?

Joby tried to console her, but his cuddles always ended in sex and she tensed up when he was inside her.

'What is it?' he asked. 'Does it hurt?'

'No, it's not that.' She wasn't sure she could explain.

'We'll have to start another babby,' he said, without missing a beat.

The thought horrified her. She couldn't go through that again.

'Can't we wait a bit?' she asked. 'I'm not sure . . .'

He looked like she'd punched him.

Which is why she didn't tell him when she went on the pill, hiding the packets between the pages of her books.

And then she realised, she might have wanted to be a bride, but she wasn't so keen on being a wife. So much sex those first few months – that fuck jar would soon be full – but so much cooking and cleaning.

Joby seemed to catch a whiff of her discontent. Sometimes she'd find him looking at her with a dark expression clouding his face. Perhaps it was suspicion, or perhaps it was just the way the light fell.

She didn't like lying to him, but she knew she didn't want to be a mother until she'd seen a bit more of life.

In the end, she saw too much.

23

Del has asked Maria to go straight back to Elsie's rather than to her bedsit after the Balogan cleans from now on, because he *can't be spared at work*. Essential work, flogging overpriced insurance and bank loans with crap interest rates, but someone's got to do it.

Maria doesn't even get a chance to lie down for half an hour that Saturday morning, because, after Elsie's breakfast, someone bangs on the front door so loudly it makes Elsie flinch.

'Jesus H. Christ!' she cries.

'I'll get it,' says Maria, irritated.

She opens the door to a stocky woman who shouts in her face, 'Where is he? He's back here, ain't he?' And before Maria can say a word, she barges her way into the house.

Maria shuts the door and rushes after her.

The woman is already in the kitchen, demanding of Elsie, 'Where is he? I know he's here! Nick! NICK!'

'No he bloody ain't here!' Elsie bellows. 'You think I'd have that bloody waste of space back? Get out! Go on, bugger off!'

'What's going on?' asks Maria.

'It's her from the betting shop,' Elsie clarifies.

'*Her*'s got a name!' snaps the woman, although she doesn't give it.

Nick was ten years younger than Elsie – her 'toy boy', as she sarcastically referred to him – although he was six-ty-six. His 'girlfriend' looks to be pushing fifty, but she might just have had a hard life. She sports a denim jacket at least a size too small, displaying an admittedly impressive if crinkly cleavage, crispy dyed black hair, and a heavily lined smoker's mouth. She wears huge, hooped earrings, like the gypsy girls.

Betting Shop Woman stands over Elsie, yawping. 'Oh, you think you're *it*, dontcha? Well, you can tell him from me—'

'He's not here!' roars Elsie.

Maria knows women like *the betting shop floozie*, as Elsie's refers to her, and she knows they're trouble. She won't go quietly, that's for sure. But she will not let her upset Elsie. She moves to stand between the mouthy visitor and Elsie's chair, just in case she lashes out, and says, 'We've not seen Nick. Neither of us.'

The woman whirls round to face her. 'And who the fuck might you be?'

'He's not been here,' repeats Maria, ignoring the question. She needs to get this woman out of here as soon as she

154

can. She prays Elsie doesn't blurt out Nick's resting place in a moment of anger.

'Is he upstairs?' asks the interloper, making a move as if to go and hunt for him.

'Don't even think about it!' warns Maria, really annoyed now. 'He's not here!'

'And I say he is. You calling me a liar?' she challenges.

'You'd better go,' says Maria, moving closer to her.

'Really? You gonna make me, are you?' The chest inflates with indignation.

Maria tenses. This has escalated pretty fast.

'You—'

Maria sees the slap coming a mile off. She ducks the blow, pushes her attacker against the kitchen wall and at the same time brings her knee up, connecting with the woman's pubic bone. Her opponent gasps and bends double.

'You give her what for!' whoops Elsie, clapping her hands in delight.

'Get out,' says Maria.

'Fuck-a-duck,' groans the woman. She pants, trying to get her breath.

Jesus. What if she goes to police and reports Maria for assault? Although an ABH charge would be the least of it.

'You tell him . . . tell him we're done.' She points at Elsie. 'I've had enough of his disappearing acts, the shady bastard. You're welcome to him.'

She limps away, spitting a final, 'He's not worth it!' behind her, and Maria slams the door after her.

Back in the kitchen Elsie's delighted. 'Oh, that was better than watching a bust-up in Albert Square, that!' she enthuses. 'Spitting feathers, she was, but you saw her off good and proper!'

Maria sits down heavily, shaking with adrenalin. 'Do you think we've seen the last of her? Will she be back?' she asks.

'Nah.' Elsie shakes her head. 'Nick was never that good a catch. Do you want a cuppa, darlin'?'

Maria's taken aback by how easily Elsie dismisses the altercation. She seems blissfully unbothered that the girlfriend could cause more trouble. And *trouble* hardly covers the fact that Maria might face life imprisonment if the police take an interest in the garden.

'I'll make the tea,' says Maria, sighing heavily. She gets the mugs. 'Are you okay, Elsie? She didn't touch you?'

'No. Fine and dandy, me. Bit of entertainment.'

Maria is far from entertained. Just because Elsie doesn't rate Nick as love's young dream doesn't mean the girlfriend won't worry about him and go to the police.

She asks, 'Elsie, what about Nick's mates? Are they likely to turn up or report him missing?'

'Since he retired he only knocks about with bloody winos,' snorts Elsie. 'If he's not buying a round, no one will give a toss.'

Maria's not convinced. The visit has rattled her.

She's shocked by her kneejerk response to the threat – as if that night of horror with Nick has unleashed some long-buried killer instinct.

She's worried – she's probably a poisoner as well.

And she's furious – Del's used all the semi-skimmed and not replaced it.

'We need milk, Elsie. I'll go and get some.'

Outside, she checks to see if there's any sign of her adversary, but the woman seems to have disappeared.

But who else might come looking for the husband rotting under the roses?

24

Del has the day off the next Tuesday and he grumpily agrees to take Elsie to a tea dance at the community centre down by the Angel.

Maria sets off early to Brian's. He's texted saying, *Working from home. Have eclairs!* She can't wait to find out what's happened with the boss.

She hurries past the Crouch End Waitrose, staring hard at the pavement, so as not to eyeball the *Big Issue* seller. She hasn't got anything to give her – she never has any spare change and smiling at the woman won't put food on her table.

As usual, she feels anxious about leaving Elsie alone with Del while she's working. What might she say? But what else can Maria do? She can't babysit her every minute of every day. She needs to keep the money coming in.

Maria has only ever been without her own cash twice in

her life – when she was a kid, before she started earning her own pocket money, and when she was with Joby – and she'll never make that mistake again.

She's nervous when she lets herself into Brian's flat, braced in case something truly terrible has happened. Much as she wished horrible things on the boss, what if the mushrooms can be traced back to her? Surely she would have heard by now if something awful had happened. No news is good news, right?

No one would realise she'd given anything *with added ingredients* to the man. She'd served canapés to everyone that night, nothing suspicious there. No one saw her take the special plate from the top of the fridge, no one was in the kitchen when she put it back in her rucksack. She didn't have a row with the boss, only spoke to him the once, so none of the guests are likely to connect her to him, would they?

The students next to Elsie could hardly say anything either. And there's no trace left of what she used.

But . . .

Just because you're paranoid doesn't mean they're not out to get you.

Brian seems chipper and unconcerned as he makes them tea. She asks if everyone enjoyed the party – by which she means the boss but she can hardly specify. Brian says everyone loved it, apart from a few gruesome hangovers the morning after, and he goes on to tell her he's planning on doing even more hours in the office while the boss is away on holiday.

So – he's away on holiday!

The relief hits her. She takes a big mouthful of the tea

– something hot and perfumed – and to her surprise realises she's also more than a little disappointed.

Her face must change because Brian looks concerned and asks how she's doing.

'Fine,' she tells him, although she's also telling herself.

'You look a bit knackered.'

'Thanks a bunch. I'm always knackered.'

Brian's one of the few clients who seem to be genuinely concerned. Most take her at her word as she brushes off any enquiries. But he pushes on.

'Are you sleeping? Is it Elsie? How is she?'

She hesitates. It would be so nice to confide in him. Tell him what she did, ask him to find out exactly what happened to his boss to put her mind at rest.

Instead, she tells him that Elsie is doing 'as well as can be expected' and sets about the cleaning.

When she's finished she feels almost giddy.

She shows Brian the ridiculous rubber gloves Balogan bought her, and they both laugh.

'Where did you get them?' he asks.

'A client.'

'A client who's buying you presents? I thought I was your sugar daddy,' he jokes.

'It's not like that,' she protests.

'It's always like that!' says Brian.

There follows ten minutes of Brian waxing lyrical about the many charms of his new man. Alex has so many sterling attributes, he may even walk on water.

*

When she gets back to Roseberry Gardens she can tell Del is annoyed before he opens his mouth. He fiddles with his cigarettes and glares as Maria swings her backpack on to a chair. Elsie beams up at her as Del purses the thin lines which pass for his lips.

'Well? How was the tea dance?' she asks.

'It was a bloody embarrassment, if you must know,' he pouts.

Boris tries to climb on Del's lap, but he pushes him down. Not a huge fan of the fur family, is Del. The cat hurtles out of the catflap pursued by invisible demons.

'Why? What happened?'

'She wouldn't leave the singer alone. Kept trying to sing along with him and grab him and stuff.'

'She likes singing.'

'There was this bloke there with his shirt off,' pipes up Elsie, word-painting with her fingers wiggling. 'Like Iggy Pop – that pickled . . . pizzle. Like one of the . . . them bleedin' bog people.' She laughs.

Del ignores her. 'And she wouldn't leave this other bloke alone – some dodgy geezer dressed like Elvis.'

'Fat Elvis,' clarifies Elsie.

'As long as she enjoyed it.'

'Wouldn't stop laughing,' says Del, as if this was a bad thing. 'Laughed at Elvis. Laughed at the singer.' His tone changes. 'Kept laughing and saying Nick would never dance again.'

Maria thinks, *For fuck's sake, Elsie!*

Elsie hoots and announces, 'He's only narked cos we didn't win the raffle.'

Del turns to face Maria, arms crossed. 'What did she mean?'

'What do you mean, "What did she mean?"' she tries. She's about to make herself a tea when she startles, noticing Boris at the bottom of the garden pawing near the rose bushes. For a second, she wonders if he's trying to dig up the old man, as if Nick has been summoned by the mention of his name, but then she realises the cat is just taking a shit on him.

'Why won't Nick dance again?' presses Del.

'I have no idea.' She forces herself to keep eye contact.

Del waits. It is hard not to fill a silence.

'Perhaps he might have hurt his foot?' supplies Maria, turning away and cringing as she says it. *Pathetic!*

'Really? When was this? Because the thing is, he's not got back to me about the lock-up. He said he'd give me a ring as soon as his mate got the keys. He knows I need to get the off-road parking sorted before my permit runs out. *She's* no bloody use.' He nods towards Elsie. 'I've asked around and no one seems to have seen him for weeks.'

Maria shrugs.

'He can't hurt no one no more,' chirrups Elsie, clapping her hands in glee. 'No-no no-no no-no!'

'Fuck's sake,' says Del, irritated with everything that comes out of Elsie's mouth.

Maria bustles around the kettle, willing Elsie to keep schtum. If she carries on like this she might as well put an advert in the bloody *Metro*.

'There's a brew on already,' says Elsie, making the shape of steam with her fingers.

Good. Keep her rattling on about tea, her favourite topic.

'Do we need fresh? It's not stewed, is it? What biscuits do you fancy?' asks Maria.

'Where do you reckon he might have gone, then?' presses Del. 'Seeing as he's hurt his foot, like?'

Sarcastic. What's he angling at?

'I know! I know!' squeals Elsie, her hand shooting up like she's back at school.

'The Chocolate Digestives?' tries Maria, rummaging in the cupboard, eager to distract her.

'He's—'

She grabs the Digestives and Ginger Nuts. Behind the abandoned Rich Tea, which Elsie saves for people she doesn't like, Maria finds the good stuff. 'Jaffa Cakes!' she announces. They might save the day.

Del stares at Elsie, who is bouncing up and down in her seat.

'He's gone. For *good*!' she crows. 'Ding-dong the witch is dead, the wicked witch is—'

'*Jaffa Cakes*, Elsie!'

Ignoring Maria, who is shoving three packets of various biscuits in Elsie's direction, Del takes hold of his aunt's hand, which causes her to turn and face him.

'Where's he gone?'

'He's . . . he's off . . .'

'Elsie, come on, let's choose . . .' Maria sounds like a demented kids' TV presenter, but if Del notices she's laying it on a bit thick with the biscuits, he doesn't say anything.

'He's off to see the wizard, the wonderful . . .'

Del crouches down so his eyes are the same level as

164

hers and makes his voice kind. 'Auntie Elsie, where is he? Where's our Nick?'

Maria sees Elsie's eyes flick to the window and back. Her brow creases.

'He's . . . he's under—'

'Elsie!' Maria's voice is screechy.

'Under . . . the moon of love!'

Del won't give it up. 'Stop arsing about,' he snaps. 'Where is he?'

'He's under . . . that woman from the bookies!' proclaims Elsie.

'Her?!' Del tuts. 'Again? Has he got bloody shares in Viagra?'

Maria exhales. Is Elsie remembering the recent visit from Betting Shop Woman, or is she deliberately crafting a cover story? Maria puts biscuits on a plate for something to do. When she and Elsie are alone, they eat them straight from the packet. If Del buys the yarn about the woman from the bookies, luck might be on their side.

'She was round here the other day after some of his stuff,' says Elsie.

'Yes, she was,' Maria confirms. It's the only true thing either of them have said about Nick since his death.

The interrogation fizzles out. Thank God.

When Del finally leaves, they watch TV and then Maria starts getting Elsie ready for the night. She's in high spirits and there are several rousing choruses of 'Over the Rainbow' before Maria can get her to clean her teeth.

When she's settled in bed with the special puzzle book recommended by Comfort – 'to keep what's left of my brain ticking over', as Elsie puts it – Maria goes back to the kitchen and pours herself another brew. She must be fifty per cent tea by now.

She gives the cats a fuss before shutting the kitchen door on them overnight – so they can stay indoors if they want, or get out of the catflap, but not pester Elsie. She strokes the little bald patch on top of Sweetie's head, fuzzy as a peach, worn thin with love like the Velveteen Rabbit.

The feline family used to sleep on Elsie's bed until recently. Maria would go into Elsie's room and find the old woman contorted around all four of them: Boris tucked behind her knees; Sweetie under one armpit; Spotty snuggled in tight next to her sister; Harry on the pillow, on top of Elsie's head, or nestled between her neck and shoulder.

But Maria started to worry that the tortuous shapes Elsie got herself into accommodating the cats wasn't doing her creaking joints any good. She also worried they might smother her in her sleep, although that was probably just an old wives' tale.

After some negotiation, it was agreed the cats would sleep in the kitchen and luxurious new beds were provided.

Now Maria worries that Elsie misses them.

Eventually, she forces herself to go up to bed.

She doesn't sleep more than a few minutes at a time without the new and improved worries along with the dark old memories dragging her back to the surface.

25

Maria liked the caravan at first. It was snug. Sure, she had to focus on putting things away in their right place – Joby nagged her if anything was left out, saying she might have had a messy bedroom when she was a kid, but it wouldn't work if she didn't keep things 'spic and span'. But he wasn't angry if she forgot. Not then.

He had his little rules. He didn't like her brushing her hair inside. He wasn't keen on showering in the wagon either, preferring to use the leisure centre or have a 'sluice down' outside with the bowl like his dad. He rarely used the indoor toilet apart from at night.

He liked her to cook outdoors with the Calor Gas if the weather was okay. He was the far better cook, but now that was to be her job. He had his own jobs – sorting the generator and the water and the rubbish.

He'd say things like, 'You're a woman now – a married

167

lady. My queen!' He wasn't even taking the piss.

Maria never felt like a queen.

She had to leave a lot of things back in her bedroom at her dad's – her old toys, clothes that had gone out of fashion that she couldn't bear to throw away.

Frankie immediately started a campaign to let out her room to a lodger.

The other thing that took some getting used to was that there was nowhere to go when you had a row. At her dad's she could stomp upstairs and shut herself in her own room to sulk, but what was she supposed to do in a caravan? Sometimes the atmosphere felt like the whistling pressure cooker in Uncle Nugget's wagon, threatening to explode at any moment.

Maria missed school. She thought they'd be off travelling now there was no baby, and whenever she questioned him, Joby promised they would – at some unspecified point in the future, 'when the time's right'.

She also assumed, if she wasn't at school, she'd get a job. But Joby didn't want her to work. Her new position in life only required that she keep a clean wagon and cook.

It was *sooo* boring.

When she told him she wanted to go back to do her exams, he snorted, 'How many married women do you know in a school uniform?'

And she had no answer for that.

He mocked, 'My dad didn't go to school. Now he's his own boss. You don't need a piece of paper to get on with your life, girl.'

Joby's dad might run a business, but Maria noticed how

he had trouble reading and writing, although she knew better than to bring that up.

She tried, 'I liked learning, Joby. And my mates are there.'

'You learn more from the university of hard knocks than you'll ever learn at school,' he pronounced.

They had a row about it and she cried and then Joby apologised for shouting and said, 'You know I love you, girl.'

'Love is what you do, not what you say!' she countered, feeling really wise, like Alanis Morissette or someone.

She spent a lot of time on the flash new phone he bought her, chatting to her schoolmates when they got off lessons. He introduced her to the girls on the site who he suggested might be her new friends. The girls chatted about the usual – fashion and where to get good knock-off designer gear; they gossiped about celebrities and made bitchy comments about other families. There seemed to be various vendettas with clans from across the country. It was the sort of stuff Maria recognised, if not the history.

Two *married women* were younger than her by a few months, and half a dozen had two or three kids by the time they were twenty. Photos of the little ones were on display in the caravans, mothers and daughters wearing flash matching outfits. The children might run wild on the site, but in the photos they were in their Sunday best, the girls with big bows in their long hair like Victorians.

While Joby was at work she'd spend time in Lily's wagon or go over to see the Maine Coon cats bred by her neighbour, Rosa, who lived in the biggest static caravan on the site. Most people were friendly, at least to her face. Rosa's youngest, Chanel, was not.

'We're calling her Chanel, cos she's number five,' explained Rosa. 'Youse best get on it soon if youse two are to catch us up on the babby front,' she grinned.

Lily had started on at Maria the day she got back from hospital, giving her advice about 'starting another', talking about the best time to 'do it', providing herbs. It was exhausting.

Anthony took to popping by on his lunch breaks. The way he looked at her made her feel uncomfortable, so she tried to make sure she was at Rosa's, or she did her shopping then, even though it was busier in town.

She couldn't talk to Joby about it – as far as he was concerned, the sun shone out of his brother's arse. At least she was away from Frankie. At least she and Joby could do it whenever they wanted.

Weeks passed.

Chanel seemed to thaw. She was two years younger than Maria, although she seemed much older, and she was the only one of Rosa's kids who still lived with her mum and dad. Technically she was supposed to be at school, but most of the time she just hung round the site. They had a few afternoons sunbathing together, or they played with Rosa's kittens, but then the girl called her a '*gadji*' and when Maria asked what it meant, she laughed and said it was a word for 'stupid kids who aren't gypsies'.

'But I'm married to a gypsy,' said Maria, annoyed at being labelled a kid by someone Chanel's age.

'Blood's thicker than water,' mocked Chanel.

There were things she liked.

Joby brushed her hair as she sat on the trailer steps. He

bought her a new fancy hairbrush with proper bristles and told her she should give it one hundred strokes every morning and every night.

In bed he'd spend hours on her, emerging from under the covers like a deep-sea diver.

He bought her a gold bangle, so heavy it felt like a shackle on her wrist, big gold earrings.

But . . .

She began to hate the smell of the chemical toilet and the half-hearted shower. She didn't like the dogs on the site – no one ever cleared up their shit. Same with the toddlers running round without nappies. And she didn't like the horses – huge skittish things. The uncles made fun of her when Joby took her down to the fields to see them.

Anthony encouraged her to get up on one of the mares a couple of times, which was a couple of times too many, and Joby had a go at him, telling him to lay off.

'Lady Godiva with all that hair, hey?' laughed Anthony. 'I'd like to see that.'

'Shut it,' said Joby. 'That's for my eyes, not yorn.'

But then he never seemed to notice how his brother always found an excuse to sit next to her at the pub, or how he touched her hair when she wasn't looking, making her recoil.

It was so easy to make fun of her. She knew nothing about horses, or trucks, or their way of life. She knew nothing about her new family either.

'Rosa said they do the bare-knuckle fighting, your Anthony and Nugget?' she asked Joby. 'That's still going on?'

'Yeah. Good at it, too,' said Joby, as if it was the most obvious thing in the world.

'Isn't it illegal?'

He laughed as if she was being funny.

'Are you related to Tyson Fury?' she asked another time.

'What, that *didicoy*?' sneered Joby. 'He's not one of us.'

The distinction baffled Maria.

She didn't know how big a deal Lily's mother had been as a fortune teller. She was 'famous across the land', according to Rosa. 'She had the gift.'

And until the wedding, Maria hadn't registered that Joby was nearer thirty than twenty. Almost thirteen years older than her.

His weekdays passed working on some building site or other, a drink down the pub with his dad and mates, then sex and telly, or telly and sex. His ideal weekends involved more sex and longer down the pub. If he was off at some boxing match or horse race she wasn't usually invited. He claimed it was where 'the deals' were done, but she had no idea what those deals involved. If she asked, he didn't answer.

When she moaned that she wanted a night out, he said he was too knackered.

When she met her friends down the precinct, they talked about school and netball and who they fancied, and she ached for it, even though it all felt childish now.

He started nagging her, as bad as Frankie.

'Life's all about family.'

And she nagged back – 'When can we go on the road?' – prodding, not letting it be, even when he came home late from the pub.

Anthony once heard her and said, with a filthy leer, 'She wants to spread her wings, that one.'

'I want to get away, Joby. You promised, Joby. Can't we go somewhere, Joby?'

So it was her fault really; partly her fault.

It was an accident.

If Joby hadn't been drunk, sure it wouldn't have happened, but he didn't mean it. He'd been annoyed, yes, but he'd only been gesticulating, not aiming for her. And there's not much room to flail about in a caravan.

She could tell her dad was livid when she went round to see him, her lip split. After his second tea – in the giant *Best Dad in the World* mug she'd bought him one Father's Day a million years ago – he finally looked at her and said, 'If you go back to that bastard, that's it. We're done, me and you, if you go back.'

'What?'

'Come home,' said her dad. 'Now.'

Frankie focused hard on her own tea. It was obvious she had no desire to see the prodigal daughter return.

When Maria said goodbye to her dad he didn't reply.

Joby couldn't say sorry enough. They had great make-up sex and he wrapped himself around her in bed. She was hooked on that as much as the way he made her feel during.

He promised her a puppy. One of Walt and Lily's dogs was pregnant. 'Purebred,' said Joby.

'But . . .?' All the dogs on the site were obviously mongrels.

'Sure, it'll be a purebred dog.' He winked. 'The father's a dog and the mother's a dog.'

And she smiled and he took her in his arms, and she felt safe.

It was a one-off, an accident.

26

Brian phones. 'Come round! Come round!' he trills.

'What is it?' asks Maria, feeling queasy. He usually sends a text. It is never good news when someone calls, although he sounds positively jolly.

'Come here and I'll tell you all about it,' he replies. 'It is *mind blowing*! And I've got something for you.'

She's annoyed that he won't tell her anything more on the phone, so she sets off. Del is on duty this morning and Elsie seems happy enough. It's less than twenty-four hours since she saw Brian, so it has to be something important if he needs to see her now.

When Maria arrives at Brian's flat, she startles when she sees him. He's bleached his eyebrows and dyed them purple.

'What . . .?'

'Trying something new.' He grins.

He's almost vibrating with excitement as he offers her a

concoction that looks like frogspawn – bubble tea, apparently, although it bears no resemblance to any tea Maria's ever seen. Brian sits on his beanbag and she sits on the sofa and he gets sidetracked telling her how the tea originated in Taiwan before he gets round to telling her his news.

'For God's sake, spit it out!' says Maria. She is not referring to the bubble tea.

'He's never going to bully me, or anyone else, again!' announces Brian, triumphant.

She knows immediately who he's talking about.

'There's been an accident!' He tries hard not to smile.

She doesn't have to ask who's had the accident. Her heart alternatively leaps as if it might escape through her throat and then plunges into her bowels as he talks.

'No one at work reported him missing because we all thought he was off on his *jollies*, didn't we? And his so-called chums? Didn't even think to check why he hadn't joined them on the first leg of their trip.' Brian takes a sip of his bubble tea.

Maria squeezes her hands into fists.

'His ex-wife was still listed as his next of kin. She only called the office yesterday. You okay?'

Maria is far from okay, but manages, 'What happened to him?'

'He was off his tits is what happened. Not entirely out of character. Too fond of the Bolivian marching powder, if you know what I mean.' Brian has never seemed so perky. 'The lorry driver reported seeing a man dancing along the side of the North Circular, which the dashcam corroborated, apparently. He was merrily skipping along one minute and then he flung himself under the wheels of the juggernaut, laughing his bloody head off!'

'Jesus!' croaks Maria.

'Turned out that wasn't a metaphor,' says Brian. 'They couldn't identify him from his face, that's for sure. He was completely pulped. Splattered all over the tarmac—'

'Stop!' yelps Maria. She's taken aback by Brian's unfettered delight. She doesn't need the gory details.

'I know!' says Brian, thrilled. 'I don't know whether to laugh or cry. It's so—'

'Don't . . .' She takes a few deep breaths and asks, 'When was this?' She knows all too well when this was but she needs to feign innocence just in case he puts two and two together.

'The night of my party!'

'Oh-Jesus-fuck.'

'I know! He didn't seem that out of it when he left here, did he? Must have fuelled up on route.'

She sits stony faced, trying to get a grip on her emotions. Another death! She is horrified, but also . . . What? It's a feeling like laughing in church. She has to stop her lips smiling of their own accord and she's appalled with herself. What the hell has she become? This is a different league of wrong.

'Another tea?' says Brian.

Maria shakes her head and manages to ask how the lorry driver is doing.

'Oh, he'll be fine,' say Brian. 'It wasn't his fault, was it? And it's hard enough getting drivers these days.'

Not what she means.

Am I fine? wonders Maria.

Brian seems gleeful now, but that might just be the shock. And how would he react if he knew that she had caused this? Would he still want to be her friend? Wouldn't he be horrified by what she's done?

'Just a sec,' he says.

He pops into his office, and Maria collapses back on the sofa.

How guilty should she feel? The boss's death is her doing. She's more to blame than the truck driver.

There is a running tally of things she feels guilty for. *Accidents.* Her mother, her baby, Joby, Nick. Perhaps she is cursed.

But this is a different level – premeditated; deliberate; callous. Perhaps she's evil.

Brian reappears, saying, 'And I told you I'd got something for you. Here's your pressie!' He bows, handing her an iPhone.

The gift distracts her from her weightier ruminations. It is so lovely.

'I can't take this. It's too much, Brian!'

'I've upgraded. I'm not using it. And yours is a museum piece,' he mocks. 'Go on!'

She takes the phone, thanks him, makes her excuses, kisses him on the cheek and leaves. She needs to be alone to process this news.

As she walks back to Elsie's she has an urge to go to confession, but she was never actually baptised Catholic, so mightn't that be a sin in itself? She wishes for the millionth time she could ask her gran or her mother questions like that.

She is guilty, she knows that. At what cost to her eternal

soul? But—

The truth is, she feels little for Brian's boss. She feels little for the old man lying under the rose bushes. Karma bit them on the arse. They both deserved it. She is only afraid for herself; for Elsie and herself.

And what of the other body?

What will happen if someone unearths that from its forest grave?

And—

A flash of an image.

What happened to the head?

The body she buried in Spain had no head.

27

She is walking slowly back from Brian's, deep within her dark memories, when she turns into Roseberry Gardens , but the second she registers the police car up near Elsie's, she's running.

Her first thought is that something bad has happened to Elsie. The second is that they're digging up the back garden.

One ankle winces as her feet hit the pavement. Her chest tightens with dread. As she feared, the police car is parked right outside Elsie's house and the front door is wide open. As she reaches the gate, a policewoman comes out of the house and Maria gasps, 'Where is she? Is she okay?'

Before the officer can answer, Del appears on the doorstep and says, 'She's in the kitchen.'

'Is she all right? What's happened?' She can hardly get the words out as she tries to catch her breath, bent double, her heart hammering as much from fear as the run.

Oh, *she's* fine,' he replies, looking furious.

'Her nephew's explained the situation – the particular circumstances,' says the policewoman.

Particular circumstances hardly covers the insane battering in Maria's chest.

'She attacked one of the kids next door is what happened,' scowls Del. 'He'll probably have a black eye tomorrow.'

'She did what?'

'She had a go at one of the students. No idea what set her off. One minute she was minding her own business in the garden—' At the mention of the garden, Maria's panic intensifies. She quickly looks to the policewoman, but there's no reaction on the girl's face. Del continues, 'Then I heard a bit of cursing, she came back inside, and the next thing I knew, she'd thrown a tin of tomatoes at him over the back fence.'

'Bloody hell. Is he hurt?'

'Not badly,' says the policewoman.

Thank God for that. But what was bloody Del doing while all this was going on?

'Who called the police?' asks Maria.

Del says, 'The student—'

'My colleague is next door talking to him now,' the policewoman explains.

Maria prays there's no mention of mushrooms, although that's an insane thought.

She finds Elsie sitting in the kitchen listening to the radio, like butter wouldn't melt. As soon as she sees Maria she demands tea and toast. She seems blithely unaware of the chaos she's caused, or the danger she's put them in.

Del and the policewoman walk through the house into

the garden and Maria's stomach does a flip. Luckily they stand near the garden fence where *the incident* happened, rather than poking around the bottom flower bed, but she can't make out what they're saying because Elsie continues chattering about toast.

'Elsie, why did you throw a tin at that lad?'

She's ignored.

'You know you could be in trouble if you've hurt him. We could all be in trouble—'

'I WANT MY TOAST!' screams Elsie.

Give me strength! thinks Maria.

A young policeman knocks at the front door and Maria lets him in. He joins Del and his colleague in the garden.

'Toast! Toast! Toast!' chants Elsie.

'Elsie! For God's sake, give it a rest!' she snaps, and immediately feels rotten for upsetting her.

She can bear it no longer and abandons Elsie to join the garden summit.

'Everything okay?' she asks.

'I don't think he'll need stitches,' says the policeman.

She asks Del, 'What about Elsie? Did that lad do something to make her go off on one?'

He shrugs.

'By the time we got here, he'd had a change of heart,' the policeman goes on, indicating next door. 'He's not pressing charges. And there's no point cautioning her in her state, yeah?' he asks his colleague.

'No,' agrees the policewoman. 'So we'll probably let this one slide.' She addresses Del: 'You just need to keep an eye on her.'

Maria's shoulders relax a little. She thanks the officers – for what, she's not entirely sure. She offers them tea, but they say they have to get on.

Maria asks Del to stay five minutes while she pops to the shops because there's no bread left. By the time she's returned the police car has departed. Del doesn't have to say a word. He leaves without saying goodbye, his face like thunder.

'No Mother's Pride?' bleats Elsie, outraged, grabbing items out of a Tesco bag-for-life as Maria switches on the kettle.

'No, sorry, love. Just hang on. I'll do us toast as soon as I've had a wee. You sit there.'

Obviously, there were dozens of sliced whites at the mini supermarket at the end of the road, but Maria's been trying to wean Elsie off it and get more fibre into her. She's bought a large granary loaf, hoping Elsie won't kick off about the 'bloody bits' getting stuck under her denture plate.

She's only gone for a minute. She doesn't even wash her hands – she'll do that in the kitchen – but as she comes through she sees Elsie stabbing a knife inside the toaster trying to release the huge doorstep of bread she's cut and rammed in the slot.

'Elsie! No!' Maria's voice is sharper than she intended. She snatches the knife from Elsie's hand and flings it on to the kitchen counter. Sweetie skitters across the floor and lunges through the catflap and Elsie deflates into tears.

'I'm sorry!' Maria hugs the old woman and leads her back to her chair, soothing, 'I didn't mean to shout, but the toaster could give you an electric shock. It could kill you,

Elsie! Are you listening? Please don't do that ever again.'

Maria cuts the bread thinner, toasts and butters it and, as a treat, spreads it with strawberry jam.

Elsie eats it while quietly grizzling. The sound cuts through Maria.

She has a cup of tea herself as she watches Elsie eat. Then she sets about washing up. As she wipes the knife, the image of Elsie stabbing it into the toaster is overlaid with another vivid scene from just a few weeks ago – a blade stabbing into an eye . . . The image of Nick floundering around, weeping blood.

Maria leans over the sink and brings up her own tea in one hot heave.

28

Elsie is still agitated when Comfort arrives later that afternoon.

Maria explains about the lunchtime violence, playing it down as best she can, although there's no easy way to say that the police have been round because Elsie injured a student. She's worried that this behaviour might cause Comfort to side with Del about shipping Elsie off to a care home.

Elsie seems to have forgotten the tin-lobbing incident. She's now fixated on her missing letter opener. She gets distressed when she misplaces things.

'I paid for that with my own money,' she keeps repeating. 'I paid for all the stuff in this house. I've worked hard for all these . . . things.' She jabs her finger around the room. 'I bought that, and that, and that. And the . . . that opening thing . . . letter opener. Where the bloody hell is it?'

You're best off not remembering, thinks Maria.

She offers the nurse tea.

'Please. It is cold enough,' says Comfort, who always settles herself nearest the radiator.

'But there's no snow!' says Elsie. 'We always had snow before.'

The weather is brutal – metal-grey skies and insidious damp.

'You had snow before what?' asks Comfort.

Maria expects her to say global warming, but Elsie ponders, frowns, then exclaims, 'Before . . . before *Brexit*!'

She suddenly sweeps her hand across the table, sending her mug and plate flying. The mug shatters with a crash, although the plate survives. 'Bastards!' she rants.

'Change the subject, please!' Maria implores Comfort as she gets the dustpan and brush from under the sink.

There's a hiatus as Comfort tells Elsie she is going to visit her family back in Nigeria in a few weeks' time and Elsie nods and smiles.

She then asks Maria, 'How has she been?'

What can Maria say? She sticks to small, safe things – things unlikely to cause another meltdown.

'She claimed her name was Michelle when we went to the doctors the other day.'

'She will get more confused and unpredictable as things progress,' says Comfort.

'Yes, we know. But the thing was, she told me she'd always wanted to be named Michelle because no one had written a good song about an Elsie. Then, when we got home, she suddenly shouted, "Cabaret!" out of the blue. She'd remembered there's that line about Elsie in the song, which is more than I did!'

Elsie, now beatifically calm, looks quite pleased with herself.

'Are you named for Mother Mary?' Comfort enquires.

'Probably,' says Maria. 'I think my mum . . .' The sentence dies in her mouth. *Never have I ever had the chance to ask my mum why she called me Maria.*

She throws the shards of ceramics into the bin and bustles inside the fridge until she's calmed herself.

When they say goodbye to Comfort, Elsie settles down to read the *Mirror*. She can't seem to focus on a book any longer and she used to love reading. So much of Elsie's identity is now past tense.

Maria's own ambitions to see the world also seem past tense. She thinks of what it might be like to travel to Africa like Comfort.

How she would love to run far away from what lies decomposing beneath the rose bushes; from what lies hidden in a Spanish forest; from the consequences of Brian's boss's death. How she'd love to escape. But she is tethered here by Elsie and the need to keep her crimes hidden.

And wherever she goes, she can't escape herself.

29

She wears the new purple T-shirt Brian gave her the next Friday she goes to Balogan's.

He walks in looking grey. Very early for him. She's not even started on his bedroom.

'Maria.' He acknowledges her before he sinks on to the sofa.

'Are you okay? Do you need anything?'

'That . . . is a question.' He slowly adjusts his weight and shakes his head. 'So much I need. For now, though . . . perhaps a coffee?'

She doesn't know how to use the complicated machine in the kitchen and is too nervous to ask him what to do. She opens cupboards but can't find any Nescafé, not that she really expected to, so she takes the ground coffee from the tin, and spoons it into a pan with boiling water, and hurries back to check on him. He's bent over, his head in his hands.

'Do you want something to eat?'

'No, thank you.' He sits up and smiles the saddest smile she's ever seen. He seems to be considering another sentence, but his chin falls to his chest a moment, as if he might sleep as he is, sitting on the sofa.

Maria observes him – it is easier to do so when he isn't looking at her. He has lovely lips.

He takes a breath and rallies, looks up. 'How are you, Maria?'

She hurriedly looks away. 'Me? Oh, fine,' she tries, in case it might be true.

'English people use that word all the time. It is meaningless. How are you? "Fine" or "I can't complain". It is like the word "nice". Perhaps it should be banned.' One side of his mouth smiles.

His eyes disturb her. She turns back to the kitchen, busying herself finishing the coffee, as if that might solve something.

She calls through, 'Milk?'

'A little, please.'

She sieves the black liquid into a cup through three layers of kitchen towel, adding a splash of milk. It does not look at all inviting. She pours herself a glass of water and carries the drinks through, sitting opposite him, watching as he takes a sip and winces.

'Is it okay?'

He nods his head very slowly, obviously appalled.

'It's crap, isn't it?' She sighs.

He looks from the cup to her face and says, 'It . . . is . . . fine . . .'

They both laugh. She's surprised to hear the sound come from her mouth.

'Are you sure you're okay?' she tries again.

'As okay as I can be.' He takes another tiny sip and pulls a face.

'I'm rubbish at coffee. Sorry.'

He wrinkles his nose and says, 'It tastes like . . . liquid suffering.'

She smiles. 'I'll crack on, then.'

She finishes cleaning his bedroom, in case he wants to lie down, but he remains on the sofa, dozing. It is peaceful. When he opens his eyes again she asks if she should hoover, and he tells her to leave it until next time and they say their goodbyes.

'Thank you,' he says and smiles right at her.

The image of that smile lingers as she hurries along damp pavements on her way back to Elsie's. But the further away from Balogan's flat she gets, her joy curdles, and the familiar shadow of dread settles in her belly.

She has sat and laughed with a man she hardly knows – flirted, almost – despite the bodies she has left in her wake.

That night she dreams of Brian's boss and wakes on a sickly wave of guilt.

The next afternoon at Elsie's, after she's done the washing-up and put a load on because Del forgot Elsie's overnight Tena Lady pants – again – she sits for her second tea of the day, and out of the blue Elsie says, 'You met someone, darlin'?'

'Why?' asks Maria, thrown. 'What makes you think that?'

'You seem different today, that's all. Brighter. It's nice to have a friend,' says Elsie, starting to sing 'With a Little Help from My Friends'.

Maria wonders if Balogan wants her as a 'sort-of friend' – that grey area she inhabits for customers like Bex, who seem to need someone outside of their own social circle to unload upon – or a real friend like Brian.

'I might have met a friend,' admits Maria.

'*I'm* your friend,' says Elsie.

'Yes, you are,' she replies, giving Elsie a hug. 'But you're more than that. You're my family.'

30

There was a time she might have had a real family.

Joby redoubled his efforts between the sheets. Her guess was that he wanted to get her pregnant before Appleby Horse Fair, and while she wasn't exactly complaining, sometimes she just wanted to read or go to sleep. She didn't like to think that she was playing a trick on him, waiting until he went to work to take her pill. She never forgot.

He didn't talk about it, but Lily wouldn't stop banging on about a grandchild. It exasperated Maria.

'What about Anthony?' she asked. 'Why doesn't he make you a grandma?'

'Oh, our Anthony's not about to settle down yet,' laughed Lily. 'He's not ready to be a dad. Let him enjoy himself for a bit, I say.'

Anthony was eight years older than Maria.

Joby bought himself a flash new embroidered waistcoat

for the horse fair. Gold. She loved it. He looked like a sexy snooker player. He bought her an entire new wardrobe – a huge pink fake-fur coat in case the nights were cold, a pink bodycon dress so tight you could see what she'd had for breakfast, and pink kitten-heel shoes totally unsuited to grass. She loved all of it.

He paid for her to go to a hairdresser in Ashby who piled her hair high, the first time she'd had it up like that. Proper glamorous. She had a headache after an hour.

Chanel and her youngest niece, Caress, both had the same hairdo because they all went to the same place to have it done.

Caress was five. The family had big ambitions for the child to be a performer or beauty queen and Chanel taught her little dance routines. Caress looked bored most of the time. When they dressed her up, the kid had so much fake tan and make-up slathered on her face she looked like a tiny, weary, thirty-two-year-old barmaid.

The first day at the Appleby fair was a riot. Maria didn't drink as much as the rest of them, but she was high on the occasion.

When they arrived at the site, they set up in the field next to Fair Hill in glorious sunshine, then she walked round a bit to take it all in. Everyone seemed to be in a party mood, and everyone seemed to know everyone else. Police –'gavver pigs', as Anthony called them – everywhere. She sat on the riverbank at dusk with Rosa and they watched the lads and lasses bathe after racing their horses and traps up

196

and down the road. She felt a bit horny seeing Joby stripped to the waist, holding on to the big black-and-white mare, and Anthony on the bay, already in the water, like a scene out of a picture book.

When they came up from the river, Joby stood by her and shook himself like a dog, showering her with diamonds of water until she squealed and ran away, and he chased after her whooping. He dried himself off, then they both got into their evening finery, and set off to join the others in the Masons Arms. It was rammed because so many other local pubs had closed for the event to avoid trouble.

Joby was a king then, buying rounds right, left and centre. He glad-handed men, hugged women and patted kids. As the evening progressed, he disappeared with his dad to chat to someone about business, leaving Maria standing outside the pub with Lily, Rosa and Chanel. They were busy talking to a gang of other women she didn't know, and she suddenly felt very alone. She was almost glad to see Anthony heading their way.

But as the pints went down the flirting amped up. She had to take evasive action, laughing and wiggling away and making sure she went to the loo with one of the other girls, so he didn't ambush her in the corridor of the pub.

Anthony got louder and more insistent, grabbing for her, even though the others could see. But no sign of bloody Joby. Thankfully, Rosa led her away before she had to push him off yet again.

The next morning it clouded over. Joby left her to it all day long. She watched the horses prance and parade around. As the light faded, the youngsters appeared all dolled up doing the same – girls dressed to the nines and lads doused in Lynx, strutting about, giving each other the eye. Deals seemed to be brokered for horse and human flesh alike – mothers setting up dates and monitoring the level of flirting.

There were a couple of scuffles – daft lads who'd been at the bevvy pretty much all day.

By the time she finally met up with Joby over at the pub it was getting dark, and he was pretty much smashed.

Loud chat and laughter. But while Joby talked to every-one else, he ignored her. Anthony hovered close, gazing at her like the dogs looked at Lily near feeding time, and she had a swift, angry thought that she could flirt with Anthony and make Joby jealous if she wanted.

After what came next, it's that thought that tormented her.

She saw Joby hug a girl in a low-cut blue dress – she didn't know her name – petite, pretty; long, flowing dark hair; strong dark eyebrows like they'd been tattooed on. There was a lot of messing about. He hooked his elbow around the girl's head and shoved it under his armpit. She shrieked, but not in a *get off* way.

Maria was raging.

Then Anthony was by her side with another drink. He touched her hair as he handed it to her. 'Yorn proper beau-tiful, girl,' he slurred.

'That is the least interesting thing about me,' she replied, regal.

She gulped down her drink and asked for another, deter-mined to catch up with Joby.

'For a kiss, then,' demanded Anthony.

She laughed and pecked him on the cheek. She knew what she was doing.

Until she didn't.

They were on the pavement outside the pub – just travellers, no locals. Joby started dancing, showing off stupid moves. The dark-haired girl clapped and cheered, like he was the most hilarious thing she'd ever seen. The song blaring out of the open pub doors was some old Rod Stewart number from the time he wasn't an embarrassment. Maria turned to Anthony and held his hand, and then they were dancing and laughing together. She started singing along, although the only words she knew were, 'Baby Jane' and Anthony's hands were sneaking all over her and she didn't push them away very hard.

And the next thing was, Anthony flew. His head and body catapulted back as his feet took off from the ground, and he was flung up and away from her, and before she could work out why, Joby was yelling at her, right up in her face, and she was shocked into silence.

She couldn't remember much about getting back to the trailer.

She woke to screaming.

An Appleby-sized hangover. Maria was so shaky she almost fell over as she tried to pull on her leggings.

She heard the sirens before she got down to the river and then she was running before she really knew what she was seeing—

Joby and Anthony lying on the dewy grass.

Lily screeching and wailing and hitting out at anyone within hitting distance.

Mist billowing up from the River Eden.

Paramedics kneeling like they were praying.

Joby couldn't speak. Maria had to piece together the story from the others.

The brothers had been drinking, obviously – it had carried on all night – and Anthony had been on some other stuff as well. He should never have got on any horse, let alone the flighty mare. He should never have gone in the water. Joby should have stopped his little brother, he should have kept him safe, it was his fault this had happened – this shouted by Lily, hysterical, being dragged off Anthony by the paramedic, the light of the police car flashing blue across the grass, a policewoman trying to keep the others back from *the scene*; two officers grappling with Uncle Nugget, who had no idea what to do apart from kick off.

Anthony's on-off girlfriend was surrounded by half a dozen teenagers like herself. Sobbing. Loving her time in the spotlight.

And Anthony just lay there. Absolutely still.

Rosa led Chanel away while the body was lifted, and questions were asked. Lily wailed at Joby, and Maria was left alone. She couldn't stop shaking – from cold, from shock, from the fear that she was somehow responsible. She caused the fight. What had happened between Joby and Anthony afterwards? How had Anthony ended up dead?

She picked her way through the caravans and trucks and litter and managed to get back to the wagon.

When Joby eventually came in, much, much later,

wrapped in silver foil to keep him warm, he wouldn't look at her.

She asked how Lily was, how his dad was.

'Bad,' is all he said.

He wouldn't touch her.

After they got back from Appleby, she lay in bed at night trying to sync her breathing with his, afraid to reach for him. He radiated anger, even when he fell asleep. If her hand touched his back, his leg, he shrugged her off, grunted and pushed her away. If she tried to talk to him, he yanked back the duvet, climbed over her, and stomped over to the fridge to grab another beer. Sometimes she cried quietly, so her tears slid into her ears.

Eventually it came out. Four drinks down one Friday night, Joby admitted there was a split second when he might have saved Anthony, if only he'd acted sooner. That hesitation to go into the water after him cost his brother his life.

'And we'd fought that night, you know. Proper fought. Because . . . Then— I could have saved him. It's my fault. My own brother. My own blood.'

After he said that the first time, he said it over and over.

'I killed him.'

We killed him, thought Maria.

The first time they did it *after* was vicious. She grabbed at him, clung to him, bit him, angry that he'd made her wait so long. It was over too quickly.

She had to finish herself off as he snored.

It became the pattern.

Once, very drunk, he sobbed that her not getting pregnant again was a punishment for what he'd done.

That would have been the time either to tell him the truth – that she didn't want a baby, not yet anyway; she wanted to travel first – or to throw away her pills. She did neither.

A month-long wake. Lily went a bit wild. She burned all of Anthony's possessions, piling them on to a huge bonfire in the middle of the site. Maria felt it was a waste – she should have taken the stuff to the charity shop so they'd be of use to some poor sods who couldn't afford a warm work shirt, good boots.

One Sunday afternoon, Lily banged on Joby's door and as Maria opened up, she punched her in the face. Maria was amazed that she did, in fact, see stars. As she wrapped ice cubes in a tea towel to put on her jaw, Joby stormed round to his mum's wagon to have a go. Maria ran after him and watched as he shouted at his mother through the door she'd locked against him, banging and pulling until he tore the door right off its hinges, and Lily came out then, howling, 'I'm your family! *Me!* Not *her*. She's cursed, that one!'

'She had nothing to do with it,' shouted Joby, gripping his mother's arms by her side so she could do no more harm. 'It was me. It's my fault our Anthony's gone, not hers!'

Maria stood rooted to the spot.

'All she's done is bring bad luck, that fucking gorger bitch. I told you it'd be bad. The signs *showed* you. You should never have married out,' screamed her mother-in-law in reply.

Maria had already lost her grandmother, her dad, her baby. She'd already lost one mother, and now, with a sinking feeling, she realised she'd lost another.

Silently she agreed that yes, she was indeed cursed. It was what she deserved, these losses. And her heart wizened to the size of a crab apple.

31

She sees Balogan again on the Friday night. She's just finished when he lets himself into his flat looking as tired as she feels.

'Maria,' he acknowledges her. He comes up closer. 'These shadows?' he indicates the dark circles under her eyes. He asks nothing more, but she finds herself telling him.

'The old lady I look after. Elsie. One of her cats has been ill. I didn't sleep well.'

'You dealt with it?'

'Yes.'

'When our dogs became ill, my father would deal with it.' He makes a swift throat-slitting gesture.

'Oh, God. No! Not like that! The cat's in hospital.'

'There is a hospital *for cats*?' He shakes his head as if this is ridiculous. 'For dogs, I understand. They are working animals. But a hospital for cats?'

He's making fun of her.

Sweetie was rushed to the vets when she suddenly stopped eating. Del had to drive the cat across to the animal hospital for an emergency operation. A blockage. Elsie is distraught.

Maria asks Balogan, 'Do you want a drink?'

'A coffee. Come. We will attempt to elevate your last attempt.'

He leads her into the kitchen and shows her how to use the sleek coffee machine. She's acutely aware that he is standing close to her, his meaty arm brushing her own.

They take their drinks through. Maria sits on the sofa and Balogan stands by the window.

He remains looking at the view for a long time. Maria doesn't move after she's finished her coffee. She doesn't want to disturb his stillness. She doesn't reach for her rucksack, although she's ready to set off. He seems sad.

Eventually he says, 'There was no hospital when my mother . . . was ill.'

Maria remains silent, unsure of what he is telling her. After a pause, Balogan walks across to sit next to her, sinking into the cushions with a sigh.

'My father was a big man.'

'Like you?'

'I mean he was a big man in a small town. He – how do you say? – *looms large*? In our home. He was a strong man, a hard man in some respects, but also a good man. Most of the time. He came to Sweden a refugee. With nothing. I was born there. We had very little when I was growing up.'

'What did he do?'

'Do?'

'What was his job?' she asks.

'He ran dog sled teams – trained them. I helped. This is before these sorts of dogs became *pets*.' He says the word as if he's disgusted with the concept. 'I see so many of these dogs in London. These animals need to run for many miles every day. It is no life for them here! They are working dogs! They are bred to work.' More quietly he says, 'We are all bred to work.'

Maria notices how he sips his coffee. He has nice manners. No rough edges like her own father, or Joby. It surprises her in such a large man.

'Perhaps we would all do different work if we had a choice.' It seems he is talking to himself. He turns to her. 'What are you looking for, Maria?' he asks.

She glances around the room, unsure what she might have mislaid.

'I mean, in life?' He smiles a tired smile.

She shrugs. She doesn't feel comfortable acknowledging her ambitions out loud.

'What do you do in your spare time?'

'What spare time?' Her laugh sounds bitter.

'What do you do when you are not cleaning?'

'I look after Elsie.'

'When you are not working?'

'Elsie's not work. Well . . . not really.'

He takes another sip of his coffee, and his leg relaxes against hers. Maria surreptitiously inches away from him. The closeness in the kitchen was comfortable – this contact is too intimate.

'My mother had big hopes,' he confides. 'She wanted the

big love story. She wanted too much, but she was destined for a small life.'

Me too, thinks Maria.

'It was difficult with my father. Not all people *welcomed* him as a refugee. And not all people were happy that the Swedish girl married the foreign man. He had friends, of course. I am named for one of those friends, a fellow refugee. He was from Nigeria. But there were many people who were not friends.' He sighs heavily and adds, 'It weighed greatly on my mother. She died twelve years ago. Today.'

'I'm so sorry,' says Maria.

He stands again and walks to look out the window. He is very still. He says quietly, 'She killed herself.'

Maria hears herself say, 'Oh!' She can offer him no more because his pain is too much for her to deal with on top of her own: the harrowing memories of Joby; the current, barely controlled panic about Nick's body; the worry she'll be linked to the death of Brian's boss; her fears for Elsie and the future.

If Balogan wants her as a friend, she's already proving a bad one.

Both of them are silent for a time. Finally, she gets to her feet, and leaves with a small, 'Goodbye.'

The lift opens on the ground floor and Balogan's neighbour, Cass, is waiting.

'Hi,' says the girl.

'Morning,' replies Maria.

Cass doesn't move so the pair stand for a couple of seconds before the lift doors start to close again.

'Would you like to get that coffee with me today?' asks Cass. The way she asks is . . . needy.

Maria hesitates. Del is staying with Elsie today for a change. He'll probably just dump her at the community centre – using the volunteers there as unpaid babysitters, despite it being his day off. When was the last time she had any time to herself?

'Not upstairs,' adds Cass. 'Somewhere else? My treat! Do you mind walking?'

Maria wants to walk to clear her head. 'Okay.'

Cass's face brightens.

They walk along the river. It's dark and windy and cold, but lights are reflecting in the Thames – always the party girl, the Thames – which gives the night a festive air. They cross at Waterloo.

Cass talks the entire way, telling Maria about the gigs.

'There's not, like, a lot of money in the sort of stuff we do – kind of a jazz-funk fusion – but I love it. Performing, you know. Small venues. We do have a following, though. Mal's really famous in certain circles!'

Jazz-funk fusion – no wonder there's no money in it, thinks Maria.

It's relaxing for Maria to listen to the girl chatter on. She's not required to ask questions because Cass hardly takes a breath, excitable as a child.

'We have all sorts of influences – you probably heard the drum and bass, yeah? Soz! And Mal's parties! Legendary!'

Cass leads Maria through to Soho, where she buys them both a coffee in a small café that is already surprisingly busy. The Friday-night crowd still out from clubbing are firing themselves up on caffeine for the next leg of their journey, night cleaners like Maria are trudging their way home, and the early shift workers are plodding the other way.

'Do you want to come to one of our gigs? I can get you tickets.'

'Perhaps,' says Maria, with zero enthusiasm. Seeing how Cass's face falls, she adds, 'It's just that cleaning isn't my only job. I usually care for an old lady overnight, so it's hard for me to get away.'

'Oh,' says Cass. 'Bummer.'

She chatters on. Then Cass buys another coffee.

Maria takes advantage of a short pause to ask, 'What's the story with you and Mal?'

'What? The arguments?' Cass laughs. 'Oh, it's always been that way. Don't worry about it. He's, like, got a few problems, you know – anger issues –but haven't we all!' She sounds almost jolly. 'It's good of him to let me stay there really,' she continues. 'I cramp his style, you know? But he only wants what's best for me, and—'

Before Maria can ask what she actually wants to ask – *Does he hurt you?* – her phone buzzes. It's Del. Ridiculously early for him. Her heart sinks.

She answers, then says to Cass, 'I'm sorry, I've got to get back. Elsie, my old lady, has flooded the kitchen.'

As crises go, this is hardly a big one – and it's irritating that Del bothered calling her at all – but Maria is keen to get away. She finds it uncomfortable listening to Cass when she's sharing so much, and she's giving her nothing in return.

As Maria gathers her things, Cass stands and flings her arms around her.

'Thank you for this,' says the girl, as if having a coffee together is a marvellous gift Maria has bestowed upon her. 'It's, like, such a relief talking to someone, you know. Mal's friends are all well old.'

'It was nice,' says Maria, disentangling.

'Can we do it again?'

'Of course.'

She doesn't really mean it. She hurries away.

On the bus back her thoughts drift. Along with her more pressing anxieties, she fears for young Cass. An older, controlling man with anger issues – she knows where that can lead.

32

Del leaves as soon as Maria arrives back at Elsie's.

After Maria has cleared up in the kitchen, she settles Elsie with Spotty on her lap.

'Don't you worry, your sister will be coming home,' croons Elsie. 'Let's hope she'll be back soon.'

Maria gives up on any idea of a sleep and pours herself a tea. If she's lucky, she'll get to bed early tonight. She watches the old woman stroke Spotty's fur with the cat brush, both cat and owner mesmerised by the action.

Elsie's face relaxes.

Maria is far from relaxed. One man lies rotting in the back garden, just a few metres away from where she sits. Another has been ground to a pulp beneath the wheels of an articulated lorry. Yet another is buried beneath a pile of rocks in Spain.

Whether Sweetie survives her operation is the least of her worries.

It might be tiredness, it might be the coffees she's already drunk, but Maria is jittery. She imagines what it might be like to do a runner. If it wasn't for Elsie, she'd do it in a heartbeat – pack and leave London; disappear. She craves some sense of freedom. Everything is piling on top of her and she can't bear it much longer – she might scream, or lash out, or throw herself under the wheels of a lorry.

Apart from that, it's an uneventful day.

Del collects Sweetie from the animal hospital that afternoon and brings her home. Elsie dissolves into noisy tears, crooning to the cat how much she's missed her. 'Lovely girl, my lovely girl,' she says over and over.

The cat stares at them from her plastic prison – probably imagining ripping out their throats, given her expression.

'Let her out. Let her out!' bleats Elsie. 'I know just how you feel, mate. My poor baby.'

Sweetie looks more than a little discombobulated when Maria opens her carrier. She emerges, tries to leap up, misses the chair, then crouches on the floor, confused.

'She's off her tits!' says Elsie.

Maria lifts the cat on to the kitchen table so Elsie can stroke her, ignoring the face Del makes.

'Look, they've shaved her! Look at my Sweetie's belly! Oi! Have you done this?' she challenges Del.

'Jesus wept,' he mutters. 'I can't. I just can't. She's doing my head in.'

'Bugger off then!' snaps Elsie.

'You sort this, yeah?' says Del. This is directed at Maria.

'I'll sort it,' agrees Maria.

Del does as Elsie suggests and buggers off.

'My Sweetie,' says Elsie, gently picking up the cat's front paws and nuzzling into her neck, squashing the cone of shame. 'Me and Maria and Spotty and Harry, we've missed you so much. And . . .' She trails off. Maria wonders if she's forgotten, but Elsie adds, 'And Boris! We've all missed you, girl!' Then she nods towards the garden and says, 'No one misses *him*.'

Maria winces. Sometimes Elsie remembers too much.

Elsie turns as she hears Del's car start in the drive. 'Who was he? That bloke?' she asks as he drives away.

She continues stroking Sweetie, who eventually purrs a greeting. It looks like Elsie might purr too.

Maria goes up to shower, leaving Elsie to her reunion. When she gets back downstairs Elsie's still gazing adoringly at the cat, who sits on the table, gazing back. The scene might have been one of quiet meditation, except for the fact that Elsie is pouring milk into an overflowing tea mug and it's dribbling on to the floor. Maria takes the carton from Elsie's hand and wipes up the mess.

'I don't know what I'd do if I lost this one,' says Elsie. And then she looks up at Maria. 'He doesn't get it, Del. You do.' She pauses, then continues, 'We couldn't have kids, me and Nick,' she says, wistful. 'But you – you're like a daughter. Thank you. For everything you do for me.'

Any reply catches in Maria's throat.

When Elsie goes to bed that night, she asks Maria if Sweetie can stay in with her. Of course, that means Spotty wails piteously until she too is allowed access to the inner sanctum of Elsie's room alongside her sister.

Maria checks on them later.

'There's a sight,' she says, smiling at the girls nestled alongside each other, both snuggled up to Elsie.

'Bad as the Kray twins' mum, me,' says Elsie. 'Don't be fooled, babe. They might look innocent, but all cats are serial killers at heart.'

Me too, thinks Maria. The thought gives her chills.

33

Balogan is already at home when Maria arrives late for the Tuesday overnight clean. He greets her then disappears into his kitchen. When she's finishing the bedroom – shaking out the feather duvet and plumping his soft feather pillows – she hears the microwave. The smell of meat wafts through the apartment.

He reappears holding two bowls – steaming meatballs and gravy, red cabbage on the side – just as she's cleaning his bar. He places them on his big round table, indicates one bowl and says, 'For you.'

'Oh, thanks, but I couldn't. I've only just started in here—'

'Join me,' he instructs rather than asks.

She has little willpower to refuse. She sits across from him and spoons in a mouthful. God, the taste!

'I am sorry I don't have bread,' he says, between his own spoonfuls.

'No worries. This is delicious!'

There's a companionable silence. She is surprised to find herself in this cosy situation, but she can't restrain herself to eat slowly and finishes at the same time as him. Rich meat and gravy – when did she last have a meal like this?

'Where did you get these?' she asks, as warmth and nutrition flood her system. 'They're amazing.'

'Get them? I made them.'

'Oh. What's in it?'

'Lingonberries. They are from the mountains.

'What's the meat?'

'Reindeer.'

'What?' she splutters. 'I'm eating Rudolph?' It is unusual for her to joke with most clients, but she's shared a meal with him.

Balogan smiles and then brings over a bottle of spirits from the fridge and two small glasses. She wonders if they're shots, but he sips his, so she follows suit. A taste she's not experienced before.

'Mm. What is this?'

'Aquavit. The predominant flavour is from the caraway. From home. From Sweden.'

It makes Maria nervous to be around people when they're drinking, but she's never seen Balogan drunk.

She understands why he might like to be in control.

He starts talking. He tells her magical things about his homeland. He conjures the Northern Lights and the brutal cold which can turn steam into snow. He tells her stories from his childhood, tales of shapeshifting creatures which live in lakes and woods which can lure a man to his death.

She's heard of trolls, of course, but not the *vittra* which exact a terrible revenge on anyone who disrespects them. She didn't know of the forest soul eaters seducing men to their deaths, or the sad, wretched unborn zombie children who haunt forests, yearning for a decent burial.

She shivers. There's a chill to these tales, but it's also fun, like her friends telling each other ghost stories when they had sleepovers as kids. She would love to visit the icy forests of his childhood, to travel over frozen expanses in a sledge pulled by dogs. What she wouldn't give to see the Northern Lights!

The aquavit makes her feel relaxed. Him, too, by the looks of it. He smiles as he reminisces, his face soft.

He tells her about coming to London. 'I arrived here with the clothes I stood up in,' he reveals.

'Why?'

'Problems,' is all he says in reply. 'I slept in bus stations and on the Circle Line. I got a job in a hotel kitchen and worked through the nights. It is a habit, this, to sleep in the day, one that I have not yet given up.' His smile is almost apologetic.

'You slept rough?'

'For a time. This . . .' He indicates the expanse of his flat. 'This has taken a long time.'

'It's a beautiful home,' says Maria.

'It has taken its toll.'

Before she can work out what he means he asks, 'What was it like for you, when you first came to London?'

★

219

After Spain, the first place Maria stayed in London was more basic than her current bedsit. A hostel. Wood Green is a little better, although there's no sign of any woods, and little green.

The first day she arrived in London, before she unpacked the few possessions she'd been given by the charity, she sat down and struggled to get the new scissors out of the packaging. She thought, *You'd really need a pair of scissors to do the job*. She had to use her teeth.

Then she stood in front of the small rectangle of mirror in her room. Most of the wounds on her face were healing by then. She noticed how her cheekbones jutted out like Lily's because she'd lost her puppy fat along with so many other things. She'd become scrawny, bruised shadows beneath sunken eyes, the missing tooth. She looked about forty. She wasn't even twenty back then.

When she'd finally liberated the scissors, she wove her hair into two heavy plaits, hacked them off and kept hacking. Her reflection looked demented.

She shaved off the rest with the Bic razor she'd bought for the purpose. She did it slowly, but still managed to nick her scalp a couple of times.

Now she uses a trimmer. She's never completely got used to the buzzcut. But it keeps certain men away. She'd had enough of her hair being mauled by Joby and the others.

Maria took the job with the cleaning agency, started work, tried to blot out the past by keeping busy and physically exhausting herself. At night she wondered if her body would ever feel like her own again. She dreamed of the hospital – being prodded and punctured and screwed back together – and woke panting.

London is hard with nothing to fall back on, but she felt she'd be better hidden in a city, and she'd always wanted to live in the capital. It was the polar opposite to a small town.

She feared what Lily might do when the phone went silent, when there was no word from Joby. And because of that she couldn't go home; she could never go home.

But it was tough. She had to swallow any shred of pride she might have left, and she went to the church and the community centre on foodbank days – and she still has to when money's tight now. Sometimes if she saw a woman with kids in tow, she couldn't face it and had to walk straight back out again.

She waited outside Pret and Costa as they were closing, hoping for out-of-date sandwiches and cake. She wasn't the only one – small groups gathered at these places like flocks of sad seagulls.

Her dad would be mortified if he knew that she'd stooped so low.

When she felt enough time had passed, when she felt she was back on an almost on an even keel, she plucked up the courage to call home.

Frankie answered. And in a torrent of abuse, she learned that she'd killed her own father.

'How bloody long has it been? Without so much as a bastard postcard . . . Never got in touch . . . Thought you knew better, din't you . . .? He hadn't a clue where the fuck you were . . . Worried sick . . . Died of a broken heart because of you . . . You selfish . . .'

She listened to Frankie rant at her for almost ten minutes before she quietly ended the call.

She wandered about London in a daze for weeks after that call. Numb. Her father was dead, and she hadn't even known.

He'd had a heart attack six months before she'd returned to Britain. If only she'd left Joby when she first thought about it, rather than doing nothing, she might have seen her dad before he died. He might not have died at all. But she couldn't torture herself like that.

She would go to sleep and dream of her dad – the nice times they had together in Skegness, down the Miners' Welfare, watching the deer and peacocks in Bradgate Park. When she woke, the loss would hit her again like a punch.

She considered calling her old mates to get more details, but she couldn't bear it. Stress was a cause of heart attacks, she knew that much. Anyway, her schoolfriends might have moved away by now, or most likely had their own kids, their own lives to worry about. And if she called they'd ask where she was and it would get out and then . . .

There was no way she'd try to contact anyone on Joby's side – what could she possibly say? They'd never go to the police, even if they were worried about Joby being missing, but they'd come after her in a heartbeat.

If she thought of Lily it made her gasp. Losing two sons! The guilt hit her as hard as the grief.

It was too painful to think about her dad or Joby, so she didn't. She used all her energy to put that part of her life aside, refused to revisit those memories, although the dreams that wake her now are full of the past.

Her eyes open with the thought of Joby hot on her skin – a flush of shame, a flush of horror. Her eyes open full of tears for her father.

She'd saved a little money by the time she had the plate in her ankle removed, but her stash of cash disappeared soon enough. She was hopping on and off buses a month after the operation, urgently needing to start earning again, although, at the hospital, they'd told her to wait at least six weeks before she went back to work. Cleaning took twice as long because she had to drag a chair around with her, sitting to take the weight off as she hoovered.

She lost two jobs because of that.

The only thing that stopped her topping herself on the worst nights was the thought that some other poor cow would have to clean up her mess after her.

So, she worked.

For years she's worked, the same old thing, the same old guilt.

Then the job with Elsie came up. She was the first customer who was kind to her.

She tells Balogan an abridged, sanitised version of this time. It is still more than she has revealed to another living soul. She doesn't mention her dad – too raw, even all these years later. Too private. Balogan listens, really listens. Even better, he doesn't comment. He gives her space. Eventually, after she's finished, he talks again, telling her how he misses his home.

He says nothing more about his own family, but he tells her more of the myths and the legends – of the creatures who drive people insane with their music.

Maria laughs, nodding to the wall where the neighbours'

drumbeat faintly pulses through. It isn't too bad tonight, but Balogan takes out his phone and sends a text, and the music immediately stops.

She laughs, and says, 'That is impressive.'

'I am both their landlord and their employer,' he replies. His smile changes as he adds, 'I have the power to destroy them.'

She doesn't think she's heard right. There is a sudden jolting change in atmosphere which makes her feel slightly sick.

Her face must register shock, because Balogan seems startled, either by her reaction or by what he's said. He stands quickly, looming over her as he reaches for her bowl. 'They will be no more trouble,' he adds, clearing the glasses, his face blank, closed off.

She asks, 'Is it okay if I go now? I can catch up next time.' Nervous.

He grunts in agreement.

She gathers her things, says goodbye, hurries out.

On the bus back from Balogan's, she goes over the weird exchange. Did she misunderstand? This morning the heater makes the back of her calves hot and the thrum of the engine beneath her makes her sleepy and she drifts. She leans heavily against the window. She can't keep her eyes open. Perhaps it's the alcohol.

She sees a man looming above her, moving against her, rocking back and forth. It's a pleasant sensation. She may even smile. But this isn't Joby's body on top of her. This man is huge, meaty, silver-haired. The face—

The bus jolts to a stop at temporary traffic lights.

Maria has to get off at the next stop and walk to rid herself of the images. She walks quickly until she reaches the bedsit. She needs to go back there to check her post.

She has never thought of Balogan like that before. She feels no desire for him when she's with him, does she?

She tries to cauterise that kind of thought – look where lust had got her before. But occasionally those feelings sideswipe her, as if she has no control over her own body. It appals her.

She feels ashamed and guilty, although of what, she's not entirely sure. She has bigger things she should feel guilty about.

Her feelings for Balogan are complicated. He is not a father figure, nor is it the brotherly affection she feels for Brian. It is not just a case of fancying the man either. There is something about his controlled manner which attracts her as much as the physical. There's a coldness, a steeliness within him, that she recognises. And it's as if she can see herself as he sees her – someone who does a good job; someone he can confide in; someone he trusts.

There's a sense that somehow they're alike.

34

Maria wakes from a lurid dream, drenched, wrung out. Another grave. A huge moon hanging low, tangled in the branches of twisted trees. The caress of an owl's wing.

Are these dreams or memories or flashbacks? So often now, it's as if time folds back on itself and her past is as close as her breath—

She sees the bull – a huge, red-tinged beast; savage; a creature of cave paintings – and she knows deep in her bones that it will kill her. It breathes fire. It comes for her.

She smells its sharp sweat. She feels its hatred.

And she fights for her life, the sensations visceral. Her muscles strain as she hacks at the beast's muscled neck, the axe heavy in her hands.

And she gasps and it roars and the blood spurts and spurts and spurts.

The relief when it's over! She has slain the minotaur.

Then, digging and sweating and scrambling to cover the body, nails bloodied, sliding down the mountain slope, branches clawing at her face, breath ragged, her heart battering . . .

Desperate to escape that place, she forces herself awake, and comes to, shaking.

The bull is not real, she knows that – a figment of her imagination, a denizen of her nightmares. That does not dilute the terror. But the grave is real enough, although she could never lead anyone back there; she would never be able to find the place again.

Pray no one else unearths it.

She is trembling as she leaves the bedsit and sets off to Elsie's early. There was no post. So much nothing in that room. She has only spent three hours in her own bed.

Del seems happy enough staying over with Elsie on the extra night Maria is now cleaning for Balogan, as long as she gets back in the morning before he goes to work. This is probably due to the fact that he can't stand the two blokes he shares a house with in Walthamstow, as much as altruism. On one of the rare occasions he spoke to Maria about anything other than his aunt, Del admitted that he hates both his housemates and Walthamstow. Perhaps he has his eye on Elsie's as a place to live rather than selling up?

Might that mean Maria could continue as she is? Wouldn't Nick's resting place be safe if Del moved in? Surely he isn't a keen horticulturalist?

She considers mentioning this plan to him, suggesting he

moves in – cheaper for him, he won't have his annoying housemates to contend with, and she'll still do the bulk of the care duties – but when she arrives at Roseberry Gardens she bottles it and decides to wait for a better time, because Del informs her that Elsie didn't recognise him last night.

'She might have been winding you up,' she suggests.

He considers it and says, 'Yeah, good point.' And he sets off for work.

Twice, recently, Elsie hasn't recognised Maria.

'Who are you, then, darling?' she asked, although she seemed blithely unbothered that someone she didn't know was in her kitchen making her breakfast. Another *muddied brain* day, she called it.

Maria informed her she was her cleaner. 'Lovely jubbly,' replied Elsie, continuing to stroke each of the cats in turn. Maria couldn't explain what else she is: carer, friend, surrogate daughter, husband killer. Beyond the call of duty.

She's dreading the day when Elsie takes against her. She's seen it happen, watched Elsie lash out when she took her to a café for a treat and there was no chocolate cake left, or when she had a go at the doctor for keeping her waiting. The language could be hair-curling. If Elsie detected a shop worker being rude or insincere, she let them have it with both barrels, the part of her brain in charge of politeness and social niceties eaten away – although Maria guesses Elsie never suffered fools gladly, even before all this kicked off.

This morning, Elsie is confusing Maria with her long-dead

sister. 'Vi. Vi!' she says as soon as Maria appears in her room. 'Don't tell Mum!' she whispers conspiratorially.

'What shouldn't I tell her?' asks Maria, opening the curtains.

'You know!' Elsie winks.

She might be remembering a long-ago tryst or some small secret from their childhood. Or is it the fact that there's a bloody big secret buried in her garden?

Spotty and Sweetie set about a pair of Elsie's bed-socks. The old woman smiles, watching them indulgently. The fur might already be starting to grow back on Sweetie's belly.

'He never took to them, you know,' says Elsie.

'Who?' asks Maria, laying out Elsie's clothes for the day. This downstairs room, now her makeshift bedroom, is where Elsie used to do her union work. Spotty jumps up on the little desk.

Elsie continues as if she's not heard her. 'He wanted kids at first – said he wanted 'em. But he was a Jaffa. Fired blanks. Him, not me, though I took the blame for it. So, cats.'

She lists a dozen or so cats she's had over the years before trailing off. Maria wonders how Elsie can she remember all the cats' names, but one night last week she'd tried to clean her teeth with her comb.

As Maria helps her dress, she sees the remains of bruises on Elsie's arms where Nick grabbed her. They're much fainter now, but it takes so long for them to heal at this age. Maria remembers the bruises decorating her gran's face after the fall and pushes the picture out of her mind.

Fur grows back, bruises fade – eventually. But how long

will it take before the images of what caused those marks on Elsie's delicate skin disappear?

'Vi! Violet?' shouts Elsie, even though Maria's right next to her.

Maria shouts back, 'Yes! Yes, love! What do you want?' and Elsie giggles.

Comfort says it's sometimes easier to play along. What else would she do? Remind Elsie that her mother, her father, her sister Violet are all dead, long gone, just so she can relive the pain of losing them again and again?

'Let's have a dance, Vi!'

Maria goes through to the kitchen to turn on the radio.

Elsie whoops as she hears 'You're The One That I Want', joining in on the 'Ooh, ooh, oohs'. Maria goes back to finish helping her dress, to see Elsie bopping around the room, shimmying her bony bum in time to the beat. The hip above one cheek is adorned with a tattoo of the CND symbol, the other with the Anti-Nazi League arrow.

Seeing her so happy makes Maria smile – a small, weary, sad smile, but a smile, nevertheless.

'What do you fancy for breakfast?' she asks. There's been a recent fatwa against porridge.

'That bloke off of *Call the Midwife*,' grins Elsie.

'Behave!'

She thinks for a moment then says, 'Tapioca.'

'Isn't that a kind of fish,' replies Maria.

'You behave,' says Elsie.

After breakfast, out of the blue, Elsie pauses with her mug halfway to her lips and says, 'She's gone, ain't she?'

'Who?' asks Maria.

231

'Our Vi. My Violet.'

'Yes. I'm sorry,' says Maria.

Elsie sighs heavily and says, 'Not your fault, darlin'. You live long enough, you lose everyone you love.'

35

Mid-afternoon, Elsie informs her that she's 'cream crack-ered' and Maria takes her through to her bed so she can have a nap. She fully intends to get the washing on, but she sits on the sofa – just for a minute – and the lack of sleep the previous night gets to her. She feels things coming towards her as sleep beckons, but there's nothing she can do. Exhaustion always wins.

And suddenly she's under, slipping back to that Monday night here at Elsie's: the night of the owl; the night of the fox's scream; the night of the bleeding carcass of Elsie's husband.

She'd only popped to the local shop to get fresh milk. She'd joked to Elsie that they should have bought shares in a cow . . .

*

Maria let herself in and immediately knew something wasn't right. She paused, waiting to make sense of the sounds she was hearing.

A soft cry. Elsie. Another deeper voice. Then a yelp.

Maria rushed through to the bedroom they'd made up for Elsie next to the kitchen. The little desk by the sofa bed was on its side, pens scattered on the carpet, and the letter opener, blotter and cat-shaped stapler were strewn across her duvet, envelopes and paperwork flung all over the place.

Nick was gripping Elsie by her upper arm. The old woman was whimpering.

'Think you're so clever, don't you?' he sneered. 'This is my gaff as much as yours. I'm entitled.'

'It's my home,' bleated Elsie. 'Mine! Get out of here! Go on – do one!'

'You're fucking loopy,' he laughed. 'Full-on loony tunes. You belong in a bleeding institution! You might have bought this house, but until we're divorced, *sweetheart*, I've got as much right to live here as you.'

Maria saw a rip in the seam of Elsie's nightie where Nick was grabbing the material so tightly.

She shouted, 'Get off her! Leave her alone!'

Nick slung Elsie away from him and she staggered back and fell on the bed. He span round to face Maria.

'What's it to you?' He scowled. He'd obviously been drinking.

Maria dodged round him and knelt by Elsie.

'Are you hurt, love?'

She shook her head.

'What's going on?'

'Don't let him take my money,' whispered Elsie. 'The bastard's trying to steal my stuff.'

It was unlikely that Elsie had much worth stealing, but whatever Nick was actually doing, Elsie was distraught.

Nick ignored them both and started pulling out the desk drawers, rifling through letters and notebooks and files.

Harry and Spotty both wandered into the room, curious to see what was happening.

'Can you go, please?' said Maria, trying a different, more pleading tone. 'You're upsetting her.'

'It's got nothing to do with you,' he snapped. He took an official-looking envelope and pushed himself up to standing but tripped over Harry in the process.

'Fucking . . .'

He grabbed Spotty, who was blameless, hauled her up by the scruff of her neck, and threw her out the door. Harry scarpered after her.

'Things are going to change round here. All these shitbag cats can go for starters,' he threatened. 'And she can fuck off and all!' He jabbed a finger at Maria.

'You leave Maria alone,' said Elsie.

'Why? You think she gives a toss about you? She's only after your dosh.' He snapped at Maria, 'Fucking cuckoo!' Then he smiled, slow and nasty, as he turned back to Elsie. 'You either give me my half, buy me out, my dearest darling, or I'm moving back in.'

'No! You can't!' shouted Elsie. 'I don't want you here!'

'Try and fucking stop me you—'

Everything else seemed to happen at once—

Elsie grabbed the glass of water Maria had left next to her bed and threw it at Nick's head. It missed.

Nick went for Elsie, lunging across her on the bed.

Before Maria knew what she intended, she'd grabbed his walking stick from the floor where he'd dropped it and started hitting his shoulder, trying to get him off Elsie, and he was roaring and trying to hit his wife, and Maria swung wildly and caught him hard across the side of his ear.

He crumpled and rolled off the side of the bed.

Elsie wailed, 'Who is he? Who *is* he?'

Maria dropped the stick and sat on the bed, trying to soothe Elsie. She turned too late. The punch caught the back of her head and dizzied her for a second. Then a flurry of jabs and obscenities rained down on her.

Dazed, she brought her arms up to protect her head from the blows. He might have a rubbish knee, but Nick had been a boxer in his youth. She tried to think where his walking stick had fallen so she could hit him again.

But suddenly, like he'd been shot, it stopped.

Maria inhaled, forced her eyes open. Wished she hadn't.

Elsie was kneeling up on the bed making guttural sounds that might have been a growl.

Nick had reared back away from her, hands limp by his sides, his face red on one side where Maria had caught him with the walking stick, his mouth hanging slack. One eye was wide open in surprise.

And Elsie's ancient letter opener from the little desk next to her bed was deep in the other eye socket. Rammed in. Right up to the hilt.

36

Her phone wakes her. Her neck is stiff from where she's dozed off on Elsie's sofa.

I need to see you. ASAP! It's Brian.

The phone buzzes again: *We need to talk!!!*

She sighs. One of the most terrifying sentences in the English language.

I'll be right there, she replies. She doesn't bother asking what it's about, but she adds three kisses just in case it's not what she thinks.

Elsie is happy to go next door and watch *Some Like It Hot* with the widow for the umpteenth time – it's their favourite film.

Maria walks quickly, trying to leave the vile images from the night Nick died behind her. She's sweating by the time she arrives at Brian's, but there's no offer of tea, which immediately tells her something is seriously wrong before his face does. He brings her through to the living room and sits with his legs crossed on his beanbag, which is no mean feat.

'Everything okay?' she asks. 'You and Alex fine? Did he get that new job he went for?'

Snippets from other people's lives usually fall out of Maria's head as soon as she leaves the homes she cleans. In the same way, ask them, and few of her clients would even know her surname. But Brian is different. She's genuinely interested, and she genuinely cares.

She also wants to delay the inevitable.

'What did you do to him?' he asks. His tone is accusing.

'Who?' She swallows, turns away, rummages in her bag so she doesn't have to face him. Of course she knows who he's talking about.

'They found high levels of psilocybin in his toxicology report.'

Maria braces. She feels sick.

'What?'

'The police came round here.'

Oh God. She considers denying everything. She can't risk admitting it to anyone, even Brian – where the hell could that lead?

'I don't know—'

'Alex saw you.'

'Saw me what?' she challenges.

'You gave him those vol-au-vents.'

Bugger. 'And . . .?'

'Come on, Maria! Mushroom bloody vol-au-vents. What the bloody hell have you done?' She's never seen Brian angry before.

She pauses, considers, then says, 'It was an accident.'

It wasn't, though – not really. She caused it.

'You didn't give those to anyone else, did you?'

'Of course not!'

'For fuck's sake!' says Brian.

'But you hated him. And I didn't throw him under that truck.'

'You might as well have.'

True. She asks, 'What are you going to do?'

'I don't know. I've not decided yet.' He looks scared. Then his eyes catch hers and his expression changes.

She's never seen him look at her this way before – like he doesn't trust her; like he doesn't know her at all.

This is what she feared. She has enough trouble reconciling the way she feels about her own actions, let alone guessing how Brian might reconsider his friendship with someone who does something like that.

She thinks about saying it's good that his boss is dead – the man was scum. She did Brian a favour. But she decides it's probably better not to say a word.

There's a long prickly silence.

'You didn't consider that the police might have me down as a suspect, being as it was my bloody party?'

'No! Of course not!' It honestly hadn't occurred to her. How stupid! Too self-obsessed.

'They didn't say as much but that's what they were angling towards. I've not been able to sleep. I've been sick with worry.'

'I'm sorry. I really didn't mean—'

'It's a bit late to be sorry now.'

'I thought I was helping you. I am so—'

'Helping me! You're joking, aren't you? I didn't ask you to poison him, for Christ's sake.'

'Well, he didn't die of poisoning,' she reasons. She waits, watching the set of Brian's purple eyebrows for clues. 'You're not going to say anything, are you?'

'I don't know—'

'Oh God, please don't! Please—'

'I don't want to. Alex doesn't want me to. But what am I supposed to do if they come back asking more questions – *piecing together his movements the night he died?* Everyone knew I hated him!'

They regard each other warily.

'Do you still want me to clean?' she asks. As questions go, that's the most innocuous she can think of.

'I can't think about that right now,' says Brian.

'Great. So I'm now going to lose my job over an *accident.*' She exhales heavily.

'*That's* your takeaway from this? *Please!*'

'I'm sorry.'

'You don't sound sorry enough! You don't sound sorry at all!'

That's shamingly accurate. She says, 'I'd better go.'

'Yes,' says Brian. He shakes his head. 'I cannot believe you!'

He doesn't say goodbye. She tries to close the door as quietly as she can on her way out, although she actually wants to slam it shut.

She storms back to Elsie's, stomping along pavements, dodging round other walkers. She refuses to feel guilty about Brian's boss. He's not worth it!

Her conscience is clear!

The same with Nick, too – it was self-defence, wasn't it? She was trying to protect Elsie, *saving* her. She will not feel guilty! She shouldn't feel guilty about any of it!

37

Whether she's awake or asleep, Maria can't get the images out of her head . . .

Elsie on the bed, up on her knees, snarling.

Nick like a horror-show unicorn, the letter opener sticking out of one eye, the other furious.

Maria couldn't breathe for a second, immobilised by fear.

Elsie made a low growl then slumped back against the wall.

Nick stood silent, swaying slightly. Then he roared, a wounded animal noise, and took two staggering steps, lurching towards Maria, a vicious zombie, one eye wide with violence, intent on murder.

She grabbed the walking sick from the floor, drew back and swung it at his head like a golfer. Not like the Crazy Golf at Skegness – hard.

Nick keeled over like a felled redwood, sending everything

in his wake flying. And she might have stopped at that point. Called the police. Called an ambulance. He was down. It would have been self-defence, then.

But she didn't. Couldn't.

She stood over him, and she drew back the stick and hit him again. She had to make sure he'd stay down. She had to protect Elsie. And she got into a rhythm, whacking and whacking him, smashing his skull with the walking stick again and again. Just to be really, really sure.

At some point she must have stopped – and then there was no more movement.

Elsie was keening softly to herself on the bed, tugging at her nightie, trying to pull it down over her knees. She was oblivious of Maria standing panting over Nick's body on the floor. Maria couldn't help but worry how Elsie's knees would feel in the morning – a stupid thought.

Maria went over to put her hand on the old woman's arm.

'Elsie? Are you okay? Did he hurt you?'

'I've killed him! I've bloody killed him!' gasped Elsie.

We've killed him, thought Maria.

She dropped the walking stick, sat on the bed, and put her arms around Elsie. She hugged her against her chest, rocking her as she trembled, repeating, 'It'll be all right. It's all right,' saying it for herself as much as the newly bereaved wife, until she felt the old woman's breathing calm and her muscles start to relax.

'I've killed him,' whispered Elsie.

'No,' said Maria. Although perhaps the letter opener had pierced his brain. Perhaps his movements had been involuntary, like a headless chicken. But she'd had to be sure.

'No, I killed him,' she said.

And she was glad.

When Maria's anger subsided, the first clear thought that came to her was that she had to clean up the mess. She reassured Elsie as best she could. 'Don't you worry, I'll sort it. It's all okay.'

Nothing could be further from okay.

When Elsie finally rested against Maria, heavier with sleep, she gently lay her down and tucked the duvet around her, cocooning her against the night and the sight of her husband seeping blood and fluids on the floor right next to her bed.

Then she dragged the old man through to the kitchen, in case Elsie woke and freaked out. The cats skittered and fled for their lives, thundering through the catflap like demented cannonballs, which for once, was an appropriate response.

She hoicked Nick's body on to his chair to get him out of the way and on automatic pilot she ran the hot tap, scrabbling for bleach and cloths under the sink, then she started to clean the floor next to Elsie's bed. She didn't think the rug could be saved, but she did manage to get the blood stains out of the carpet. The scrubbing felt almost normal. But when she returned to the kitchen, after ten minutes or so mopping, she had to put a tea towel over the old man's head, because she couldn't bear the sight of that one accusing eye.

And then she buried the old bastard. She threw the walking stick and the rug in with him. The letter opener was still attached.

38

If it wasn't for Elsie, Maria might flee the country. She's thought about that a lot since Nick's death. She thinks about it again now – the police sniffing round Brian's and his face giving her no reassurance he won't tell them everything.

But wherever you go, you take yourself. She learned that when she went to Spain with Joby—

After his brother's death, Joby would clutch Maria round her waist and sob in her lap.

'We'll have a babby. A boy, another boy, yes? Our first son is up there with his Uncle Anthony now. But we'll have another boy.'

Nothing was more of a turn-off.

If she did have a baby with him, her *husband* – this man she didn't really know – she'd be stuck with this sentimental shite, stuck on this grim site, with this life. The thought appalled her.

But finally, Joby arranged his face into a rictus grin, and he agreed to take Maria away for *a little holiday*. He told his mother he needed to get away to clear his head.

Lily glared at Maria between her tears. 'My only living son abandoning me!' she wailed.

Maria wondered what Joby might do if this jaunt didn't end in a pregnancy – everyone holding their breath for her to start a new life to replace the one lost.

The day they set off, Maria sat beside Joby, riding high in the SUV, the wagon towed behind them. She waved like the Queen.

They were going travelling!

Late-flowering blossoms from some tree she couldn't identify were frothing with optimism as they pulled away, stirred up by the wheels like bridal confetti. Magpies chattering goodbyes.

She genuinely believed it was a fresh start, a new chapter. She was so excited she sang along to songs on the radio as they drove, and Joby laughed with her.

The crossing was brutal. Joby went up on deck, but she lay like a gutted fish on the bed in the cabin. More than once, she wished the bloody ferry would sink.

She fell asleep briefly, until she was jerked awake by a dream of Anthony waving them off.

As soon as they stepped on to foreign soil at the port of Santurtzi, Joby's mood lightened. They parked up and spent a day in Bilbao, which was full of life – *cosmopolitan* – a proper city! The highlight was the giant floral puppy outside the Guggenheim Museum. Joby snapped photos of her posing in front of it.

She was thrilled. She called her dad, but Frankie answered, and the phone went dead.

Joby drove up a mountain, Maria afraid the weight of the trailer would drag them backwards. They made camp off the beaten track, near a forest that looked like it came out of a fairy tale.

And he'd laughed! He was happy. Well, he seemed happy. Happier.

And she was beloved.

She felt like an actual gypsy girl, dancing around a real fire in a long sequin-trimmed skirt as the sparks flew up into a molten sky and the smoke flavoured their food, and her life was suddenly new and challenging and exciting. He'd bought her the skirt – red and orange, like the flames.

Joby was obsessed by the fire, even though it was so warm they didn't need it at first. He chopped wood, stripping down as he did it, swinging the axe, looking like some poster boy. He tended it as if it was his child, whispered encouraging words, coaxing the flames higher. Sweat ran down his chest like lava. She wanted to lick it.

At dusk they took turns to swig rough red wine from the bottle, the light of the flames playing across their faces, and they dragged the duvet out to sleep under the stars, as if they were in some film. They made love and it was amazing.

They were in a new country!

She hoped the old Joby might return. How hard she'd loved him.

And he did talk more, opened up to her. He told her how much he wanted to make his dad proud of him, how much he wanted his own family. He said he'd only feel whole again if they had a baby – to fill the gap in his heart left by his brother.

'That's all there is, girl. When the chips are down, your family and your community – it's everything.'

Maria didn't really have a sense of community, but she didn't say so because she didn't want to dampen his mood.

He told her again and again how much he loved her. Weren't they having a great time? There was no stopping them!

But then one night she drank too much and twirled too fast, and she tripped and fell, badly twisting her ankle. He strapped it up for her and applied poultices of mashed-up herbs and made *there-there* noises. But it hurt when he was on top of her, and he caught her hair under his elbow as he tried to take his weight off.

He went down to the village to get painkillers and an ice pack to help with the swelling. He didn't come back for hours, and when he did, the stink of spirits was on him.

But it was still okay. Then.

Barely there clouds, a dusting of vapour. Intense blue skies. She'd watch him tend the fire – sunburned nose and burnished torso. His muscles look great in the sunshine. He'd never looked better.

But he soon got bored waiting on her and took to roaming the woods in daylight hours. Him, the hunter-gatherer, hiking down to the village for supplies, setting rabbit traps, going off to fish.

Her throbbing ankle kept her awake at night as she lay alone in bed waiting for him to come back from the village bars. She had never heard silence like it.

When her ankle had healed enough for her to put some weight on it, and after she'd grumbled enough, he drove her down to the village in the valley.

The bar was small, loud, hot.

She noticed the guy straight off – small, intense. He wore a leather waistcoat over a bare chest, hard sinewy muscles, like polished wood. He had one gold tooth, which put her in mind of a pirate.

Maria stared. The man smiled at her. It must have been her hormones or being on holiday or something, because despite herself, she felt a thrill, which turned sour as soon as Joby noticed. The pirate man walked over to their table. She tensed, wondering how Joby would react.

'Madre Mari!' he exclaimed, opening his arms as if she was the most wonderful vision. And he bowed to her with a deep flourish, a ridiculous display, but she couldn't help smiling.

Joby bristled.

'English? American?' enquired the man.

'English, but citizens of the world!' Joby answered for her, and she excused herself and went through to the loos. There were models of witches hanging in the windows that made her shudder.

By the time she got back, supporting herself by holding on to the backs of chairs, she was surprised to see Joby laughing, a fresh drink in front of him, and the guy had his arm around his shoulders.

'Maria, meet Itzal.' Joby grinned. 'Itzal, mate, this is my missis.'

Mate. Surprising.

Itzal chatted to them in heavily accented English and shouted across to his friends standing at the bar in some weird language that sounded like he was bringing up a hairball. Not Spanish, *Basque*, she was informed.

As soon as Itzal appeared on the scene, Joby redoubled his efforts in bed – some macho instinct, staking his claim.

'Let's make that babby, girl!' he'd laugh, and he'd thread his hands in her hair and lean her head back to bite her neck.

And, God, she liked that. But sometimes it went on and on – him pumping in and out like some mechanical bull as she just lay there, knowing it was never going to happen.

That phase didn't last long. As the drinking with Itzal amped up, the fire got more attention than she did, and his hangovers soured their mornings.

A couple of times a week she'd go with him to meet Itzal down in Miren's Bar and they all drank too much and ate *pintxos*. Itzal warned them to avoid those with mayonnaise that had been sitting out since breakfast.

Tipsy, she declared that she'd try to learn Basque and Itzal snorted. He translated for the others in the bar, and they all laughed at her.

Maria never bought a round, which was fair enough, but it would have been impossible for her to do so, given that she had no money of her own. Joby paid his share with a stash of Euros. Maria was never invited to go with him to the bank.

Never have I ever had a bank card.

At night she lay sweltering, strange noises creeping into her dreams. If Joby wasn't back, she lay rigid, afraid of what might prowl in the twisted limbs of the forest. Or perhaps she was afraid of what she was turning into – something bitter.

She was in a new country, but she saw nothing of it. Her days were spent cooking and cleaning and sunbathing. Sometimes she wanted to scream.

She was lonely and resentful. Joby spent more time with Itzal, his new 'best bud', than with her.

'I didn't think you liked him,' she challenged.

'Keep your enemies close, girl,' he replied with a wink.

'What's that supposed to mean?' she asked, but he was already snoring.

Itzal came up to the trailer with a girl on the back of his motorbike. She had blonde dreadlocks. Maria thought she looked great and mimed her appreciation.

'Shall I try mine like that?' she asked.

Itzal shook his head. She flinched as he reached over to stroke her hair, but Joby seemed cool.

'You keep your hair just as it is, girl. Best thing about you,' said Joby.

It felt like a backhanded compliment.

'Wood pigeons. A delicacy!' beamed Itzal, bowing as he handed a package to Maria like he was making an offering.

She had no idea what to do with the tiny, bloodied bodies.

Itzal plucked the birds. Handfuls of feathers flew up into the hazy heat of the night. He sliced them open and ripped out their entrails, wrapping the guts in paper.

'There are wolves here.' He smiled, his gold tooth glinting in the firelight.

Maria wasn't sure if he was mocking her.

He soaked skewers in water, then impaled the pigeons, roasting them over the fire. She couldn't eat them.

They talked all night.

She asked Itzal about the models of witches hanging in the windows of houses and shops and the bar.

'They ward off the bad.'

'And all the owls?' Owl ornaments were everywhere in the windows of the village houses.

'Good luck,' he explained.

Joby got bored and fell asleep.

Itzal told her the region was special. He talked of the old gods, each with their own special powers, like superheroes; much older than Christianity: controllers of nature, of the weather; an icon with golden hair holding a red rose in her hand; pagan goddesses, precursors of Our Lady.

She loved the stories. She liked listening to his husky voice as he explained.

They all drank too much and when Itzal and the girl

kissed, Maria felt a flash of frustration.

Joby woke and they drank some more, and everyone laughed.

And then things got really bad.

39

She bumps into Cass again as she's on her way into Balogan's building. The girl is sitting on the floor crying by the lifts in the foyer. Maria walks over to check if she's all right.

'Cass? Hello, Cass?' She puts her hand on the girl's shoulder.

'Sorry,' says Cass, gazing up and attempting a smile. The single word hooks Maria.

They travel up in the lift together and by the time they're at the top, Maria has agreed to pop into the flat next door for a quick drink before she starts the clean.

'Don't worry, Mal's not in,' says Cass, wiping her nose on her sleeve as she opens the door.

The place is in chaos. The flat is in desperate need of a cleaner.

Cass walks through the debris into a filthy kitchen and hands Maria a cold beer from the fridge.

'No, thank you,' says Maria, 'I've got a long night ahead.'

The girl opens the beer for herself but doesn't offer Maria an alternative drink. She clears a space and hops up to sit on the kitchen worktop, swinging her legs. She reaches into an abandoned KFC box and takes out a chicken nugget.

'Don't eat that,' says Maria.

Cass laughs and hurls the nugget across the room. 'Goal!' she cries as it lands in the sink. Her mood has shifted suddenly and completely.

'Your hair is cool. Like velvet!' smiles the girl. She reaches up with her greasy hand to touch Maria's skull. 'I'd like to cut mine like that, but Mal wouldn't like it.'

That's the point, thinks Maria.

She witters on about the band's gig that night and then abruptly changes the topic and asks if Maria's met Balogan. 'What's he like? Mal works for him. And he's, like, *scared* of him,' she confides. 'But he's sexy, don't you think?'

Maria shrugs. She guesses Balogan wouldn't want her gossiping about him.

'Are you married?' asks Cass.

'No,' says Maria, adding, 'I'm going to have to make a start cleaning next door.'

'I want to get married,' announces Cass dreamily.

'To Mal?'

'No!' She laughs as if this is the most hilarious thing she's ever heard. The laughter is manic. Drug fuelled, Maria guesses.

The mood shifts again and Cass suddenly whispers, 'I hate him!' And she hurls the KFC box towards the bin. It misses and the remaining nuggets scatter across the cooker.

'Does he hurt you?' asks Maria.

Cass stops laughing abruptly. 'God, no!' She fiddles with the label on her beer. 'No, it's not like that, at all. No-no-no-no. You don't understand. Look, if he finds you here there'll be trouble. Don't say anything, will you?'

'Of course not. Anyway, I've got to get on.'

Cass surprises Maria by hopping down from the counter and giving her a hug. 'Come again?' she asks. 'I'll make us . . . pasta!'

Maria nods, although she doesn't mean it.

She opens the door to Balogan's flat just as he walks into the lounge damp from the shower, only a bath towel round his waist.

'Sorry!' She quickly looks away, looks back. Blushes.

'Not to worry,' he replies, disappearing into his bedroom.

She has almost finished in the kitchen when he reappears wearing a dark suit. He carries it well. She finds it hard to look him in the eye and feels embarrassed by her reaction.

'I have an engagement,' he explains.

'Oh. Right.' She dodges past him to clear up in the bathroom. He smells lovely, something green and woody.

She doesn't answer when he calls a goodbye. She doesn't trust her voice.

She starts to hoover. And she thinks of both Balogan and Cass next door as she works.

An hour after Balogan's left, the electricity goes off and the flat is plunged into darkness.

Maria uses the light from her phone to get a torch from one of the kitchen drawers and then she goes in search of the fuse box. She locates it in a small cupboard under the stairs to the roof garden – she'd like to go up there one day to see the view.

As she's about to close the cupboard she notices a beautiful pale blue scarf at the back. It's an odd place for it. Balogan is usually so organised, so neat. She reaches for it to put back it in his wardrobe. The material is soft – cashmere, she guesses – but something hard is wrapped inside it.

She takes it out, unfolds the scarf.

And that's when she sees the gun.

40

She is lucky with the buses on the way back from Balogan's, for once. If it turns out to be a nice day, she might take Elsie for a walk in the park later, if the weather holds. Get some daylight and fresh air down them both – as fresh as London allows. She needs to think.

She's seen guns like Balogan's on TV. When she held it, she knew it was real – not a toy, not a replica, not a cigarette lighter. It looked and felt very different from the air rifles Joby and his uncles messed around with. Heavy. Lethal.

What should she do about it? Should she say something? Should she stop working there? Should she ignore it? Who is she to judge? But it puts her on edge. Why does he want to keep a gun in the flat?

That morning there's a visit from the washing-machine repair man at long last – he's only cancelled twice. The lad seems nervous as soon as he arrives, and keeps staring as

Elsie roars lines from, 'Hit Me with Your Rhythm Stick' She is shuffle-dancing around the kitchen.

It might have been worse. Elsie delivers a fine rendition of the opening lines of 'Plaistow Patricia'. She'd once done that in the middle of the big Sainsbury's and a fellow pensioner had almost fainted in the fruit-and-veg aisle.

'Can she stop that?' says the engineer, rolling his eyes as Elsie belts out, 'Hit me, hit me, hit me!' again and again.

'She likes singing,' says Maria, wishing she'd simply taken their washing to the laundrette.

'She keeps staring at me!'

Elsie grimaces. She knows the lad's talking about her.

'She's just interested in what you're doing. She doesn't mean anything by it, do you, Elsie?'

'She not all there?' he asks, right in front of her, like Elsie can't hear him, like she doesn't count. Maria wants to do him serious harm.

It's as if a switch flicks. Elsie's face, so happy while she was singing, blanks. She sits at the kitchen table and vanishes somewhere deep inside herself and she doesn't really seem present for the rest of the day.

Elsie goes to bed early. Her body clock seems to be slowing down and she's been sleeping longer over the last couple of weeks. Maria heads upstairs to read. It still feels like this is Elsie's room, even though Maria's spent so much time in it lately.

She can't focus on the pages. She turns off the light, wondering what sort of business Balogan's involved in that would require a gun. And then she falls into an exhausted sleep.

★

Sudden, like a shot, a memory of Joby jolts her awake. Not one of the yearning dreams, where she relives the good times. A terrifying 'shroom flashback—

Joby's head – she can see it clearly. The body is some way away.

She dry-heaves, throws back the duvet. She stands under the shower, the water as hot as she can bear.

That time seems so long ago, but it's also is as close as her heartbeat.

She scrubs her skin hard. She's done this so often she's worn the sliver of soap into a razor-clam shell.

41

She hasn't made her mind up what to say to Balogan, if anything. But the next time she's at his flat, the gun is all she can think about as she cleans.

Is he keeping it for someone else? Are guns more common in Sweden? Is it legal? Why was it hidden? Why would he need a gun in a London nightclub?

She jumps when she hears the door. Balogan comes in cradling his elbow, holding himself at an angle, as if there might be an injury in his side as well as his arm. She stares, her mouth open. Blood is dripping from his cuff to the floor.

He hurries through to the bathroom, grunting a greeting, bringing the chill of the night in with him.

He's in there a long time.

Maria gathers herself, then sets about cleaning up after him using the professional stain remover on his white wool rug. Oxygenated bleach. Rubber gloves. She's always judged that rug – so impractical.

She's still on her knees when he eventually comes out of the bathroom, his jacket off, his ruined shirt rolled up and a fresh bandage on his left forearm. He offers no explanation.

'You have done a good job.' He indicates the rug.

'It's easier if you get to it immediately. If it dries it takes longer to shift,' she replies. She doesn't tell him how she knows this.

There's a long pause as they watch each other.

'How are you, Maria?'

'Fine, really,' she tries, very much doubting that she looks fine.

'Hm.' He eases himself on to the sofa. 'Come, sit.' He gestures to the space next to him.

Awkwardly, she walks over. Maria doesn't like sitting when there's work to do. She's also uneasy about both his injury and the gun.

'Tell me, what is it?'

Maria sighs. 'I'm just tired.' An understatement; she's shaking with fatigue.

'A bad night?' he enquires.

It's easier to talk about Elsie than her other more pressing concerns. Saying, 'The old lady I look after. I'm worried about her,' is so much easier than saying, 'I'm worried that I've killed three men. Why do you need a gun?'

'This woman, she is a relative?'

'No. But . . . She's like family to me.' Maria finds trying to explain her relationship with Elsie difficult. She can't even explain it properly to Del.

'Why are you worried about her?'

'It's her mind.'

Maria can't stop looking at Balogan's injured arm.

'What is the problem? With her mind?'

'She's losing it,' says Maria, annoyed that her voice sounds wobbly as the words came out. Stating the fact so harshly is upsetting.

He nods, as if he understands. 'My grandmother had problems too, with her mind. It is sad to see, yes?'

Maria nods, unsure of what else might come out of her mouth if she answers.

'How are you coping with this?'

Maria has often talked to Del and Comfort about Elsie – the practicalities of caring for her – but no one has ever asked Maria how she feels about it.

Because she's not proper family.

She's annoyed to feel a prickling of tears threatening and swallows them back. She starts to get up from the sofa, but Balogan reaches out, laying his hand on top of hers.

'This can be difficult. If you love someone.' She is very aware that he's looking at her, his eyes piercing. 'A lot of stress, yes?'

She tries to say yes but fails. She manages to deflect his concern by asking, 'What happened with your grandma?'

'Ah . . . My little *mormor*. She got lost.' He shrugs his massive shoulders. There's an expression on his face she hasn't seen before. Tender, almost.

'Lost?'

'She went out and didn't come back. One night. There was a search – the neighbours, the police – but . . . They found her the next morning. At the back of her old school. By the railings. Like she was waiting to go in for lessons.' He takes a deep breath. 'The nights in Sweden are unforgiving. She was frozen.'

'God!'

Balogan rubs his jaw.

'I'm sorry.'

'You have nothing to be sorry for,' he answers. He holds her gaze with those ice-blue eyes. She sees the hurt in them. She finds her hand reaching up to touch his face and she leans in towards him—

Balogan registers the movement, and he gets up so abruptly he knocks one of his cushions on the floor.

It is like a slap.

'Oh. Sorry. I'll just finish up,' she croaks.

She avoids him in the kitchen. When she returns to the lounge he's back on the sofa and he seems to be sleeping. She quietly cleans around him, snatching quick looks to check if his eyes are open.

When she's finished she creeps to the door calling a soft goodbye.

He does not reply.

She hurries to the lift, keen to be out of the building.

The flush of shame keeps her warm on the way home, even though the heater on the bus isn't on.

What did she expect? He doesn't see her like that. She hacked off her hair to stop men seeing her that way.

It is best not to complicate things; best to keep things purely professional. That sort of relationship would ruin everything.

And whatever business Balogan's really into, it's got to be bad.

She's mortified that she tried to kiss him, despite the gun.

Or did she try to kiss him because of it?

42

She goes straight back to Elsie's because Del wants to get off to work first thing. She manages an hour's doze on the sofa before Elsie wakes up.

They've already had their breakfast by the time Del comes through to the kitchen.

The other week he claimed he'd found 'somewhere' that took pets. He was very careful not to mention the words 'care home'. Comfort isn't coming round today, but she calls Maria to tell her that she has now looked into this place, and she's discovered that only one cat, or one small dog, is allowed.

Maria is the one who has to break the news.

Elsie immediately starts ranting about 'Sophie's bleeding choice!' and Del's face falls.

Maria can't bear the thought of the old girl being without her furry family, so she finally tries to talk to Del about a more formal arrangement – her moving in to look after Elsie full time.

'I just think she'd be happier, and it would be easier on you if I stayed here on a permanent basis rather than you having to come over all the time.'

'But you're not a qualified carer. And you're not her family,' says Del, which is the truth, but it hurts.

When he leaves for work, Elsie says, 'He's just in a bad mood, darlin'. Take no notice of him. Let's have a cuppa.'

Now and then, out of the blue, Elsie pipes up with something like, 'I want you to have this house.'

Today she says, 'I mean it, Maria. You've done more for me than that bastard Nick ever did. Or our Del, come to that. You should have this place.'

And Maria wonders what it would be like to have the house. To have somewhere nice to live at last. To feel secure that no one would dig up the roses and what lies beneath. Or, if Elsie left her something in her will, to have enough cash not to worry about what she eats; to have enough money to do a runner.

The thoughts shame her. She's a terrible person.

She isn't sure who has power of attorney for Elsie's affairs. Nothing to be done if it's Nick. If it's Del, Maria knows it will be over his dead body if she ever sees a penny.

She catches herself – *over his dead body*. The phrase makes her feel nauseous.

Leaving Elsie would break Maria's heart.

But that's what she'll have to do when Del finally sends Elsie away and puts the house up for sale. And Maria knows it is a case of *when*, not *if*. What happens when the new owners do a spot of landscape gardening? She'll have to flee London, change her name, go on the run, work cash in hand somewhere new.

In some ways it might be no worse, really. She's always looking over her shoulder as it is, afraid that one of Joby's friends or family will catch up with her and make her pay – although how they'd track her down she has no idea.

If Del sells up, she'll have to get out quick. Perhaps go to another country, start again? But the fresh start in Spain didn't go so well, did it?

43

The pain in Maria's ankle nagged, keeping her awake, and her mood became brittle. She grew brown and sullen as her hair turned white-blonde in the sun. She scrubbed and she scoured like she hated the wagon floor, trying to erase her anger.

Joby returned from the village too drunk to fuck.

'You wanted to travel. We're travelling. Jesus, girl, nothing I do makes you happy,' he snapped.

'I am happy we're here but—'

'Then tell your face, you mardy bitch.'

Sometimes he would cry in his sleep. Grief and guilt are not sexy.

Sometimes he'd try – digging his fingers into her thigh, shoving his tongue in her mouth, rolling on top of her. But he didn't get hard.

When she tried to kiss him, he'd pull away or change the

tone of the kiss, laughing and tickling her, other times he'd say, 'Stop pestering me, girl!'

Days bled into weeks. Joby showed no interest in her and no interest in returning to England. She wondered how long his cash would last.

She was sitting on the steps outside the caravan chopping vegetables for their dinner when Itzal arrived. He came alone. He sat next to her and helped, and they talked. He told her how he loved his country.

'I don't love my country,' she laughed. 'Why do you love Spain?'

'Spain!' He made an angry gesture. 'We are not Spain. We are Basque! People here have died for this land. I have friends in prison because they are true Basques.'

She didn't understand his passion for the accident of where he'd been born, but she liked the conversation. And she liked the warmth of him next to her.

He told her of a time he'd lived in Morocco.

'Ooh, I'd love to go there,' she said. 'I've always wanted to see a desert. It seems so . . . romantic.'

'It will kill you,' he said, looking serious. 'The sun will scorch you in the day, but at night you will die of the cold. People write poetry about such places to keep them warm at night. It is beautiful, but also the loneliest place in the world.'

'I'm lonely here,' she confessed.

'I would not leave you alone.' He smiled.

He gave her the look.

She leaned into him a little.

'Your hair is like the sun.' He gently brushed it out of her eyes. Corny. But . . .

He took her face in his hands then and he kissed her.

She took his hand and led him up the steps into the wagon.

That's how Joby found them when he came back from the village.

The men swore and fought and Itzal roared off on his motorbike half dressed, and she and Joby fought, and he screamed that she'd ruined his life and she went for him with a pan and as she tried to hit him he pushed her away and she fell awkwardly on her weak ankle and, as she went down she knocked out her tooth on the corner of the cupboard.

She never found that tooth.

She decided she'd leave. But she did nothing. And she continued to do nothing even as her bones told her to run.

He disappeared for two days. She wondered if he'd fallen and broken his neck in the woods. She wondered if she'd care if he had. The opposite of love isn't hate – it's boredom.

He returned bouncy with excitement. He seemed to have forgiven her for Itzal. He was all smiles, telling her he had a surprise for her. Then he busied himself in the tiny kitchen, brewing up one of his potions.

'What's in that?' she asked, with little interest.

'Magic.' He grinned.

'Where were you?' she asked.

He didn't reply, just handed her a mug sprinkled with what looked like tree bark and gestured for her to try it.

'Come on, girl. You a chicken?'

She took a sip, wrinkling her nose. It tasted of earth and dead things.

'What is it?'

'You're always after seeing new places. Well, this is the best getaway you'll ever have, girl.'

'Drugs?'

'All natural. Go on.'

She took another sip. Nothing happened.

He started burbling, telling her about the fantastic time he'd had with his new friends – she had no idea who they might be – extolling the virtues of the *'shrooms*.

At least he was excited about something. At least they were doing something new together. She took one more sip. She finished the brew. Nothing happened.

And then she slid into a different world—

A Disney world!

The colours! She reached out and she was there, right inside it, *Nature*!

And she forgot her swollen ankle and she danced by herself as he tended the fire.

The birds called, and she answered.

And at dusk, she flew with the owls.

He sat on the wagon steps looking misty eyed. And she realised she loved him so much! She sat on his knee. He tried to push her hand away, but she undid his zip. His smile evaporated and he stood up abruptly, spilling her on to the ground.

She started laughing – as much about the fall as about his sad limp dick. He glared at her, but she couldn't stop.

The laugh caught her, and she cackled and whooped; tears in her eyes; a glorious laugh that shook her and left her gasping, juddering, but on it went.

She watched her laughter spool up and away from her lips and she saw each sound slap him – HA! HA! HA! Stab! Stab! Stab! – pierce him, crawling into his ears, slicing him, burrowing under his skin, poisoning him, but it was so delicious. The laugh filled her up entirely and there was nothing she could do to stop herself.

At some point, a wood pigeon cooed its way into her sleep. It was joined by others – a symphony! Then the trills and chirps and squawks of different colours sifted through her fingers and turned to morning shrieks which hurt her head and she felt like she did on the ferry. She heaved.

The mushrooms became his 'side hustle'.

The weather changed. The sun was all for show – fierce light, no heat. Like his smile – it wasn't real; his eyes a million miles away.

The heater packed up and the wagon was an ice box as soon as the sun went down. She wondered if she might be the only person to freeze to death in bloody Spain.

So many stars bloomed at dusk. The beauty of the mountain still caught her breath. The owl was her companion then. No answer to its call – the loneliest sound in the world.

★

One night Joby cooked for her for a change and the food he prepared was spicy and warming. Moments like this gave her hope. He might calm down, forgive her for everything; her ankle would get stronger, and then they'd be off together.

She washed up their bowls and got ready for bed. But then she felt it starting.

She went outside and asked him, 'What did you put in that stew?' Her lips smiled of their own accord, but she was furious.

'Just a little. Come on—'

'You can't do that. I didn't want to—'

'You know you like it really. Look at you! That beautiful smile! I've not seen that in a long while. Lighten up, girl.'

After that first comedown, she wasn't keen to do mushrooms, but she had, a couple of times, just a little, to feel closer to him – as if a shared experience might rekindle what they had in those early days. But the lows – sweaty, sick paranoia – weren't worth the highs.

She'd told him she wasn't going to do it again.

He laughed at her as the fire painted shadows across his face.

'Oh, just fuck off, Joby.'

He was instantly angry. 'Talk to me like that? Like I'm a *dog*. Come here!'

'No!'

'You're my *wife*!'

'More's the bloody pity!'

She stalked off and she realised it was more potent this time. How much had he given her?

278

She vaguely thought, *I shouldn't go too far in this state.* But she found herself walking into the forest, into a dream-world, and the notion came to her – *I should leave a trail of breadcrumbs.*

Unconscious, half conscious, barely conscious.

Out. Of. Her. Skull.

She felt a surge of energy zing through her body. And she knew this power was so bright, so fearfully incandescent, she had to hide it from Joby. She had to hide her light from all the men who would want it for themselves; she had to keep it safe, otherwise they would steal it and turn it against her. Joby's mother had warned her – men were afraid of a woman's power; they were so terrified, they damned them as witches and sought to destroy them.

The fear took root, blossoming into a truth – *They will burn her alive.*

She closed her eyes, but the fire burned brighter inside her head. And then she saw the woman. A figure appeared in the flames. Her mother! But this was not the mother from the old photos she'd kept in her bedroom back at her dad's – this was a goddess, an icon, with sparks emanating from long flowing hair. A warrior. She rose from the fire with a face that was her mother's and Lily's and her own. The halo around the creature's head hurt Maria's eyes.

Hoots of birds tangled in the trees.

And she heard Joby's voice whispering, clawing inside her head: *You're to cook and clean. What's the point of you if you don't give me a babby? You're nothing!*

Were those words real? Could she hear his thoughts?

In the vision, he smiled and reached for her, pinning her beneath him as he mounted her – and suddenly it wasn't Joby but a giant bull rearing and heaving above her – and she screamed.

44

Her life is out of control.

She can't bear the feeling of being trapped and powerless, so she does one of the few things she can think to do – she calls Brian and asks to go round to see him.

When she gets to the flat, she knocks rather than lets herself in. She is surprised to see it's Alex who opens the door.

'I'm sorry,' she says, addressing them both. But she's not. Not really. She's only afraid of what Brian might do.

Brian and Alex sit together on the sofa, which leaves her with the bloody beanbag. She flounders like a beetle on its back as she tries to sit. She'd laugh on another day, in other circumstances, but Brian's expression chills any impulse to do so.

'I just wanted to talk,' she starts.

'Then talk,' snaps Brian. She's never seen this side of him.

'What are you going to do?' she asks.

'Is that the only thing you're bothered about?' He looks disappointed in her.

'He still wants to go to the police,' says Alex.

'And say what? That I murdered his boss?'

Brian's face changes from angry to sad. 'It's not right, Maria.' He sighs heavily. 'Someone died because of what you did.'

'But it happened. It's done. It's over,' she reasons. 'I can't bring him back, can I?'

'Did you mean it?' says Brian. 'Did you hope he'd die?'

'How could I have known?' protests Maria. 'I just wanted to get him back for being so vile to you. I told you it was an accident. I only wanted to make him sick.'

Her words sound hollow because she doesn't totally believe them herself. The bad part of her, the rotten part, didn't care if he lived or died.

'How can I trust someone who does something like that?' says Brian.

'Trust me? What do you think I'm going to do? Murder you in your bed?'

He tuts and shakes his head.

Maria is instantly annoyed. Here's another bloody man she's beholden to – another man who holds her future in his hands.

'I thought we were friends, Brian. Well, you're the closest thing to a friend I have. And there's nothing I can do now, is there? And even if I could, would you want me to wave a magic wand and bring him back? Really? How did he make you feel?'

'That's not the point,' says Brian. 'A man is *dead*!'

'Yeah, but *that* man.' Again, she tries, 'Look, I am really sorry. I only did it for you.'

'I never asked you to do anything for me! I would never have suggested you hurt anyone, let alone kill them!'

'I didn't know it would kill him!'

'See? I told you. How could she have known?' Alex seems more than willing to take her explanation at face value. 'For God's sake, don't get the police involved in our affairs, Brian. The next thing you know they'll be sweeping the flat for *gay drugs*.' He makes his fingers into quote marks. 'They think we're all on bloody poppers and GHB. We'll be *implicated*. They're hardly allies, are they, the bloody police?'

'It doesn't make it right,' says Brian.

'I've told him not to be so bloody stupid,' says Alex, rolling his eyes. He turns to Brian. 'What good would it do, telling the police now?'

'Oh, for God's sake!' splutters Maria. 'If you want to go to the police, go to the police.'

She stands in a huff. She takes Brian's flat keys and flings them on the table.

'If you want to throw me under the bus, then just do it.' In the circumstances, this is not the best phrase she might have chosen.

Brian doesn't say goodbye and it's Alex who sees her out.

'I'll talk to him,' says Alex. 'You know they also found coke in his system. A real party boy, his boss. That probably had as much to do with it as the mushrooms.'

'Thanks,' says Maria. It's kind of Alex to tell her that. But it doesn't mean Brian won't talk to the police about her part

283

in his boss's demise, especially if they come round asking more questions.

She nods goodbye, and leaves with a heavy heart.

She has to hope the understaffed Met have bigger things on their to-do list than hassle Brian about an *accidental death*.

45

The next morning the light is forcing its way through the trees as she softly opens the door to Elsie's room, in case she's still sleeping. The bed is messy, but there's no sign of its occupant.

Maria calls, looks around the house. Nothing. She searches the garden just in case Elsie's crouching down behind one of the bushes at the far end, playing hide-and-seek, but she's not there either.

She knocks at the neighbours, waking the students, checking with the widow, but no one has seen her.

Maria should have realised this was coming. She knew Elsie was upset after the argument with Del about the cats yesterday.

She considers searching for Elsie herself, keeping it from Del, who'll only use this as another reason to get his own way. She can't have gone too far. But . . . Maria thinks of

Balogan's grandmother freezing to death and she makes the call.

'What's she done this time?' asks a weary voice.

'She's gone missing.'

To give him his due, Del's at the house within the hour, by which time Maria has whipped herself into a right state.

'She knows how to look after herself, our Elsie,' says Del. 'Streetwise. Tough old bird. And look, I know you're fond of her, but we've got to do what's best for her, you know? I'm not the villain of the piece here. I can't be gadding about running search parties every week. I'll lose my bloody job. And it's only going to get worse – the nurse said, din't she? And now Nick's gone walkabout again it's all down to me.'

It's the most Del's ever said to her without Maria wanting to punch him in the mouth.

He drives round the north-London streets as Maria cranes her neck, looking right and left. The knot in her belly tightens with each circuit. In her peripheral vision she catches sight of another missing-cat poster tied to a lamp post and she has to turn her head away.

This happened on her watch. It's her fault. Elsie needs someone with her all the time – someone qualified; someone who can give her the sort of undivided care she needs.

Anything could happen to a vulnerable old woman round here. What might some mugger do if they found Elsie had nothing to steal? Animals prowl these streets.

Twenty minutes later, they find Elsie sitting on a pallet outside the Homebase near McDonald's, licking an ice cream without a care in the world. God knows where she got that. She has her coat over her nightie, so at least she had the presence of mind to put that on, and she's wearing her slippers.

When she spots Maria opening the car door, Elsie holds her ice-cream cone aloft like the Statue of Liberty. Hauling herself upright, she shuffle-dances towards Maria and Del like a Pearly Queen. There's a loud protest and a minor scrimmage when Maria tries to take the ice cream from Elsie as she helps her into the car.

Cleaning Elsie's sticky hand with wet wipes as they sit together on the back seat of Del's Toyota, Maria asks, 'Why did you do that, Elsie? Why did you go walkabout?'

She's ignored.

Del mumbles, 'Jesus Christ.'

'You can't do that. Elsie! Are you listening? You nearly gave me a heart attack. We were so worried.'

'No-no-no,' giggles Elsie, pretending to swerve around the corners as they manoeuvre in the morning traffic, play-fully throwing her body against Maria in the back seat and then against the car door on the other side.

At the right turn into her road, she shouts, 'Hi-ho, Silver!'

Elsie's still licking the remains of her ice cream when she clocks Del's face in the driver's mirror and laughs, whispering loudly to Maria, 'His mouth looks like a cat's arse!'

She's not wrong.

When they get in the house, Del tells Elsie to go to bed, like she's a naughty teenager being sent to her room to think about what she's done.

'Don't be daft, she won't sleep now,' says Maria.

'You can't tell me what to do!' says Elsie, jutting out her chin.

Del refuses a drink and leaves, still harrumphing, throwing back, 'This can't go on!' as he slams the front door.

Maria's heart sinks. She knows it can't go on.

That night, Maria sits alongside the sofa bed, holding Elsie's hand.

'Please don't run away again. You had us worried sick.'

Elsie nods, smiles. It could mean anything.

Maria chats to her about this and that, nothing of note, then out of the blue Elsie asks, 'How's your bloke?'

'He's fine,' answers Maria, before she's thought of what she's saying. Oh. Is that how she thinks of him, *her bloke*?

'What's he like?' asks Elsie.

'A big bugger,' says Maria. 'Huuuge.'

'Gentle giant?'

Maria pauses, fiddles with her fingers. 'I'm not sure . . .'

'He'll be sound. Same with dogs,' says Elsie. 'Terriers are the nutter bastards. The big ones – Danes, Mastiffs – soft as shit, that lot. Nothing to prove, see.'

Maria considers for a moment. 'But he could crush someone,' she says. She doesn't say, *crush me*.

'Gorillas have nests. Kittens have claws,' pronounces Elsie.

There's a companionable silence for a time.

Eventually, in a sleepy voice, Elsie says, 'Tell me a story.'

I never wanted a kid with Joby, thinks Maria, *but now I've got one – just happens she's a very naughty, very wrinkly kid.*

Elsie seems to doze for a second. As Maria is trying to think of a story to tell, something with a happy ending, perhaps, Elsie's eyes fly open, and she snatches her hand away.

'Who are you?' she bleats. 'I don't know who you are!'

Neither do I, thinks Maria.

Is she a woman who cares deeply for a vulnerable old woman? Someone reliable, a hard worker? A good friend who'd do anything for someone? A good person?

Or is she selfish and untrustworthy? A cold-hearted murderer?

46

There's no sign of Balogan that Friday night and Maria wonders if she's disappointed. She thinks of trying to kiss him. It was a bad idea. She knows he's dangerous. But there's that *frisson*. That sense of something savage under his cool exterior attracts her. She puts some elbow grease into polishing his table, to stop herself thinking of him in that way. It's embarrassing.

As she's leaving the flat, she sees the neighbours.

Both of them are staggering out of the lift as Maria is locking up. The man, Mal, has Cass in what looks like a headlock, and she's leaning against him laughing or crying, Maria can't tell. They don't notice her at first.

He must say something the girl doesn't like because she suddenly pulls away from him and slaps his face. He wrenches her arm back and half drags her towards the flat door, clocking Maria as he fumbles for his keys.

She tries to catch the girl's eye as she passes them on the way to the lift, but it's Mal who wheels round and snaps, 'You work for him?'

'What?' says Maria.

'Mal, leave it,' says Cass, her face a mess of sweat or tears.

'You work for Balogan?' challenges Mal.

'Yes, I do. Why?'

'You complained to him the other night? You said something about our party?'

'I didn't need to say anything. You could hear your music in Crystal bloody Palace!'

'Don't get clever with me!' Mal lets go of Cass's arm and comes up close to Maria. Too close. The deep lines around his mouth pull it into a snarl. 'You been in my flat, yeah? She tell you stuff?' He pokes at Cass. 'Whatever she's said, about *anything,* you keep your nose out of it, right?' he warns.

Maria's not in the mood. She stands her ground. 'Or what?'

'Mal . . .' pleads Cass.

Maria turns to the girl and asks, 'Are you okay, Cass?'

'Yeah. It's nothing,' sniffles Cass, and then her eyes go wide, and she gasps, 'Mal, NO!'

Mal is now smiling. He is now also holding a knife.

Maria freezes.

He waves the blade towards her and whispers, 'I said, keep your fucking nose out of it. Or. I. Will. Cut. It. Off.'

Maria backs away but he follows. He makes a swift movement towards her, a step, a flourish, teasing her, feints two more jabs towards her face. He laughs at each thrust.

Cass puts her hand on his shoulder and wheedles, 'Leave it, Mal. Please.' He shrugs her off.

'Got it?' he challenges Maria. 'You don't say a word to *him* about any of my business.' He gestures towards Balogan's.

'Got it,' agrees Maria.

Mal turns and strides away to his flat.

Maria forces her legs to move, gets to the end of the corridor, and stabs at the button to call the lift. Cass runs up to her as the doors open, grabs her arm and whispers, 'Please don't say anything to him, will you? Please?' She looks frightened.

'Who, Balogan?' says Maria.

The girl nods.

'About what?'

Before Cass can answer, Mal, spins round and shouts, 'Get. In. The. Fucking. Flat!'

Cass scuttles away.

Maria calls after her, 'Cass, are you sure you're okay? Do you need anything or—'

'Cass!' shouts Mal, and the girl trots after him, looking back at Maria with puppy-dog eyes. She shakes her head as if to say, *Leave it*. So, Maria does.

All the way back to Elsie's on the bus she berates herself for doing nothing, although she's not sure exactly what she could have done.

She knows where doing nothing can lead.

And even when she tries to help, like she did with Brian's boss, like she did with Nick, it can still go horribly wrong.

293

47

She woke to flames. She'd dozed, or lost consciousness, but she was still gripped by the mushrooms, back at the wagon.

The fire was a huge wigwam of branches. Joby was smiling, the flames cackling beside him.

Then she saw what he was burning.

She ran at him, trying to grab the dress out of his hands.

He held it high above his head, dancing back so she couldn't reach it.

'What the fuck are you doing? Joby! Stop!'

He dodged round her and hurled her favourite pink frock on to the fire where her other belongings were burning – charred clothes (the sequinned skirt!), shoes and pages of her books, curling and blackening and disintegrating. A flurry of sparks flew up into the air.

'Stop! Please, Joby!'

He grinned like a demon. Then his face changed. He

came closer, waving the pill packet in her face, slapping it backwards and forwards across her nose.

'Anything you want to tell me, girl?' *Slap. Slap. Slap.*

She didn't answer him. Couldn't.

He knocked her down.

She sat on the wagon steps and watched as he threw the rest of her possessions into the flames. And she stoked her rage.

A storm was brewing. The night sky looked evil, clouds, boiling in greens and purples, like a giant bruise.

He was on her out of nowhere, grabbing her right foot (not the injured one, thank Christ), hauling her down the steps, scraping her back as he dragged her along the ground.

She struggled, tried to kick him, but the jolt in her weak ankle made her yelp. He yanked her round and said, 'You're finished, girl.'

She drew herself on to her hands and knees, crouching, ready to spring away. He grabbed a large flaming branch, trailed it towards the wagon, and threw it inside.

Jesus.

Then he stood watching, his face blank as the curtains caught, flames licking upwards. He was going to burn everything.

Someone would see the smoke and call for help.

Who? There was no one.

She headed for the forest. She could hide there until he'd come down and got a grip.

But he was only giving her a head start. She heard him come after her and she pushed forwards, half running, half limping, sweating, the air close and oppressive under the trees, black as treacle.

She heard his ragged breaths behind her, then his hand shot out and he grabbed a fistful of her hair, jerking her head back so violently she felt her neck might snap.

She swung for him wildly, not connecting, the pain in her head blinding her. It felt like he was tearing her scalp from her skull. She clung to his hand, frantically trying to prise his fingers away, but they were locked tight.

He heaved her back towards the flames grunting with the effort, and she hobbled after him, trying to keep up, the pain in her head outweighing the pain in her ankle, realising too late that he was dragging her back towards the fire, nearer, the heat on her face, and then he hurled her towards it.

She fell. The flames caught her nightdress.

She can't remember anything after that clearly. She might have prayed. All she knows for sure is that she screamed. She batted at the flames licking up her body. Did she roll in the dirt? She doesn't think she would have had the presence of mind to do that. She probably did nothing to save herself.

But then, the miracle. A flash. A mighty crack of thunder immediately overhead and the heavens opened. Sudden sheets of rain. It was her salvation.

She scrambled to her feet, her scalp raw, her heart thrashing. She felt she might drown as she staggered away from him in the deluge, inhaling rain that drove into her face. She might have been screaming still.

And he came for her. And this time he came for her with the axe.

48

She notices the cold as soon as she opens the door to Balogan's flat on the Tuesday night.

In the kitchen the boiler is off and there's no pilot light. She heats water in the kettle to wash the floors. It's not that bad when she's cleaning but she hates the cold – it brings back the times she'd lie alone in bed in the trailer, high on that godforsaken mountain, trying to get warm enough to sleep.

Balogan returns before she's finished the kitchen floor.

'Sorry. I'll just finish off in here and—'

'Ah. The boiler, yes?' He mock-shivers. 'I am told, assured, the engineer will be here tomorrow. Well, later today. We will see. It is difficult to get people to work these days.'

'The power was off last week.' She is careful not to say the lights fused or mention the fuse box.

'A hot chocolate, I think?' he suggests.

'Oh. Yes. Thank you,' she replies. She is nervous of him again.

He brings through the hot chocolate as she's halfway through cleaning the inside of the windows in the lounge. He takes the drinks to the bar and pours a spirit into each steaming mug.

'Drink it while it's hot,' he directs.

'Thank you. Sorry, I'll finish these windows . . . after.'

'No need. Do them next time. The kitchen might also need a little extra work after the engineer has finished. A moment.'

He disappears into his bedroom as Maria takes a sip of the thick chocolate and brandy warms her on its way down. She sits and closes her eyes a second. The drink is like a hug.

Balogan returns with a large grey woollen banket deco- rated with geometric patterns and stylised reindeer and lays it over Maria's legs.

She jumps as his hand brushes her hip, spilling a little hot chocolate on her hand, hurriedly licking it before it dribbles on to the blanket.

'Sorry!'

'I think you might say that word too much.'

'Yes, sor—'

'You are about to say sorry for saying sorry!' He laughs. It is a good, deep sound. He comes to sit next to her, pulling the blanket over his legs as well as hers.

'And how is Maria?' he enquires amiably.

'Tired,' she answers honestly.

'And your friend? The old lady? How is she?'

'Elsie? She's, sort of . . . as well as can be expected.'

'This is an odd phrase, "As well as can be expected." Another English expression. Surely, we should hope for the best?'

'Hope for the best, expect the worst, shoot down the middle,' says Maria. 'My dad used to say that.'

'Used to?'

'He died. A long time after my mum. She died when I was born.' Why did she tell him that?

'Both of us orphans,' says Balogan.

It might be that comment, it might be exhaustion, or the brandy, or a million other things, but Maria suddenly bursts into loud sobs.

They're both shocked.

She puts down her mug. 'I'm so sorry!' she gulps, fighting to get a grip on her emotions. 'I'll just get my things and go—'

Before she can get up, Balogan reaches round and hugs her to him. And he holds her there against the warmth of his barrel chest, one hand on her bristly head, the other wrapped around her shoulders.

She braces against him for a second, two, but despite everything, her muscles start relaxing and her body becomes so heavy she thinks she might rest there for ever. There is nothing sexual in the gesture, which is comforting.

It is only when his phone buzzes that the moment passes.

He reads a text, then looks up. They regard each other. She hesitates. What does she want from him? Should she even trust him?

And then she blurts it out. 'I saw what was in the cupboard. Under the stairs. In the scarf.'

His whole body tenses.

She wonders if he might pretend he doesn't know what she's talking about, bluff it out.

Instead, he asks, 'Did you touch it?'

'No.' The lie is instantaneous.

'Good.' The blueness of his eyes is glacial.

'I'd better go.'

'Yes.'

She gets her coat. As she heads for the door, he calls after her, 'Maria?'

She turns to him.

'Never snoop in my things again. If you do, I guarantee you will be very sorry.'

It's like a punch.

49

Maria hears a scream. She forces her eye open. It isn't yet light.

She's not sure if the cry came from the past or the present, from her own mouth, or if it's Elsie. She pushes herself up to sitting. The wail comes again.

Elsie must have forgotten she sleeps downstairs now. She's probably tried to get up to her old room, because when Maria rushes to the landing she sees Elsie sprawled at the bottom of the stairs. The angles of her body are all wrong.

Oh God! Is this a replay of her gran? Maria hurtles down, two steps at a time.

'Elsie! What happened? Where does it hurt?'

Elsie's fingers dig into Maria's arm. She tries to move and screams again.

Maria modulates her voice and says, with a good deal more authority than she feels, 'You need to stay still, love.

You might have broken something. You're going to be okay. You fell. I need to get help.'

'Don't leave me,' cries Elsie.

'I need to, just for a second while I get my phone. Hang on!'

She shouts through, telling her everything will be okay, trying to calm her as she calls for an ambulance. She calls Del but it goes straight to voicemail. Of course, any normal person would be asleep at this time.

Elsie whimpers, on and off, for best part of two hours – two hours cutting through Maria like an accusation, until finally, the ambulance arrives.

Del eventually turns up at the hospital, although Elsie doesn't seem to recognise either of them by that time. She's probably confused by the new surroundings as much as the effects of the painkillers. Maria knows this is to be expected, but it still makes her wince.

Del seems less rattled. Maria suspects he's relieved that Elsie is temporarily someone else's problem.

They're told that doctors may replace Elsie's broken hip, risky though the procedure will be at her age..

Outside the hospital Del starts making noises about Elsie having, 'a little holiday' when she gets out, by which he means a trial run in a care home, although he doesn't say so, probably because of the way Maria is looking at him.

It will break Elsie's heart. It will break Maria's heart. Maria wonders if Elsie will ever return to her own home. Will she be able to manage her little dances round the kitchen – chicken arms and Babs Windsor vibes with 'The Lambeth Walk'. The attempted high kicks always worried Maria, and if she saw Elsie try to twizzle, she'd shout at her to stop, but the enthusiastic 'Oi! Oi!' at the top of her lungs always made Maria smile. What about the gentler shuffle steps of Flanagan and Allen's 'Strolling'? Will she even be able to do that again?

Maria hates hospitals. They bring back bad memories. Her gran. Her own time in Leicester Royal after the baby; in the Spanish hospital, after Joby.

Hospitals make her want to die.

50

She can't remember sitting down, but she must have done, just for a moment, because now she's on the sofa looking up at him, and Balogan's sitting next to her, holding her hand and asking, 'Maria. Are you ill? Maria? Can you hear me?'

'Oh God, I'm so sorry. I felt a bit dizzy. I'm not sure . . . It won't happen again.' She stumbles to her feet, mortified.

'No. Sit.' He doesn't seem angry with her, just concerned. 'What happened? Are you not well?'

'No. Sorry. I didn't get any sleep last night.'

'The old woman?'

'Yes. She's in hospital.' Her voice sounds pathetic.

'I am sorry to hear that.'

His face is so different when he's not frowning – kind. But this is also a man who keeps a gun in his flat; a man who makes threats.

The music from the neighbours is loud – another Friday-night party.

She gathers her rucksack and coat, pulls on her hat, and prepares to head out.

'I've finished everything. You need more toilet roll.' As she turns to leave, she adds, 'I'm sorry about . . . before. The fuse box...'

He nods, inscrutable.

He might have been about to say something else, but they are interrupted by a scream from next door.

Balogan shoots up from his seat and storms past her. Maria's never seen him move so fast. She stands and follows, hesitating as he bangs on the door to the neighbouring flat. The music silences. The door opens and a man starts shouting, 'This is nothing to do with you. This has nothing to do with business. This is between me and her.'

It is not Mal's voice.

Maria puts Balogan's door on the latch. She doesn't feel able to walk past the altercation to go home.

Balogan stands in the neighbours' doorway and says something so quietly she can't make it out.

Suddenly a man hurtles out into the corridor. He seems a lot younger than Mal. He has a man bun and, given his belligerent tone, an unlikely sweatshirt proclaiming *Peace, Love, Harmony*. Maria notices he's also holding a baseball bat by his side.

'It's got nothing to do with you or Mal. Back off!' he threatens. 'This is about me and Cass.' His face is furiously twitchy.

He starts waving the bat around. His movements are

wild and some of the swings seem very close to Balogan's head.

Balogan dodges and says, almost calmly, 'One shot.'

The lad hesitates a second and then flails at him.

The movement is so fast she almost misses it, but Balogan swerves, catches the bat in one huge hand, grabs it with both, and yanks it away. His attacker is unbalanced by the action and the next second Balogan has him on the floor, with the bat pressed against his throat.

The lad makes a strangled sound somewhere between a croak and a gurgle and a girl's squeal comes from inside the flat. It sounds like Cass.

Maria steps forwards and Balogan notices her.

'A moment, Maria.'

He turns back to the youth sprawled on the corridor floor beneath him. 'You will never get a second chance. I suggest you leave.'

Maria finds it more chilling that Balogan doesn't shout, doesn't swear, doesn't actually strike him – but the look of terror on the youth's face as he scrambles to his feet and flees towards the lift tells Maria everything she needs to know.

Mal sticks his head out of the flat now, addresses Balogan. 'We good, yeah?' He looks nervous.

Balogan nods.

From inside, Cass cries, 'Let me go after him!' but, as Mal slams the door, he shouts, 'Shut the fuck up, Cass.'

Maria asks Balogan, 'Is she okay?'

He sighs. 'Yes.'

'Are you sure?'

He regards her coldly. 'You doubt my word?'

'No . . . Sorry. I need to go.'

She is very careful not to catch Balogan's eyes as she slowly edges around him and then walks quickly to the lift.

She gets no further rest – on the bus, or back at Elsie's, where she has to feed the cats. She's too wired.

After half an hour lying down with her eyes closed, she knows there's no chance of sleep, so she gets up, strips Elsie's bed and puts on a load. She sees to the cats, puts out the bins, the recycling, and sets off for the hospital.

As she walks, Maria berates herself. How stupid is she! She said sorry to Balogan for finding a gun?

What does she want from him? He doesn't want her *like that*. She changed her appearance so no one would want her like that. All that brought was trouble. Now, she's good enough to clean and that's it.

And why is she interested anyway? The man's an animal. So are the neighbours. They're all off their heads on drugs and they work for him.

And they're scared of him. She should be scared of him too.

Where men are concerned, perhaps she is cursed.

As she crosses Crouch Hill, distracted by her thoughts, she steps out in front of a van. The driver slams on the brakes and the horn. He makes an angry gesture indicating she is insane. Maria is well aware of this.

She attracts violence.

Joby's mother said she was cursed. Perhaps she is.

Or perhaps she is the curse itself.

51

With Elsie in hospital, there's a conflab back at the house: Del and Ann discussing Elsie's future over mugs of tea. Ann has invited herself round after Del called to tell her about Elsie's fall and she's now appointed herself the *expert opinion*. Maria isn't exactly included in this discussion – she says her piece, but her views aren't called for because she isn't *family*. Her role is reduced to supplying the tea and biscuits, although she doesn't put out the box of Fox's (Elsie's favourite) because she's saving them for when Elsie gets back home – if she ever does.

Harry, not reading the room, winds his way round Del's legs, pushing his whiskers against his trousers.

'This lot will have to go,' says Ann, making a face as she indicates the cats loitering around the kitchen in the perpetual hope of food.

'No!' says Maria. 'You can't do that!'

She's ignored.

Maria had hoped there might be a reprieve. At the hospital one of the nurses said it would be better if Elsie recuperated at home, where she felt safe and comfortable and knew the layout of the house. Both Elsie and Maria had been included in that discussion and Del had nodded as if he was on board. But now, with Ann in his corner, he's changed his tune.

And he's just announced he's going to put the house on the market.

Which means Maria is going to be out of a job – although in the grand scheme of things that's the least of her problems.

Maria sits silent and sickly as Ann says, 'If our Nick turns up, he'll have to have his say. He's still her husband – on paper, if nothing else.'

'Yeah. But she made me the power of attorney. It's up to me what to do,' says Del.

'Fair dos,' says Ann. 'But he'll want to have a say anyway. You know our Nick.'

'Still no word?' asks Del.

'Not a bloody dicky bird,' says Ann. 'One of his mates reckons he's gone to Tenerife with that bit from the betting shop.' (She pronounces Tenerife to rhyme with beefy.) 'She's disappeared as well, by all accounts. Left her job. Might have had a win. If he has, I won't see any of it.' She sniffs.

'You thought of contacting the police?'

Maria's bowels contract further.

'Don't be bloody stupid,' snaps Ann.

Maria wonders if Ann still has Nick's drugs in her cellar.

There's more talk of what the house might fetch and the lock-up Nick had promised Del and, as they chat, Maria sits and contemplates her life falling further apart.

After Ann and Del have left, Maria washes up and feels sorry for herself. Both of them have homes to go to. Ann has the luxury of an actual council flat; Del his house-share in Walthamstow, and while he can't stand the blokes he shares with, at least he has a roof over his head. She can't bear to go back to her sad bedsit, even though it's recently been rebranded a *studio apartment*, according to the ad in the local estate agent's window – they're renting out one of her neighbours' places. For what it is, the rent's obscene.

She doesn't think she'll manage to sleep when she finally puts her feet up. But stress burns out the adrenals. Her eyes close of their own accord.

And her current anxieties, the recent flashes of violence, dredge up worse memories from a different time.

52

Maria is wrenched back to the Basque mountains.

The taste of smoke in the back of her throat.

The moon a dispassionate eye watching a woman flee for her life.

The owl's lament.

Why is she running from him? Why does he want to harm her? He's the love of her life!

She is so focused on trying to make out the way ahead in the darkness of the forest that she can't see him charge at her and he spins her round and the wood of the axe handle smashes into her face. Her cheek explodes in agony.

She prays then – not to Christ or his father, but to the older gods of the region, the ones Itzal told her about.

Madre Mari, keep me safe.

Joby raises the axe to finish her.

She wants to close her eyes against this final blow, but

they are wide with terror, and she sees the rage in the set of his jaw, the violence in his eyes. And she realises it is not personal, this hatred, it is the archetypal fury men aim at women – they try to destroy what they fear. His own mother predicted it.

The metal of the axe catches the moonlight, and she tries to make herself small, to scuttle away, but a tree is at her back and her face is on fire.

Bile is spewing from his mouth, raining blame down upon her – blame for his brother, blame for her betrayals – but her own lips are also moving, forming an incantation that she feels in her gut rather than understands with her mind.

And, as he swings the blade up and back – to cut off her head, like all the queens before her – the branches above them creak and twist and claw at the axe. And Joby's face contorts with confusion. He can't hold on. The axe is caught; the branches seem to rip it from his hands – and he loses his grip as he stumbles with the momentum of his swing, floundering, falling backwards over a gnarled tree root.

And she is lifted by a strange raw energy, springing forwards, lunging for the axe where he's dropped it on the forest floor. A force possesses her, and she rises to her full height, standing above him.

Joby's on his back, his neck turned to a weird angle – like an owl's head turning round on itself to see what might be creeping up behind it.

The moon is huge. And she is full of rage.

She feels the power like electricity in her body. She brings the axe high, mother moon glinting in anticipation, and then she swoops the blade down. There is a manic joy in the action. After so long imprisoned in the smallness of the caravan, doing nothing but waiting, shrivelling, becoming more helpless and pathetic by the day, by the hour, she is freed by this momentum.

The first slice is delicious.

And then she is hacking and hacking – the blade chewing through flesh and bone and gristle and tendons – putting her back into it, all her will and fury, savage, and she is drenched with spurts of his blood as she slashes at his neck. She can't stop.

Until – a last clean cut and his head comes away from his body.

She is covered with gore, splattered with his blood and her own.

Blood has no colour in moonlight.

She falls to her knees – for a moment, for an aeon. She might howl.

Then she takes off her nightdress and wraps his head in it, almost tenderly.

The earth is soft, swollen with the blast of heavy rain. She claws at the ground with her bare hands, nails ragged, grabbing a sharp branch, hewing out a hollow. It is a shallow grave.

She places his axe by his side like one of the ancients.

And she buries him.

Hauling and dropping rocks on top of him, feeling her flesh tear, dragging more branches, an upended sapling, on and on until she can lift nothing more.

The mound like a cairn.

And then she can breathe; then she is free.

When she finished, she had no words to say over him.

She staggered away, and as she walked, she cradled his head to her heart, no real idea of direction but always downhill. Slow progress, her limbs rebelling, shaking. Somehow, she put one foot in front of the other.

Freezing. Naked.

She was the girl who danced for him. She was Salome.

Stumbling and limping until she could barely walk.

She heard water. Her throat raw from smoke and screams, she scrambled forwards, carefully placed the head on the bank, and leaned over to drink, but she pitched forwards into the stream.

The shock brought her back to herself. She scrubbed her body in the icy water, washed him off her face, her hair – she needed to get all traces of him off her – shaking violently, and then she dragged herself out on to the bank and leaned against a tree.

She told herself to keep moving. She berated herself for resting – if she stopped now, she would fall asleep, and hypothermia would take her. But she was too shattered to care. She closed her eyes.

The cold burned so deep she was on fire.

And she rose from the flames. She forced herself to stand. She stretched.

In the tree trunk above her there was a deep hollow. She stood on tiptoe and put her hand inside, wondering if an animal might bite or tear her fingers with its beak. It was empty. And she knew that was the perfect place to leave the rest of him.

She kissed his lips one last time and pushed the head inside – an offering of sorts. She rammed her ruined nightdress in after him.

Then she washed her hands of him.

She walked until she could walk no longer. Down and down.

And then she crawled.

A Basque couple found her early in the morning. She heard them call to her, but she couldn't stop clawing her way forwards. The man had to jog up to her before she paused.

He leaned over her then quickly stepped away, stunned. She was probably baring her fangs.

The woman took off her jacket and wrapped it round Maria to cover her as the man jabbered into his phone.

The rest was a blur.

People came. Lights pulsed. She was wrapped in a cloak of silver and probed and placed on a bed that moved and loaded and pricked and lifted and...

She woke in a hospital in Baracaldo. Bandages on her hands and feet. Stitches in her face. A metal plate in her ankle tight as a shackle.

She couldn't answer their questions. It wasn't only that she couldn't understand the Spanish, she just could not speak.

What could she possibly say?

She loved him. She killed him. She buried him.

They asked who she wanted to call. She phoned Itzal. He helped her with all the questions.

The police seemed very interested that she'd been found naked, but unconcerned that she was off her tits on drugs – personal use of mushrooms wasn't illegal in Spain, explained Itzal. It also made sense that she'd taken too much, panicked, and staggered on to a mountain path – that accounted for her injuries. There was no evidence of sexual assault, no evidence of a crime.

She said she'd been travelling, partying too hard. She couldn't remember where, no. She'd lost her suitcase with her money and passport – no, she couldn't remember when. No, she'd not been robbed or hurt. Nothing to see here, please move along.

Itzal backed her up. These things happen, he smiled. Stupid foreign New Age tourists. As bad as the hippies dancing naked at Woodstock. Mad dogs and Englishwomen. Ha ha.

Kind people in Spain helped her heal, helped her with new clothes, new shoes, papers to allow her back to Britain. She had to give them an address. She gave them details of her school, begged them not to call her dad. She said there'd been an estrangement. She had been travelling around with gypsies and staying with friends, sofa-surfing. No fixed abode.

They were probably glad to be rid of her.

She was terrified someone would find Joby.

She told Itzal Joby had left her and gone off with some Spanish girl. If Itzal worried where his English friend had disappeared to, he didn't show it. He didn't report it. That's the thing with drugs, it makes you unreliable.

She didn't mention the burned-out caravan. No one asked her about it.

She decided on London. She felt she no longer had a home in the Midlands and she couldn't face her dad, or Joby's community.

Itzal gave her a lift to the ferry port. He tried to kiss her goodbye, but she turned her head, so it was only a peck on the cheek. She was done with all that – romance and passion and desire and *wanting*.

She stood on the deck of the ferry back to Britain like a figurehead, untroubled by sickness. She may even have laughed.

53

Del calls before Maria sets off for work, informing her that Elsie is out of surgery and it's gone 'as well as can be expected, considering' – a phrase not overly reassuring. Maria plans on going straight to the hospital the following morning, after she's finished at Balogan's.

Her nerves are already jangling as she starts to clean and the music coming from the flat next door is louder than ever. She's pretty sure that no one else lives in the adjacent flats, or they must be either deaf or night workers like Balogan, because the noise from this particular party is off the scale. She tries to block it out, hurrying through her work, keen not to bump into Balogan right now because she can't deal with the conflicting emotions he stirs up.

The music continues for hours. On a Tuesday night! The pulsing beats are so insistent Maria doesn't initially distinguish the banging outside. When she becomes aware of it, she realises it's a different sound, an urgent sound – some-one is battering at Balogan's door. Her heart hammers in response as she hurries to open it.

Cass is bent over, sobbing. 'Please—' is the only thing the girl manages to get out before stumbling against the wall. Maria takes her arm, helps her inside, supporting her as she leads her through to the bathroom.

As the girl leans against her, Maria feels her shoulders heaving. She's tiny, like her boyfriend; she weighs practically nothing.

When she raises her head, Maria sees her face is destroyed.

'Do you want me to call an ambulance, Cass love? Are you hurt anywhere else? What happened?' she asks, although she can guess.

There's only a groan in reply.

Maria carefully blots the injuries she can see with kitchen roll, to avoid damaging Balogan's towels. As she gently dabs, Cass suddenly lunges forwards and kisses her full on the mouth, then winces. Maria pats her head and continues wiping the secretions away from the battered face.

'Sorry, sorry,' slurs her guest, her face twisted with pain and ruined with tears, snot and blood.

She notices the girl's skinny arms are also a mass of bruises and scabs. She's a total mess – a swollen eye, scratches across her cheek and eyebrow and there's a tear in her top which—

Suddenly the music next door abruptly stops. They both startle. The girl looks terrified.

'If he comes round, I won't tell him you're here,' promises Maria.

The phone in Cass's jean pocket starts ringing. For

perhaps ten minutes Maria holds the trembling girl as they sit propped against the bath together, both wondering what will happen next as the phone trills, stops, then rings again.

Then the shouts start.

'CASS! CASS!' He kicks the door to Balogan's flat.

'He knows I'm in here,' she whispers, gripping Maria's arm.

'Do you want me to call the police?'

God forgive her, but she's relieved when Cass shakes her head.

The slams continue. Ridiculously, Maria is concerned for Balogan's woodwork.

'Cass, CASS! I'm warning you! I'm calling your fucking mother. I'm doing it. Now!'

The girl springs up, unsteady as a fawn, and bleats, 'No, Mal!'

Maria has no idea what's going on.

'Your mother?'

'Yeah. He'll make me go back there. Please don't let him send me back there!'

'He can't make you do anything. You've got to leave him.'

'I can't leave him. He needs me. He loves me, really he does.'

'This isn't love!'

'You don't understand. It's not like that.'

Another kick at the door. 'CASS!'

Cass stands, stumbles and lurches towards the door, shouting, 'Please, Mal! Don't, Mal!'

Maria says, 'No! Ignore him. Don't open it—'

'I've got to! He's my dad!'

Maria is so startled she doesn't move for a second and then Cass is at the door.

As soon as the door opens a crack, Mal thrusts in, grabs Cass's arm, and wrenches her out of the flat. As he drags her along the corridor she cries, 'Please, no, Mal!'

Maria puts Balogan's door on the latch and rushes after them, with little idea of what's going on or what she intends to do.

She hurtles into the neighbouring flat, Mal too messy to shut the door behind him. The room is in chaos – takeaway containers, clothes, bottles, a broken chair, drugs in a bag, a discarded crack pipe. No one else seems to be there.

Mal slings Cass on the floor and she lays curled on the filthy carpet as she shrieks, 'No, Mal! Please, Mal!' over and over, like a mantra.

He looks up and notices Maria has followed them. His sneering expression does not change, but he abandons Cass and slumps down heavily on the sofa.

Maria stands framed in the doorway, as if she's on pause.

'She's done this,' says Mal.

'Done what?' Maria is playing catch-up here.

'She did this to herself. She never knows when to stop, do you, Cass? Fucking idiot.'

Cass snivels. She looks up at Maria and says, 'Just go. Please. You'll only make it worse.'

And it might have stopped there. Maria might have left them to sort things out between themselves. How could she help Cass? But as she backs away, despite her misgivings about Cass and what Mal might do to her, she spots a black sports bag on the floor next to the sofa where Mal sits glaring at her. The bag gapes open. And it is stuffed with cash – more money than she's ever seen in her life – so naturally she stares, she can't help it. And Mal notices her do so.

Maria half turns to go, trying to pretend she's not seen anything.

'Wait!' he snaps.

Maria looks to Mal – and despite herself, her eyes track to the bag on the floor and back up again.

Cass whimpers, 'Mal, no!' And both women watch his hand reach down the side of the sofa. He doesn't take his eyes off Maria as he brings out a gun.

The gun is more mesmerising than the cash.

Mal gurns. It in no way resembles a smile.

'Move!' he instructs. He gestures for Maria to get away from the door, but her legs don't seem to be working.

He stands and takes a step towards her, pointing the gun at her face.

Would he really shoot? If he shoots, would anyone come? Maria considers the possibility, almost like she's not in the room, almost as if this isn't happening to her.

Mal walks towards her, kicks the door shut and brings the gun up to the side of Maria's head, pressing it into her temple. It feels cold, hard, like the gun at Balogan's. Probably real, then.

She tries to compute the half-thoughts flitting through her mind. Should she promise that she won't say anything? Should she threaten him with Balogan? Should she beg?

But she can't move. Any words stay lodged in her mouth, and she stands silent as a statue as Cass pleads, 'Mal, please. Stop!'

He brings his lips closer to Maria's ear and asks, 'You said you work for him, Balogan, yeah?'

With the gun against her skull, Maria makes the smallest nod possible.

'What do you do for him?'

From the floor, Cass says, 'She cleans for him.'

'You're his cleaner, yeah? You're only the cleaner?' He laughs high and nasty. His expression changes and he says, 'You're dead.'

As soon as those words are out of his mouth, Maria finally forces herself to move, ducks, lunges and grabs the first thing she can, which happens to be one of the acoustic guitars propped against the wall, and she swings it in front of her to keep him away, which she knows is ludicrous because she's brought a guitar to a gunfight.

He laughs, probably thinking the same thing, but in that split second when he forgets himself in the laugh, she swings the guitar back around and it slams into the side of his cheek. The wood splinters with a satisfying crack where it connects, and he staggers back, losing his footing over Cass, who's still curled on the carpet looking up at him, petrified, and he trips sideways, scrabbling like a cartoon animal running off the edge of a cliff before he falls on to one knee.

She smashes the guitar down on his head once more to make sure he stays down, and again, because he's still holding the gun, and again, for taunting her with the knife that time – each blow a heavy *thwack* as it connects.

When the guitar disintegrates, and he's face down on the carpet, she grabs a bottle of tequila from the coffee table and continues hitting him until the gun skitters away.

It's like hitting Nick – it takes on its own rhythm.

Until he's still.

And the girl on the floor is quiet at last.

54

She comes back to herself. It takes her a few seconds to feel connected to her body once more. She has a splinter in the palm of her hand from the guitar.

Mal is a sickening mess on the floor. The gun has skittered away under the coffee table.

Maria stands motionless above him, holding the bottle, holding her breath.

Cass unfurls and crawls over to Mal, touching what is left of his face.

Maria galvanises herself, bending to check, as if his lack of movement, given the state of him, might be a vile joke. The two women look at each other, horrified.

Maria notices the stain spreading from his head, bleeding into the floor beneath him. She'll need to see to that.

A high-pitched noise escapes from Cass. The girl shoves her knuckles in her mouth to stop it and looks up at Maria, eyes huge.

'Cass. Get up, you need to go. Get away from this. Now. I'll sort it.'

The girl is too dazed to answer.

Maria takes the girl's hand and helps her to her feet. She holds her arms and makes herself talk calmly.

'You need to leave. Just go. You were never here. Okay?'

They nod slowly at each other.

Then, like a robot, Cass walks to the bathroom on wobbly legs.

Maria hurries back to Balogan's for her cleaning kit. She stands in the hallway a moment, takes a few deep breaths, gathering herself before going back inside Mal's flat.

She puts on her rubber gloves and starts to wipe down the remains of the guitar with bleach as she tries to make sense of what Cass has just told her.

Her *father*!

Cass reappears from the bathroom a minute or two later and seems a little more together. She sits on the sofa, folding her feet underneath her like a lamb, and scratches at her skinny arm.

Maria stops cleaning for a moment. 'Cass, I'm so sorry.'

'I'm not,' says Cass. She sounds matter-of-fact. 'Don't be sorry. I'm . . .'

'But—'

'I hated him. He was always trying to control me, you know?'

'But he was your *dad*?'

'Yeah.'

'How old are you?'

'Eighteen. He had me, like, when he was my age.'

'He hurt you?'

Cass snorts. 'Like you wouldn't believe . . .' Her thoughts seem to drift away.

Maria gets up and takes the girl's coat from where it's been discarded by the side of the sofa and wraps it around her shoulders.

'Are you okay? Will you be okay?'

The girl pauses, then nods. 'Yeah. I'm fine.'

They both sit staring at the floor for a few seconds, then Cass says, 'What are you going to do with this . . .?' She nods to the carnage at her feet.

'I'll clean it up,' says Maria.

Cass unfurls herself from the sofa and steps carefully around Mal's contorted form.

'I'm going now,' she announces. 'I'm taking this.' She snatches the bag of drug paraphernalia from the coffee table, hugs it to her belly like it's a child.

'Where will you go?'

'To my boyfriend's. Me and Mal had loads of fights about him!' She laughs, coughs. 'Or to a mate's – anywhere but my mum's.'

'Why not?'

'No way! Don't make me go back there! Please!'

'Of course. No one can make you do anything, Cass. But, why?'

'I can't breathe when I'm around her. She so fucking *needy*! She can't let me be. Totally toxic. She's a control freak – worse than him! She hates my boyfriend. She hates the drugs, but she can talk.' She snorts a sharp laugh. 'She hates Mal. She hated me staying with him – kept saying what a terrible person he was. What a bad influence.'

She had a point, thinks Maria. She says, 'It can't be that bad at your mum's.'

The girl shakes her head. 'No! She used to sing with him. She's jealous of me!'

There's an awkward silence.

'Families are complicated,' sighs Cass.

Maria says, 'I need to get on and clean this up. Are you sure you'll be okay?'

Cass considers. 'Yeah. I'll be hunky dory.' She heads for the door.

'Wait,' calls Maria, nodding to the bag of cash.

'Oh God, no. No!' Cass gasps, shaking her head. 'It's not mine. Mal collects for him. It's *his*.' She indicates Balogan's flat next door. 'He'd kill me if I took that. I told Mal not to. He was skimming off the top. I kept telling him. I didn't realise how much – all that in there. But now . . .' She trails off.

'Mal was stealing from Balogan?'

'Yeah.'

Maria stares at the stash of money in the bag. If Balogan hadn't already realised the money was missing, perhaps he wouldn't miss it now . . .

No. Bigger things to sort out first.

She hugs the girl goodbye, looks her in the eyes and asks, 'Cass, I need to know . . . will you tell anyone? About *this*?'

'Are you mad?' She starts laughing. It's almost as disturbing as if she'd said she was going straight to a police station.

She hurries out of the flat without saying goodbye, still laughing.

As soon as she's gone, Maria checks rooms, the wardrobe. There's no one else in the flat.

Then she lays the empty double bass case next to Mal's body, lifts him up, rolls and rams him in. She puts the gun next to him and closes the top by sitting on it and bouncing until it clicks shut. A stroke of luck. If Mal had been bigger, she wouldn't have got him in.

For the next hour and a half, she scrubs the carpet, every surface, anything she might have touched. She leaves the smashed guitar near the broken chair. She's sure she's wiped her fingerprints off the neck of it. The tequila bottle she wipes clean of blood and puts into her backpack – no point wasting that.

She puts the cleaning stuff back in Balogan's flat and gets her coat.

She hoicks up her rucksack, zips shut the holdall of money and slings it over her left shoulder before wheeling the double bass carrier out of the flat – down the long corridor, into the lift, willing it to descend quickly, down, down, down to the basement. This is much later than she usually leaves, but her luck holds – she sees no one as she steers the case through the underground car park, unlocks the storage room and shoves it into a corner right at the back, where she covers it with old boxes – some empty, some housing spare bulbs, mop heads, nuts, bolts screws, wood, who the hell knows what – stashing them carefully on top of each other, creating a wall. Finally, she props the giant floor polisher and a stack of old paint tins against the tower. Not ideal, but she has no better plan right now. She'll have to leave it here until she can think of how to get rid of it, where to dump it.

She wonders if she should leave the bag of cash alongside it. But—

She could use it for so much: a deposit for Elsie's house as soon as Del puts it on the market; a nest egg so she can stay with Elsie rather than leaving her to go out to clean; an escape fund.

She checks the car park. Only a few cars are ever parked here and there are no security cameras as far as she can see. But how many people have keys for this room? She has no idea. Few flats are occupied, so hopefully not many.

On the bus, she surreptitiously peels off her rubber gloves. She drops them into a wastebin as she walks back to Elsie's.

Under the bridge by the bus stop she sees a youth kick at a dead pigeon. It isn't the worst thing she's seen that morning by a long shot.

55

The dawn has seeped into a dull grey morning. The rain has almost stopped but Maria guesses it will be one of those soupy days of apathetic drizzle where it never feels like proper daylight, and you get just as soaked as you would in a downpour.

Three posters of missing cats on her way back. *Reward! Chipped! We miss him so much!*

Missing people on the radio news. So many things mislaid, including basic human decency.

She is bone tired, soul tired.

She showers and changes, everything in her body aching and heavy, then she goes to the hospital, hating to leave Elsie by herself in the ward despite the horror of her own long, gruesome night; despite being desperate for a sleep she knows will not come easily.

Del hasn't bothered visiting, according to the nurse, and

she can't really blame him. He's most likely already gone to work because, like her, he needs to earn a living, and Elsie is so out of it, she's no idea who's there and who isn't. All language seems to have deserted the old woman, which is terrible to see – a foreshadowing of what it will be like at the end.

Perhaps it's already here.

She treks back to the house, dumps her jacket in the hallway, and just as she's about to switch on the kettle, she stops dead. There's someone at the bottom of the garden. A man. Her heart starts battering as she creeps closer to the window, trying to make out what he's doing.

He's got a spade. He's digging up the rose bed—

She drops the packet of teabags she's just picked up, grabs a kitchen knife, and scrambles for the door, not sure exactly what she's shouting.

As she tears out of the kitchen, the man turns, spots her, and legs it towards the bottom gate. She runs after him. He twists away when she tries to grab him and runs up towards the house, panicked, Maria hurtling after him screaming like a banshee.

She manages to clutch the back of his damp hoody, and he squeals, 'Stop! Stop!', swinging round and holding the shovel out in front of him for protection. 'Gerroff me, woman!' he gasps.

'Who the fuck are you? What the fuck are you doing?' challenges Maria. She guesses she must look deranged, given the man's reaction. She's still holding the knife.

'Del sent us,' he gasps.

'What?'

338

'Del. His auntie lives here, don't she? He wanted it tidied up a bit before the old girl came home.'

'Del did what?' *Elsie's coming home?*

'The garden, innit? *Del* said.'

She takes in the man's gardening gloves, notices there's also a gardening fork lying on the grass next to a big bag.

'Din't get chance to call before. Who are you?' asks the bloke, gathering himself.

'I look after Elsie.'

'Oh. Yeah. Well. Del gave us the key to the garden gate. Got these for the old girl. She's in hospital, innit?' He indicates half a dozen rose bushes in the bag by the garden fork that she'd failed to register. 'Those ones there are well fucked, mate.'

Del doing something really nice and thoughtful for Elsie!

When Maria finally gets rid of the would-be gardener, assuring him that she will plant the new rose bushes, and yes, he can still claim his twenty quid from Del, she has difficulty making her tea.

She sinks on to the sofa, lays back her head and wonders what truly terrible things she must have done in a former life to deserve this. Now, on top of all her other worries, she has another bloody body to dispose of.

A short, fractured sleep shreds her.

What to do?

She lies rigid on the sofa, waiting, dreading a bang on the door from the police, or Balogan turning up on Elsie's doorstep, materialising like a dark angel demanding retribution. She hadn't realised she was so afraid of him.

She took his money.

She can't have been thinking straight.

She knew the people next door worked for him; knew he was their boss. What will he do if he thinks Cass has stolen from him? She can't forget the look on the girl's face when she suggested she take the bag – she was terrified.

What might he do if he guesses Maria has it?

But how would he know?

Should she tell Balogan she took the money for safekeeping? Although if that was true, why didn't she just put it in his flat?

Because she wants it for herself.

If it wasn't for Elsie she could flee, using the money to start again somewhere new, a different country. Del's not said anything more about selling the house, but it's coming.

She feels totally wrung out – too tired to move, too exhausted to work out what she should do next.

The irony is the theft makes her feel worse than killing Mal, killing Nick, killing Brian's boss. What a fucked-up moral compass she has.

But a cover story for stealing Balogan's money is the least of her problems when there's the contents of the double bass case to consider. She has to move that as soon as possible.

So stupid to leave it there! What was she thinking?

She calls the cleaning agency, claiming she's ill, although she can't explain what sort of sickness ails her.

She paces around the garden and regards the new rose bushes left by the gardener Del sent round. The labels show pink blooms, although now they're just stubby sticks with thorns and a few tiny buds.

She wonders if Elsie will ever get to see them flower.

And she wonders if she could bring the bass case back here and bury Mal's body in another part of the garden. As bad as Fred West.

She has to get back to Balogan's as soon as possible. What the hell will she do if someone's found the body?

Her whole life is now a series of questions. It's all bloody unravelling.

She takes the tube back to the South Bank to save time. It's a mistake. It's so crowded she's hemmed in by bodies on all sides, the crush suffocating. She feels herself panicking and has to get off three stops early, emerging into the daylight like a survivor of a zombie apocalypse.

Could she wheel the double bass case down to the Thames and dump it in the water? Somehow find a dark secluded place along the riverbank where there are no people and no security cameras? Does anywhere like that even exist in London? Wouldn't the evidence be washed up on some shore?

Or should she wheel it back to Elsie's? Deal with it there? Nothing else comes to mind. *Think!*

The only thing she knows for sure is that she'll have to remove the case from the basement room. A caretaker (not that she's ever seen one), builders, electricians, other flat owners, anyone could have a key. Is she the only cleaner who has access? The agency gave her the key along with those to Balogan's flat so she could use the heavy-duty carpet cleaner for a deep clean when she started.

As she arrives at Balogan's she feels lightheaded, and her knees aren't at all keen on her making her way across the car park to the storage room at the back. She jumps like she's been tasered when there's a movement to her right, and a skinny rat scuttles across the floor in front of her, minding its own business. She unlocks the door with clumsy fingers.

She takes a breath, steels herself, switches on the light, and stops breathing.

Is she losing her mind?

Before her, all the supply boxes have been stacked neatly on top of each other against one wall. The paint cans are similarly piled up alongside them and the floor polisher has also been moved to the side.

She has to put her hand on the wall to steady herself.

There is nothing else in the room. The double bass case – presumably along with its contents – is missing.

56

Before Maria's stress became specific – an entirely fitting response to the number of bodies littering her path – she sometimes wondered what she was so afraid of. What kept her awake at night even as a kid? The fear of dying?

Right now, dying seems like it might be a huge relief – an end to this churning anxiety.

An assault of questions, the most startling being, *Where is the bloody double bass case?*

Has Balogan moved the body? How would he even know it was there? And if not, who the bloody hell did? Why would anyone throw out a double bass case? Would the bin collectors even take something that size? What if they looked inside? Did Cass come back and find it?

For a fleeting moment she wonders if attacking Mal was some sort of warped flashback. But it went on too long. And the holdall of cash is real enough.

Jesus. The money!

She has stashed it in Elsie's airing cupboard, right at the back, covered with the sheets and duvet covers. Del never bothered changing his own bedding when he slept over, and he hasn't stayed at the house at all while Elsie's been in hospital.

Even now the bag nags at her.

Maria has always thought of herself as a basically good person. Despite all the evidence to the contrary. What a joke. She has never considered herself a common thief. It doesn't sit right with her.

She leans on the wall by the storage room, trying to order her thoughts.

Balogan is dangerous. But he's the only person she could talk to about what happened at the neighbours' and the missing bass case. And although he terrified Cass, that's not why she thinks she'll have to give the money back to him. She just can't keep it. It's something to do with him trusting her with his things, with his memories, confiding in her. She would rather ask for a loan than steal it.

She feels she's made a choice. It may be the wrong one.

She sets off back to Elsie's, gnawing at her nails on the tube. In a tunnel she sees herself reflected in the window – her eyes look wild.

She's almost crying with fatigue as she collects the bag. She daren't sit down or have a drink, because if she did she might collapse. Instead, she forces herself to set off again immediately. She's sweating as she clutches the sports bag close to her chest and trudges back to the tube. What would happen if someone found her with all this cash? What would happen if she was robbed? Wouldn't that be ironic.

She sees someone in a hoody and for a second thinks it's Cass before the girl turns to reveal a different face.

She ricochets across London once more.

She feels sick as she approaches Balogan's building and her guts plummet as the lift travels up to the top floor.

Her mind is so preoccupied, it's only when she arrives at the flat that she realises she's not thought this part through properly. Too tired, too distracted.

She has no way to get back into Mal's flat to leave the bag there, which was one idea she came up with on the way over. *Pathetic*.

How will she explain why she has the money?

Perhaps . . . claim they left their door open and – what – she just found it? It's a bit, *A big boy did it and ran away*.

She hesitates in the lift for so long the doors close in her face and she has to press the exit button again.

There's no noise at all as she walks past Mal's flat, which is more disturbing than the music ever was. She finds she is walking more slowly than usual down the corridor, and she's shaking as she knocks, as a courtesy, but before she gets the keys in the lock, the door opens, and her heart makes a bid to leave her body through her ribcage.

His face looks weary and unreadable as he gestures for her to come in.

It seems pointless to play out a charade – she doubts she could even if she wanted to because she is beyond tired – and as soon as he shuts the door she immediately thrusts the bag towards him and blurts out, 'I'm sorry. I didn't mean to take it.'

Balogan takes the bag, but doesn't react, waiting for her to continue. His silence is frightening.

She edges into the room. He motions her to the sofa. Maria's legs obey before she's consciously computed the request. He places the bag on a chair and remains standing.

There's a long pause. Maria squirms.

He sighs and says, 'I think you understand I am now in a difficult position.'

She repeats, 'I didn't mean to take it.'

'But you did.' His eyes are glacial.

She'd have been better keeping it and saying nothing.

Out of habit she glances around the flat. There is no mess in the room.

There is, however, a gun on the counter of the bar.

Maria was never called into the headmistress's office at school, she was rarely in trouble back then. She was a good kid. She wonders if this is what it might have felt like, waiting for your punishment – minus the gun, obviously.

Balogan stands, watching her. The silence expands.

Eventually he says, 'You stole from me.' Not a question.

She has to look down at the rug to avoid his eyes.

She tries to breathe through a wave of dizziness that swells and threatens to overwhelm her, until she can bear it no longer. She opens her mouth, considers fudging some version of the truth, but simply says, 'Yes.'

'But you brought it back. Why?'

'It was wrong. I'm sorry.'

'You must have known it was wrong when you took it.'

'No. Not really. I . . .' It doesn't even ring true to her. She blows out a big breath and says, 'Yes.'

'So why?'

'I didn't really think. I just . . .took it.'

'What for?'

'To look after my old lady.' It sounds weak. 'She needs it.' And, more honestly, 'I need it.'

'This woman is not your family.'

Of their own accord, her eyes keep glancing back to the gun. Balogan notices where she's looking, walks over to the bar and picks it up. He doesn't try to hide it.

'This was a betrayal.'

'I understand if you don't want me to work here any more.'

He makes some noise that might signify amusement or annoyance. 'It is much more than that.' He doesn't point the gun at her, but he continues holding it by his side. 'How can I trust you now?'

She tries to explain as best she can. It comes out garbled. 'I am sorry. Really sorry. It was a bad decision – a spur-of-the-moment thing. It was just sitting there, in the bag, on the floor next door, and I thought . . . I'm not sure what, exactly.'

It's strange that he doesn't ask her how she came to be in the neighbouring flat or how she knew it was his money.

She flounders on. 'All I was thinking was how much good it could do – to help Elsie? I wanted it for her. Because she'll need full-time care when she gets out of hospital. I want her to be able stay in her own home with her own things around her. As long as she can, anyway. Her nephew wants to sell her house and put her in some care home, without her cats – and I know they're just cats to him, to most people, but they're important to Elsie; they're her family. She can't be without all the things she's worked so hard for over the years. Everything she knows and recognises! It's not fair on her! She doesn't deserve that. But . . . but I can't look after her and do all my other work. She needs a nurse, a professional. And care homes, I just can't . . . But. I'm sorry. I really am.'

He walks over to the window. 'This is not your concern. It is not your responsibility, this woman.'

'But she needs me. If you knew her, you'd understand.'

'You are fond of her, yes. But she is not your family,' he reiterates.

Fond is too small a word. Softly, Maria says, 'I love her. She is all the family I have. I know what losing everything feels like.'

Balogan looks out over the London skyline, like he's considering.

'This woman would have good care – twenty-four-hour care – if the house was sold, yes?'

She shrugs. 'Perhaps.'

'You could visit.'

She nods.

'Then—'

Words emerge. 'It's not just that. I can't let him sell her house.'

'It is not your house. It is not your decision.'

'No.'

He waits rather than pushes.

She waits longer.

He finally sits. He rests the gun on his thigh, but he keeps hold of it.

'You are allowed in my home. I have told you things I have not told anyone else. You now know things about me I would not want others to know. You have become aware of some of my . . . weaknesses. I trusted you. I do not trust many people. And you stole from me.' He stares at her, his blue eyes impaling her, pinning her to the sofa. He speaks quietly, 'I do not tolerate disloyalty.'

She doesn't know what she's going to say until the words are out. 'It's not just Elsie. I don't know what I'll do when he sells the house – he's just put it on the market – Del, her nephew – and I couldn't possibly afford to put in an offer because houses in Roseberry Gardens go for about a million and because... Her husband's buried in the garden.' She takes a breath. 'I buried him in her garden.'

And the truth comes spilling out.

57

She tells Balogan all of it. A confession – her part in killing
Nick, Elsie's part; what she did, what she felt. It clarifies
things for her. When she's finished speaking, it takes her a
few minutes to feel she is back in his flat, the sofa against
her thighs. She watches his face. He does not seem shocked
or sickened.

She waits for his response. She is now at his mercy.

What is she hoping for by confessing? That he might trust
her now that she's revealed a secret, her own weakness?
That he might forgive her for taking his bag of cash? That
he might put down the gun he's still holding?

'Take that off.'

She startles a moment, then realises he is gesturing to
her rucksack. She slips it from her shoulders and hands it
to him. He searches through the contents and removes her
mobile phone.

Balogan walks to the door and indicates she's to follow him, holding the gun inside his jacket as he steps outside. He watches her as she locks the flat behind them.

Why hasn't he asked for his keys back? Perhaps he'll take them back when he's finished with her.

As they pass the door to Mal's flat she wonders again, why didn't he ask her how she got the money?

They walk down the hall together, get into the lift and he presses the bottom button. As they travel down to the basement level, no words are spoken. What would she say? *Are you going to kill me?* Balogan escorts her to the far side of the car park. She tries not to look at the room where the bass case was as they near it. He gives no indication of any emotion as they walk past it; instead, he stops next to a black SUV parked in one of the few occupied bays nearby.

'Get in.'

Maria's stomach does a sickening flip. She immediately notices the shape under the tarpaulin in the back – a double-bass-case shape. Is he going to get rid of the body now? Is he about to discard her, too? She daren't ask.

Balogan climbs into the car and puts the gun inside the glove compartment. Maria clambers in the passenger side, wondering if she might be able to lunge for it if it comes to that. Why didn't she keep Mal's gun? It might have come in handy right now.

He locks the doors, switches on the ignition, and Taylor Swift's voice starts in the middle of 'Shake It Off' as he pulls out of the garage.

Unlike London buses, it's a smooth ride. A light

drizzle makes the night roads glisten. There's little traffic. He switches off the radio.

No one has driven her anywhere for years. Despite everything, the motion starts to lull the knot in her belly.

Another half-mile or so and he says, 'You have, perhaps, done me a favour.'

'I'm sorry, I don't understand.'

'I think you do. But you should not have stolen from me. No one steals from me.'

She feels sweat prickle at her hairline. She does not look away from the road ahead.

She knew in her gut she should never have taken the money. But it was just too tempting. Now she fears she's going to pay dearly for that choice.

She figures saying nothing might be safer, so she sits, pressing her feet against the car mat and her back against the car seat for balance. Another wave of fear clutches her and feels she might be sick. She opens the window, sticking her head out like a dog.

Within minutes it's too cold and she closes it again.

She tries to run through her options, can't think of many.

The thing with physical exhaustion is that it is totally demanding. The body snatches at rest whenever it can. The car seat warms her back, the headrest supports her. And, yes, there is a gun in the glove compartment – just there – and perhaps he is toying with her as a cat might a dying vole, but still she feels her eyelids grow heavy and she is dragged under into a dark syrupy sleep.

★

By the time she judders awake, they are going past the turn-off sign for Bristol. He drives exactly at the speed limit.

The night streams past the car windows. She sits cocooned inside, warm, comfortable, protected from the cold.

They pass a few camper vans, one caravan. Miles between the headlights coming in the opposite direction.

She stretches, making tiny incremental movements, rounding and arching her back in the warm seat, pointing and flexing her toes, clenching and releasing her fingers, until she's fully awake.

Balogan pulls into a service station, parks, gets out and indicates she should follow him inside. He does not take the gun with him.

In the Ladies, she stretches some more, wondering. Could she tell someone? What would she say? Is she being held against her will? Is she in danger? He's not made a specific threat. Should she make a run for it now or take the gun from the glove compartment as he drives, and finish him, or perhaps finish them both as they skid off the road?

The small animal part of herself is still afraid, but to her surprise a deeper part is calm. There is a steady growing confidence. She has no idea what he intends to do with her – but she also feels, after what she's been through, she is more than a match for him.

He doesn't know what she is capable of.

She waits by the car. Her jacket is too thin for the night. Her ankle nags, reminding her how it hates the cold and the damp. When Balogan returns, she sees he's brought her a coffee along with his own.

They climb back into the car. He starts the engine for

warmth, and they sit a moment. It is almost companionable.

'Did you really mean to kill him, the man in the garden?' he asks.

She takes a sip of her drink. 'I was protecting Elsie.'

She sips her coffee. He sips his.

'Have you killed anyone?' she asks.

He doesn't reply.

He finishes his coffee before pulling into the petrol pumps.

Maria is shocked that anyone would pay motorway prices for fuel.

58

Maria's chronic fatigue is not simply due to the physical toll of repetitive labour; the thankless work – surfaces filthied again as soon as she's cleaned them. Eat, sleep, clean, repeat. Her life's work, utterly pointless. Women's work.

A large component of Maria's exhaustion has been the result of keeping so many secrets – the effort of forcing a beach ball under the waves, pushing it down every morning as it merrily bubbles up again each night.

The weight of so many unspoken words – words describing her guilt and crimes and the terrible memories and her *fury* – has settled heavily around her heart; words looping and knotting themselves in the dark recesses of her mind, dragging her down, imprisoning her.

She tried to make herself small. She is not small.

Telling Balogan about killing Nick has made her feel lighter, stronger.

She takes another sip of coffee.

And very quietly she says, 'I killed my husband.' A final confession before the last rites, perhaps.

She flicks a quick glance across to check on his reaction. It's enigmatic, as usual.

He drives on. Eventually, he asks, 'Why?'

How can she explain that? Would it make Balogan more or less likely to dispose of her if she tells him of her life with Joby, the drugs, the visions? But what has she got to lose?

So she tells him the truth. All of it.

And as she talks, she is unchained, buoyed up with a new feeling of relief.

She talks for miles, looking only ahead at the road. The unburdening is cathartic.

Balogan listens without comment.

And as she talks, she feels a dark energy stirring deep in her gut and a lightening on the crown of her head. She feels she is expanding; an experience as if she is becoming larger than the confines of her body. And she embraces this strange new feeling of aliveness.

It is surprisingly good coffee.

They pull off the A30. The roads get narrower, twistier, trees embracing each other overhead. It feels ancient here. She notices a bloody mess smeared across the tarmac that suggests a former badger, more unidentifiable roadkill a mile or so on. Balogan drives down a track only just wide enough for the SUV, thorns scratching the side of the vehicle, bony fingers reaching out for them, the only passing places verges and farm gates. He takes another tight turn and pulls off the track up on to bumpy grass.

He switches off the engine and the headlights. It is suddenly pitch black. They wait a moment until their eyes adjust. Wherever they are it's deserted.

'Why here?' she asks.

'You do not shit on your own doorstep,' he replies, getting out of the driver's side.

As she emerges she tastes brine in the air, feels a sea breeze on her scalp, an expanse above her. She rolls her shoulders a little and finds she can stand taller. The ache in the small of her back has eased, possibly thanks to her revelations, probably due to the warmth of the car seat.

'There are cameras on motorways,' she comments.

'At this time of year, many people travel down from London for the Easter holidays. When I first came to this country, I worked in a hotel near here one summer.'

They wait.

Her ears catch a rumble of waves somewhere to her right.

He also seems to be listening, or perhaps sniffing and testing the air. It is probably too early for dog walkers.

He does not instruct her, but she follows his lead.

He removes the case from the back of the car, standing it upright. The ground is too uneven to roll it and Balogan lifts the bottom end and she takes the thinner top part. Together they move, taking small steps over the rough ground. She matches his pace as he walks backwards through a gap in a gnarled hedge, up a small incline. As they reach the crest, the sound of waves gets louder, angrier. They steadily make their way towards what can only be the edge of a cliff.

She wonders if she should bide her time, wait until they are nearer, then thrust the case towards him, sending him hurtling over the edge along with it. She wonders if he's had the same idea – is he planning to toss her into the sea after the body, silence her, leaving her smashed against the rocks, rotting down with the rest of the garbage bobbing around the world's oceans?

He manoeuvres so they're facing each other on the precipice. 'Bend your knees. Brace your muscles,' he advises.

She nods. She cannot distinguish the expression on his face.

'Ready? On three,' and they swing together – one, two, three – sending the terrible neighbour over the edge, spinning down into the churning water below.

They do not hear a splash.

She remains tensed, waiting for what might happen next, alert to his movements. If he goes for her she is prepared to lash out.

It is just as disturbing when he comes close enough for her to see he is grinning – it brings to mind a crocodile.

59

As work goes, it was not the worst. They walk back to the car.

'Do you want to drive?' he asks.

'I don't have a licence,' she confesses. It seems such a ridiculously tiny thing when the list of her larger transgressions grows by the day.

He twists side to side, releasing his back, and then he gets back into his seat.

As she climbs in he says, 'The radio reception is poor here. Would you mind music?'

'No.'

He fiddles with his phone. Something starts playing – Swedish, she guesses by the language – a combination of heavy metal and folk, if such a thing exists.

As he drives her mind drifts, not unpleasantly. She considers whether she could return to this spot, do the same with the remains in Elsie's garden. What might digging that up be like?

At Bodmin, he offers, 'You are very good at what you do.'

'Thank you.' She's not sure what he means but she realises she might be smiling.

'Strong. Meticulous.'

The road gets busier as he drives east.

As they start to cross the Tamar he says, 'I have a work proposition for you, if you would consider it.'

'What work?'

'I would like you to clean for me.'

'I already clean for you.'

'Let's say . . . a more advanced clean.'

As they pass the sign for Devon he adds, 'Similar work to tonight.' A pause. 'And next door.'

'Next door?'

'I have cameras in my neighbours' flat,' he says, by way of explanation.

She lets that sentence percolate for several miles.

You'd imagine people would notice them. She'd seen nothing, although she'd not been in the neighbours' flat long, and she was more focused on other things. Perhaps Mal knew and didn't care. Perhaps they were more focused on other things. Hidden cameras can't be legal . . . She catches how ludicrous that thought is, given the circumstances, and she suppresses a snort.

Of course, he saw her take the money! What might have happened if she'd kept it and continued lying to him?

'I have cameras for all my tenants,' he eventually continues.

'They are people who work for me. I do not generally trust people who work for me.'

'I work for you.'

'Hm.' One side of his mouth twitches. 'But it is different.' He turns down the volume on a particularly angry riff. 'The people next door, for instance. He worked for me. Past tense, obviously. You did a good job cleaning up that . . . unfortunate mess. I would like you to do more work of that kind.'

Maria has no idea how to answer.

'Think about it.'

She does.

'I would require you to drive,' he adds a mile later.

'I can drive. I've just never taken a test.'

'That would need to be rectified. Do you have a passport?'

'Not any more,' she answers.

'You would need one. My work is not confined to London. Or the United Kingdom.'

He's offering her a job with travel!

Jesus, what kind of person is she to see that as a positive?

By the time they reach London, the traffic is already jammed and irritable. And by the time Maria gets out of the car back at the underground car park, her body feels stiff, but she is also very awake.

'Are there cameras in the storage room?' she asks.

'No.'

'Then how did you know . . .?'

He walks her across the garage and points up. 'Here.'

On a sign above them saying *Do Not Leave Possessions in Your Car* there is a tiny hole.

363

'There.'

'CCTV? But there's no light.'

'You have heard of a *hidden* camera, yes?'

Is he teasing her?

'In my line of work, it is good to see who might be visiting. If you work for me you would need to be more aware of such devices.'

They travel back up to his flat so she can collect her phone.

It is the first time she's seen the flat in daylight. The view is beautiful.

'I would need your answer soon.'

'Why?' she asks.

'I need to make plans.'

'Okay.' She shrugs on her backpack. 'And if I say no?'

'We will come to an arrangement.'

'The sports bag?'

'Trust can be earned.'

As she walks towards his door, she turns and chances it. 'I don't know if I trust you either, you know.'

One side of Balogan's face smiles.

On the bus back to Elsie's her phone pings with a text from Brian – *I've found a new cleaner.*

It makes her sad. Another person she's lost. Perhaps she'll try to talk to him. Or she might leave it, give him time to calm down.

She yawns, both overtired and wired. She can't work out if she's nervous or excited.

The phone pings again. Brian – *I won't say anything.*

She'll have to take him at his word. But the more time that passes, she guesses the harder it will be for him to do so.

As soon as she's fed the cats she climbs into bed without getting undressed, falling to sleep almost instantly. It feels like she's still moving, as if she's still travelling in the car, almost as if she's floating.

And she dreams of Mal, seawater flooding in through the cracks in his musical coffin.

60

Elsie's being released from hospital. She's coming home!

Maria has cleaned the house from top to bottom in preparation for her return. She's picked a small bunch of forget-me-nots from the front garden and has made a posy for the kitchen and another for the little desk next to the downstairs bed. Elsie told her they symbolise love.

Del is annoyed when the cats push their way around the walking frame trying to get to Elsie's legs as soon as she steps into the hall.

'Get them buggers away. They'll be having me over as well as her and that's all we bloody need!' he grumbles.

'What's that?' demands Elsie, spotting the newly installed child-gate in front of the stairs.

'It's to stop Sweetie going upstairs until her belly fully recovers,' improvises Maria. A little white lie. As if a gate would stop a cat going anywhere it liked.

Maria shuts all four cats in the kitchen, then helps Del bring Elsie through to the bedroom, now with the added commode.

'Oh, please! Let them in!' pleads Elsie, but as Maria and Del help her to sit, Sweetie is already in the room, jumping on the bed, having headbutted the kitchen door open.

'They'll hurt you!' says Del, trying to keep the cat from jumping on Elsie's lap.

'He has a point,' says Maria, but Elsie won't hear of the cats being kept away from her. The compromise is each animal is allowed in for an individual supervised audience, and then removed to the kitchen with a treat. They don't protest – Dreamies will always trump their love for the old woman.

It doesn't take long for the journey from the hospital, seeing the cats, the excitement of being back in her own home to tire Elsie. Her face begins to droop.

'We'll leave you for a bit of shut-eye, hey, Auntie Elsie?' says Del. 'Will you sort her?' he asks Maria.

After Elsie has achieved the first 'christening' of the commode, as she puts it, to the accompaniment of several expletives, and she's lying settled in what is now referred to as 'my own bed at long last', Maria returns to the kitchen.

'She does seem a lot perkier,' says Del. 'Do you think she's on the mend up there as well?' He points to his head. 'She knew all the cats' names.'

'She always knows their names,' says Maria. But she adds nothing more. Neither of them really expects a miracle.

After he's gone, Maria makes herself and Elsie a mug of soup. She takes it through and perches on the edge of Elsie's bed as they sip and gossip together.

Later in the night, Maria hears Elsie cry out and hurries down to her bedside.

'Does your hip hurt? Did you have a bad dream?' she asks. There's no reply. God knows if the woman's mind can thread together a dream. Or perhaps Elsie lives among her dreams most of the time now.

She wonders if she misses Nick at all, in these small hours, like she sometimes misses Joby. But that is a shameful, secret grief. She could never tell anyone about that, not even Elsie.

In the morning, it takes Elsie a good hour to come round and a good deal of tea, toast and strong painkillers are required.

'What have I missed?' she asks as Maria wipes down the tabletop.

'I may have a new job,' says Maria.

Elsie beams. 'Oh, Violet. I knew you could do it!'

So, they're back there again.

Comfort arrives in the afternoon, more smiley than ever.

It's obvious that Elsie tires much more quickly than usual and Maria helps her through to her bed for a nap.

When she returns to the kitchen, Comfort says, 'She seems to be doing very well.'

'She's glad to be back here,' says Maria.

'And you. Are you doing well?'

'Yes. Better.' For once she might mean it.

'You are doing a good job caring for her.'

'Thank you,' replies Maria, avoiding eye contact, like all women, embarrassed to be praised. She makes a start on the washing-up.

'No, Maria, listen to me,' says Comfort, collecting her bag and coming over to the sink. She puts her hand on Maria's forearm. 'What you are doing for her, this is love, this is a true service.'

The terrible kindness threatens to undo her.

61

She has arranged to meet Balogan in the morning, on Del's day off, so he can sit with Elsie. She needs to discuss the 'job offer' in more detail. She needs to know exactly what she might be letting herself in for.

'Maria,' he greets her warmly. 'A drink?'

'Just a coffee, please.'

She waits by the window as he bustles in the kitchen. The daytime view is amazing. The skyline catches the early sun's rays, making it a city of gold.

He hands her the coffee and asks, 'Would you like to come outside?'

He leads her up the stairs and unlocks the door at the top to the roof garden. There are tubs of daffodils bobbing in the breeze, a bird feeder. It is a jolly background for a dark discussion.

'Did you do this?'

He nods and smiles. 'Come, sit.'

He moves two of the wooden chairs so they catch the sunlight. They settle themselves.

Balogan begins, 'This man next door – let's not dignify him with a name – was stealing from me. This you know. I had suspicions. I only knew for sure that night.'

She nods.

'You perhaps did me a favour. He is now no longer a problem.' He takes a sip of his coffee. 'He was not a good man for many reasons. I am not a good man either, but who can say we are, at heart, *good*?' he muses. He doesn't seem to require an answer.

Despite herself, she finds her eyes tracking away from him to the view, which always draws her.

'You could live in a flat like this,' he offers.

She barks out a short involuntary laugh.

'You like it, yes.' Again, not a question.

'I love it.'

'You are a good cleaner. Very good at cleaning up the mess created by others. I would pay you to work for me doing the same. There is also the possibility of work transporting certain packages for me. Should you wish. Bags of money, for instance.' He smiles. 'And with that comes the possibility of a home, perhaps somewhere like this.'

She almost chokes.

Of course she would like more of *this* – sipping coffee high in the sky! Who wouldn't? She wonders if she is already sliding towards the pact.

'You have thought about my offer, yes?'

'Of course.'

He waits, but she can't answer him. Cleaning is one thing.

Transporting drugs is another.

'The remuneration takes into account certain *stresses*. And there is no pension scheme.'

Is he making a joke?

A moment passes, then he asks, 'What are your ambitions, Maria?'

She shrugs.

'What do you want in life?'

She has thought a lot about her ambitions in the last few days – what she might attain given the new *career*. What she wants: *for Elsie to be okay; a home of her own; travel, of course. And perhaps, one day in the future, somehow, a family of her own* – but she doesn't share these thoughts. They're not secrets, exactly, but they're private.

Instead, she says, 'I'd like my own place. My own things. Not to worry where the next penny is coming from.'

'I have bigger ambitions,' says Balogan. 'So should you.'

'Like what?'

He ignores the question, and says, 'You can be more.'

'A queen?' she asks, sarcastic.

'A warrior, perhaps.' He grins. He takes another drink and says, 'I would need to trust you.'

'But you don't trust me really. Not now.'

'You can earn trust. You must. Trust is everything. It is bigger than faith or hope or love. Love fades.' He looks straight at her. 'Where does your loyalty lie, Maria?'

'How do you mean?'

'Your loyalty – to your people, your country, your football team?'

'I don't . . .' She thinks for a moment, then says quietly,

'Elsie. My loyalty is to Elsie.'

He nods. 'I would expect your loyalty to me also. This I would need.'

'And the cameras?' she asks. 'If I lived in one of your flats, what about the cameras?'

'For you? I have no need. I already have footage of what happened next door.' He smiles another crocodile smile.

She assumes her face also does something because he puts his hand on hers, as if to reassure her.

'If you decide to say no, as long as you say nothing about my work, this will not be used against you.'

She doesn't know if she should take him at his word.

'What exactly are you asking?' She needs clarity.

'For you to clean – in cases of unfortunate *messiness*.'

'Just clean.'

'Just clean.'

'You know next door – that?'

'Indeed.'

'That part, I don't make a habit of it.' Joby, Nick, Mal – isn't that a habit?

'A professional. No. I gathered. I saw. I am not asking for you to do that aspect of the job. It is not an everyday occurrence. But, rarely, very occasionally, it happens . . . things of that nature. The people I employ to do that part of the job, while extremely skilled in that respect – *humane* – they are not professional cleaners. I would like to hire someone who is.'

'Who would do that? Cold-blooded killing?' asks Maria. She is genuinely perplexed. 'I killed Mal because I was fighting for my life.'

But, Brian's boss . . .

'When women kill it is usually personal,' says Balogan. 'Men kill more . . . dispassionately. Only a few kill for killing's sake. I do not usually employ those types.'

He takes another sip of his coffee and she follows suit. 'The people attracted to that side of the work? They have usually been in the armed forces or similar. It does not come naturally to most people. Military training assists people to cross a certain line.'

'Have you—'

'If you cross that line once, perhaps it is easier to do so again,' he interrupts, ignoring her question, admitting nothing. 'But you need at least some intrinsic aptitude for the work . . . otherwise guilt can crucify you.'

She watches the sky, as if it might provide guidance.

'People say killing gets easier, the more you do it. It does not, necessarily,' he continues. 'You simply get better at learning how to put it out of your mind – after – to function as normal, despite the memories.'

Maria has had years of practice at that – ever since Joby.

'I have commitments,' she says, 'Elsie.' She is actively considering his offer. It surprises her.

'It is good that you continue to do your other work. Ideal perhaps. Only, you would need to be available when I ask you. You would have to be *on call*, as it were.'

'How many calls should I expect?'

'In the last year? Three times. That is more than average. If possible, I do everything I can to avoid such unfortunate circumstances. Not all of these instances have been as . . . extreme as what happened next door. Occasionally, the issue is one of . . . persuasion.'

'Persuasion?'

'Use your imagination.'

That feels worse, somehow.

'Or a certain rebuke in response to transgressions.'

His language is the management speak of the cleaning agency.

'What is it that you do? Your business . . .? Drugs?'

His silence confirms her assumptions.

She finishes her drink. He finishes his.

'Cheers!' says Balogan, with heavy irony. 'It is a last resort, an absolute last resort, this aspect of my business.'

She nods.

'It is an issue of image. In my line of work, it is sometimes necessary.'

'How so?'

'In a dog-sled team there is always an alpha. Then age – a decline in strength . . . If the others smell weakness it precipitates fights. Then a dog might have to be removed. Dealt with.'

'Harsh,' says Maria.

'It is. But we are more than brute animals. Humans also have this.' He indicates his head. 'We have to strategise.'

'What if I can't do it?'

'It is right that you ask these questions. A trial basis, should we say? At least one job. If it is not for you, you would need to say.'

'No women. No children. No animals?'

'Most definitely not.'

Bizarrely she believes him.

'Another?'

She shakes her head. 'I need a day or two . . . before I give you an answer.' She's surprised at herself. What is she doing – negotiating? 'I need to be able to trust you. I'd need some sort of guarantee – because of what you filmed me doing to Mal . . .'

He doesn't seem angered by this. Instead, he says, 'It is right that you consider this seriously.'

'Okay. And I need to make sure Elsie will be taken care of.'

'But I must have an answer soon. I have business back in Sweden.'

She walks all the way back to north London. It takes a couple of hours. The sun is hot by the time she gets to the house. The days have been so dull recently, it's refreshing to see a clear sky, feel the possibility of spring.

She wonders what reassurance Balogan can possibly give her so she wouldn't feel beholden to him? Even if he wiped the footage from next door in front of her, would she really believe he didn't have another copy? Perhaps she's walking into a trap. Perhaps, given the . . . perks, it might be worth it. And what employee isn't obligated to their boss?

Near Finsbury Park there's a squawking. Maria looks up to see a small flock of green parrots. Is she seeing things? They screech by overhead, improbable feathers and long tails catching the sunlight.

It feels like an omen.

62

Maria used to be a good girl. Her dad always said it, her gran said it, the teachers said it. She thought it must be true.

What is she now?

She didn't get a seat on the crowded bus on the way to work, and she's now being jostled by a grubby man who reeks of old sweat. Two girls sit staring at their phones, ignoring a woman with her arm in a sling.

Wouldn't it be nice to drive between jobs? Or to be able to get a taxi? Wouldn't it be lovely to choose what work she took on?

Only she wouldn't be able to choose, would she? If she accepts, she'll be at Balogan's beck and call.

She spends the night at the bedsit. She just needs some head space and Del seemed happy to step in. It feels strange being back in the single bed after spending so much time at Elsie's.

She can't sleep. As she lies tossing and turning on the unforgiving mattress, a phrase comes to her: *It is better to die standing than live on your knees*. She has no idea where she read that.

When she opens Elsie's door in the morning, she immediately senses the absence.

Del sits in the kitchen. There's an open bottle of Lidl champagne on the table.

'A bit early for that, isn't it?' says Maria.

'Don't be a killjoy,' snaps Del.

'Where is she?' asks Maria.

'Got a buyer,' says Del, resolutely refusing to look her in the face. If he had, he might have seen her pale.

On automatic pilot, she turns to fill the kettle. 'You're definitely going to sell, then?' she manages.

'Not just selling, it's practically *sold*! An offer above the asking price. A fucking cash buyer! Wants it all done and dusted pronto! It's only just gone up on the website.'

Jesus fuck! That came out of the blue. She never thought he'd get round to it so quickly. Does that mean he's persuaded Elsie, or has he done it behind her back?

'Where's Elsie?' repeats Maria.

'She's at the place. A trial overnight. Sooner it's sorted, the better,' says Del. 'Can't have you letting me down again.'

'That happened once! I told you, it wasn't my fault. It was an emergency!'

'You didn't even call.'

'I didn't have my phone on me.'

'One time too many. What if there'd been an emergency here?'

She has no answer to that.

'Where's the place?'

'It's got good reviews,' says Del. 'Big garden, lots of activities. She'll love it. They specialise in people like her – with her mind, like.'

Maria squeezes the handle of the kettle, battling the urge to smash it into Del's face.

'The cats?' Her voice is tight. There's no sign of them, although their dishes are still on the kitchen floor.

'A woman's picking them up tomorrow from the Cats Protection.' At least he looks a little shamefaced saying that.

Maria sits and glares at him.

He sits and glares back.

'What? It's the best thing all round. You know it is. Little holiday. Then we can sign her up full time in a couple of months. It's a gift horse, the sale. Don't even want a survey, apparently! The estate agent said the bloke—'

'What the hell are you doing with that?' Maria clocks the roll of notes Elsie keeps in the old tea tin next to the cat treats – five or more elastic bands around it, her *emergency cash fund* – now nestling in Del's open briefcase.

'That's just to tide me over for a bit – until all the paperwork and stuff's sorted.' He juts out his chin a little as he adds, 'Anyway, what's it to you?'

The urge to do him serious harm sears through her. Violent thoughts. Should she grab the skewer they use for their baked potatoes and ram it through his neck? Should she stab him through the heart with the garden shears?

She sits, clenching her toes.

'Look, she won't mind. She won't even know where the hell she is, will she' He laughs as if it's funny.

Maria rises from her chair and steps towards him.

He doesn't look at all sure now.

63

She lets herself into Balogan's, checks the rooms, but nothing seems to need cleaning or tidying. She sits on the sofa and waits for him.

He arrives an hour later. She doesn't even say hello, but launches into, 'Did you do it to force my hand?'

He doesn't pretend not to understand what she's talking about.

'It is an investment.'

'Bullshit.'

'I do not appreciate language like that.'

She snorts, 'What? You torture people! You pump kids full of drugs and you hire people to kill for you and you *dispose* of bodies, yet you don't like swearing? Fuck off!'

She tenses for his reaction. To her surprise, he smiles, shrugs.

'A drink?'

'Yeah. That'll solve everything.'

'Maria, please do not sulk. This is a business meeting.'

'Elsie's nephew told me. Why did you put an offer in on Elsie's house?'

He pours himself a vodka and turns back to her.

'It is an investment – both in property terms and in terms of your continued loyalty. It is a way I can trust you.'

'But—'

'It is a gesture of goodwill. So you can trust me.'

Christ. How much money does he have?

They watch each other for a time.

She says, 'How can I trust someone who . . .? I don't understand that part, the *dealing with* people.'

'It is a kindness,' he replies. 'Dogs will tear each other apart if they sense weakness. What is better?'

'We're not talking about animals.'

'You have not worked with some of the people I work with.'

There's a pause.

He sighs. 'My father told me not to get too attached to our sled dogs. They were not pets; they were working animals. But when I was a child, there was one Spitz puppy, Freja. She became our alpha. Eight, nine years these dogs can work. But . . .' He gazes into his glass. 'She could not accept that she was no longer the lead dog. There were too many fights. My father told me to deal with it.'

'Did you?'

'Yes.'

The silence expands. She finds her leg is jiggling.

'But not when I should have done. She had savaged two

other dogs by the time I accepted my responsibility. Both of them had to be dealt with as well. Three lives instead of one.'

There's another long pause.

Finally, he says, 'We are all working animals.'

She pushes her feet into his carpet to stop her leg twitching, full of nervous energy.

'Your answer, Maria? You will keep my business to yourself? You will work for me?'

'I have conditions.' Hark at her! *Conditions*! 'Elsie needs to be taken care of. I will have to get someone in first, a carer or a nurse, before I leave her to *clean* for you.'

'Understood.'

'And the footage from next door. Cass . . .'

'Ah yes, the loose end.'

'You won't hurt her?'

'No. She was blameless. But she will hurt herself.' He sighs. 'I'm afraid her hobby, the drugs, will hurt her. It is almost inevitable.'

'Yet you sell them.'

'This is not the time for a moral discussion, Maria. What difference the judge who drinks himself into oblivion with the finest whiskey, the lawyer who medicates herself with prescription antidepressants and the contents of her wine cellar? If I do not fill this gap in the market, someone else will. It is only business.'

They watch each other warily. *We both know the worst of each other*, thinks Maria.

'It will be in your name, the old woman's house.'

Her jaw drops.

385

'I have the footage. You have the property. We are equal.'

She takes a moment. Then she nods. 'Okay. Yes.'

His smile is wide. It surprises her how happy he looks.

He comes towards her and offers his hand. She gets up from the sofa and takes it. It feels strange to shake it. *Never have I ever shaken someone's hand before.* He holds it a moment too long for comfort.

'An alliance,' he pronounces. 'I had an instinct about you the first time I met you. I am pleased we will work together.'

When he offers her a lift home. She says, 'No thanks. I'd prefer to walk. Clear my head.'

She dawdles on the way back to Elsie's.

In the side roads, she notices tiny new ivy leaves, light green against the leathery dark of the winter foliage, a shine on the delicate new growth against the patina of the old.

At Elsie's, Del lies twisted, face down on the sofa. The stain on the carpet has dried in and she won't be able to get rid of it completely, which is very irritating. She sighs.

She stands outside in the garden for a moment before she deals with him. There are small tight furls of fresh brackens growing from the frayed brown fronds, a soft greening on the branches of the lime tree. One of Nick's rose bushes, as she thinks of them – one of the new ones the gardener bloke brought round – is already showing a bud unfurling.

She takes a deep breath, stretches her arms high in the sky, as if she's won a race, then heads back to clean up the mess in the lounge.

She takes the bottle and glass from next to the sofa and starts to wipe up the spillage of red wine.

Del startles awake and yawns. Seeing Maria he cringes, embarrassed, and says, 'I've just been sorting a few things. Time got away from me.' His breath is foul. He is obviously very hungover.

'Okay.' She finds she can be civil. She goes through to the kitchen and puts the bottle in the recycling bin.

He leaves while she's getting the laundry out of the machine. He doesn't say goodbye.

When Del first told her about the house sale and his attempts to get rid of the cats and turf Elsie out of her own home, Maria wasn't sure what she might do to him. But he is Elsie's nephew, after all. And now she knows she can control a violent urge.

It is reassuring.

64

Del has brought Elsie back from her 'little holiday' in the care home and has left them to it. She now has her mug of tea before her and the things in her overnight bag have been put back in the downstairs bedroom.

'What was it like?' asks Maria.

'It was nice.'

'Was it?' There's a turn-up for the books.

'Well, I didn't like the people in charge, or the inmates, or the food, or the bed,' adds Elsie, counting the things off on her fingers. 'And you weren't there. The cats weren't there. And they couldn't make a decent cuppa to save their bloody lives!'

They watch a bit of telly together. It tickles Maria – no matter how bad things have been for her, the denizens of Walford have always had it worse.

'What have I missed?' asks Elsie.

'In *EastEnders*?'

'No. What have I missed with you?'

'Had another set-to with Del.'

Elsie laughs.

'Harry brought up a hairball.' Harry brings up a hairball most weeks, regurgitating fur and evidence of his latest kill. 'And I've got the new job,' says Maria.

'A good one?'

'Not sure yet.'

They toast Maria's birthday with a glass of Lucozade each. She'd forgotten all about it until this morning.

'At least it has bloody bubbles!' grumbles Elsie, narked that she's not allowed 'a proper drink' while she's on the painkillers. 'And cheers to your new job!' she adds.

Maria's not sure if it's something she should be toasting.

The complaints about teeth cleaning commence. Then Maria helps Elsie to the loo and asks if she wants a shower.

'Nah. A cat bath. Lick and a promise. That'll do.'

Getting her into bed is a major operation, but once the swearing has died down and she's lying back on the plumped-up pillows, Maria asks, 'What do you fancy doing tomorrow?'

'Tomorrow?'

'Yes.'

Elsie goes quiet for a bit. Her face has a serious expression, as if she's thinking through all the options, then she bursts out with, 'Tomorrow's another DAAAAY!' And they both laugh.

Maria washes their glasses and loads the washing machine again but decides to leave it rather than put it on. She can do it in the morning. Or perhaps they'll wrap up warm and sit in the garden together, do something different to mark her turn around the sun in another cycle.

By the time she pops her head in to check on Elsie, she's asleep. Harry has snuck in and is curled by Elsie's feet. He looks so peaceful, she hasn't the heart to disturb him.

She goes up to bed herself, reads half a chapter of her latest book, but she's too tired.

Sleep takes her quickly.

An owl's cry—

She's shaken awake by the horror upon her again. She's kicked off the covers and she's cold. She hugs her knees to her chest and pulls the duvet tighter. Back on the freezing mountain, ancient trees the only witness—

Joby was the love of her life, but he wanted to cut out her heart and bury it in the forest, so she cut off his head and buried him instead. There was no possibility of life when she covered his broken body in soil and stones and branches.

But Nick . . . She can't be sure.

The owl the only witness—

That noise as she buried him. Was it a cry? A groan? Surely it was from a fox? Or the sound must have come from her. It was because of the pain in her ankle, wasn't it?

As she shovelled earth on top of him, it can't have come from Nick. Can it?

She doesn't want to think of that and so she doesn't.

She realises the soft hoots aren't part of her dream – they're coming from the trees outside the bedroom window. Owls – murdering machines. She smiles to herself and falls back into an untroubled sleep.

ACKNOWLEDGEMENTS

My dad was the only bloke I knew who was a member of both the Federation of Window Cleaners* and the Musicians' Union. He played double bass. Write what you know.

My mum worked her way up to become the chief de-fluffer at a knicker elastic factory.

For many years, my brother and I earned our keep cleaning floors and windows alongside them, so thanks to all the people who employed us: Tesco (extra thanks for the Green Shield Stamps), Fine Fare and The Family Planning shop in the Coalville precinct, where I read all the leaflets and learned rather too much at a very young age. I also cleaned at Boots, Halfords and the local biscuit factory.

With my day job as a fitness instructor, I'm permanently knackered, so thank you to my friends at Proud Cleaning, Mart, Gareth, Fiona and Jamie, who prevent me from drowning in bum fluff from both the cats and my Geoff.

Thank you to the bloggers and friends on all the social medias who have kept me going through yet another year of sky-high anxiety and fathoms-deep depression. Mental health issues – yay! And a big shout-out to hypnotherapist Andrew Parr who pretty much kept me alive during the worst times.

Huge hugs to my Viper family and friends who made it possible to change my name by deed poll to Published Author! Love to Nest Supremo Andrew Franklin, Viper Momma Miranda Jewess, Marketing Maestros Flora Willis and Angana Narula, my future husband** and Press Wizard Drew Jerrison, Lord of Sound Nathaniel McKenzie, Office Queen Alia McKellar and Editor and Bingo Master Therese Keating. Thank you also to eagle-eyed copy editor Alison Tulett who caught many of my daftnesses, including a 'half-hearted duster'. Despite hourly panics when The Fear is upon me, this team make me feel seen, valued and supported. Not once have they said, 'Please don't jump on that desk and sing again.'

I am genuinely thrilled by the successes of my stablemates. (*Mixed metaphors; it was a vipers' nest only a paragraph ago – Ed.*) They have been my cheerleaders and sounding boards along the way. I am proud to call people like Janice Hallett and Catriona Ward mates. I feel I have a social life when I chat online with Leonora Nattrass, Dave Jackson, Guy Morpuss and Kates Simants and Griffin; when I send love across the water to V. L. Valentine, and fangirl James Mylet's mum, Dan Malakin's dog and Nicola White's cardboard squeaky chicken***. There's also been huge kindness in the wider authorly community, with writers like A. J. West,

Alice Clark-Platts, Douglas Stuart and Marion Todd doing everything from interviews to liking my posts and feeding me cake at book festivals.

Huge respect to legendary, iconic agent Jane Gregory and her team at David Higham Associates: Stephanie Glencross, who has Zoomed me through several sobathons; my first reader, Our Lady of the Roses Mary Jones, and glamorous assistant Camille Burns.

And without the support of my Geoff and my fur babies – Tiggy P, Splodge Statham, Pinky Snowdrop and Bertie the Emotional Support Kitten (now three) – I would have sunk a long, long time ago. So thank you. Steak and Dreamies all round.

* For window cleaners, a bucket list means something entirely different, but writing a novel has always been on mine.
** Subject to contract.
*** It's a thing.

10% of the royalties of this book are being donated to Age UK. I've worked for this organisation and other charities as a fitness instructor, supporting many clients with dementia. As Mae West said, getting old isn't for the faint hearted.